SWANS ARE FAT TOO

Michelle Granas

Acknowledgement:

I am grateful to Louise Burns at Andrew Mann Ltd. for her kind support and assistance.

Notes and Disclaimers:

All the characters are figments of my imagination. All their actions—including those of the gondola-keeper—are made up. There are no Radzimoyskis (or at least that's not what they're called).

I have simplified the usual Polish spelling of some characters' names.

I have simplified many other matters as well. This is a novel and its references to past events are intended primarily to suggest the outline of a history being compiled by the characters. Sources are noted at the end of the book.

The Warsaw Ghetto Uprising and the Warsaw Uprising are different events.

This story was written in 2006.

LCCN: 2014902894
Copyright © 2014 Michelle Granas
ISBN: 9780988859289

1

Heartless, soulless, a human skeleton;
Youth! Lend me wings!
— Adam Mickiewicz,
'Ode to Youth,' 1820

"What do you think she'll be like?" Kalina turned to her brother.

Maksymilian shrugged, hiking his glasses up on his nose, and speaking in his squeaky voice. "Some *babsztyl*, I suppose. We'll get rid of her. We got rid of the last one and we can take care of this one too." He spoke with quiet determination. There had been blood and a knife and a lot of screaming. It hadn't affected him. He was ready to carry on.

"But this one's our cousin," said Kalina. "It could be dangerous..." Maksymilian shrugged again.

*

Hania Lanska, descending from the airplane at Okęcie in Warsaw, knew nothing of what was awaiting her. She had missed the funeral, she thought, as she lugged her bag along the corridor and tried to avoid being buffeted by the hurrying passengers. She was hurrying too—not that it mattered now, after the fourteen-hour delay at take-off in New York. It was so stupid to have come all this way, just too late.

"No excuses!" The image of her grandmother rose before her. A large—a vast—woman, with thin hair slicked back in a bun and piercing eyes, standing erect and ferocious beside a grand piano. "There are no excuses!" she would snap, as she rapped on the piano lid with...with what? She had always been rapping with something. A ruler? A stick to beat time? To beat her pupils? "There is no excuse for making a mistake. Concentrate!" Rap, rap, rap.

And then the music would begin again, the beautiful music emerging somewhere between the student's red and concentrating face and frantically working fingers.

She would certainly not consider Hania had an excuse for missing her funeral. And yet truly, there had been no help for it: they had been kept "for security reasons" locked in the JFK gate area for all those hours.

Only once had the airline brought round food. She'd thought she would starve. The portions on the flight over hadn't been very large either. Quick marching with her flight companions, her eyes searched the airport for a vending machine. Please let there be a candy bar somewhere, she thought, as she hurried along. She was weary, rumpled-feeling, distressed, and really, a little chocolate would have been welcome.

Customs was coming up. She felt in her bag for her passports as she walked, pushing the American one down and pulling the Polish one out. Here she was. Would she fit past the booth? Always she had this fear, but it was ridiculous really. Of course she would fit. The uniformed guard gave her a cursory glance and stamp-

stamped her passport. She was through; she only bumped the sides a little because she was tired and it made her clumsy.

She came up panting to the conveyor belt. All the suitcases were black or dark green and nearly identical. All were being snatched off in great hurry. She wondered if hers had departed with a stranger. She didn't like to push through the crowd, though, as other people were doing. If she lost her luggage, so be it, she wasn't going to join the melee.

It was so stupid to have come too late. Her arrival at this hour would no doubt cause her aunt and uncle difficulties. She had telephoned this morning, just before the plane left. She wondered if they would be here to meet her. Her aunt hadn't said, but she'd asked for the arrival time. It was dark out and late. She hadn't been in Poland since she was a teenager—seven-eight years ago, and then only briefly.

What did the streets look like now, and her cousins, and what music had they played at the funeral?

She watched as a dark green canvas bag was tipped over the end of the belt by a woman struggling with two small children and an oversized frame-case. She waited a moment till the spot cleared and then stepped quietly forward and claimed her bag. Now to see if anyone was waiting.

She walked through the doors into the gauntlet of people, the line of searching faces behind the barrier, the hugs and kisses as passengers were claimed. There was no one she knew. She wasn't sure she'd recognize her relatives anyway and they probably wouldn't recognize her. She flinched from the occasional glance that slid over her, curiosity dying. No, no one came toward her. She stopped and looked around. Already the crowd was thinning. No one had come to meet her. She had thought it very likely and yet she was disappointed. She was jet-lagged and flat-feeling and alone. Perhaps they were too busy. No doubt there had been many things to do in connection with the funeral.

'Though they would certainly not be prostrated with grief. Natalia Lanska, concert pianist, had been much admired, had been adored—by people outside her own family. If any one of her nearest kin had felt for her, it was only she herself, Hania thought—and more out of compassion than anything else. Yet she had missed her funeral.

She would just have something to eat at the little café there. She turned towards it, and as she did so she saw the closed sign go up on the cash register and some-one turned out the light.

Two men in mustaches were approaching her, asking simultaneously in broken English if she needed a taxi, ignoring one another, talking over each other. No, she wanted to say, I want something to eat! Still, it was getting on for nine-thirty and Wiktor and Anna would no doubt be waiting for her.

She liked the looks of the second taxi driver bet-ter, but nodded okay, in Polish, to the first to speak, and followed him through the glass doors into the night. The warm air wrapped around her, and the smell of diesel and pavement. Then she was in the taxi and they were speeding along the avenue—a smooth, spruced-up, any-where-in-the-world sort of avenue between trees. The potholes would begin later. She tried to look out at the city. Here it was still the outskirts. Trees and garden plots and billboards. So many billboards. What was that Ogden Nash bit?

I think that I shall never see
A billboard lovely as a tree...

Such an inconsequential thought but she smiled a little to herself and turned her gaze ahead as they came up too fast on the tail of another car and swerved at the last moment away to the right. Did the taxi driver really have to slalom so? In and out among the traffic, and wasn't that a red light they just went through? It was! She sank down in her seat. Thank goodness they were getting now into the city proper and he had to slow down some. There were streets of old buildings, stuccoed buildings with wrought-iron balconies and pilasters, and crowding behind and between, great modern constructions of glass and steel had sprung up everywhere. And here they were coming to downtown. Amazing how full the streets still were of people at this hour. Smart young men and women, with fashionable haircuts, laughing at café tables, leaning towards one another intently to tell a secret, make a point, leaning back in their seats to enjoy the joke. She almost wished she could tell the taxi driver to stop, could get out and join them, sit at a café and have a nice time with friends, have something to eat. They went on though, and soon they were passing embassies and parks, turning down tree-lined streets, and the taxi was pulling up too abruptly before a pre-war building of rather dilapidated mien.

"Here?" the driver asked, twisting in his seat to look at her in disapproval. "Are you sure?"

"Yes," she said, looking out uncertainly. Of course it was the building. She'd spent the first six years of her childhood here. It just looked unfamiliar, somehow. Perhaps it was the surroundings that had changed, been cleaned up, new buildings added, leaving No.17 looking shabby and out of place. She paid the driver and got out and as she faced the tall carriage entrance ahead of her, with its forbidding doors, she rather wished the taxi hadn't left so quickly, with a squeal of the tires. She was alone in the street. Not that she was afraid of the Warsaw night, only she felt suddenly reluctant at the thought of meeting her aunt and uncle. She was not shy, but she was very sensitive to other people's feelings—including their feelings toward her. Perhaps they wouldn't be very glad to see her. Her heart contracted a little. Deep within, a little voice prompted that she was always unwanted. It was true, she knew, but she hushed it at once. Still, she couldn't linger in the street for ever.

She approached the dark entrance. A panel of the heavy iron grillwork guarding the passage stood open. Hidden now by the night, the passage's vaulted roof held a pattern of criss-cross lozenges and large swathes of chipping paint, she recalled. Beyond was a lightless courtyard surrounded by walls of windows; the door she wanted was here though. There was an intercom, but it was dangling by its wires; obviously it didn't work. She tried the door and it swung open, letting her into a cool, black, high-ceilinged entry-way. It smelled of mold and cleaning detergent. Her grandmother's apartment—her uncle's now, that is—was on the third floor, she remembered, fumbling for the light switch—which had been here, along the wall. The light sprang on and lit her halfway to the first landing and then went out again, plunging the staircase in darkness. A small amount of light came in from the tall windows and she chugged on up with her heavy suitcases. Maybe, she thought, she would ring at the door and her aunt and uncle would fling it open with cries of delight. They would crowd around her with hugs and apologies for missing her at the airport and offers of refreshment. They would say how glad they were to see her again. They would make her feel welcome and at home… Maybe—but probably not.

Something was different here but she couldn't think what. She remembered the black art nouveau balustrade and the patched marble steps. It was probably just the late hour, and how long she'd been away. Still, it felt a little eerie.

It had been her father who had decided she should come. "Someone from the family should attend," he had said, "I can't possibly get away, but you're free. Why don't you go? It would be good for you."

When something was inconvenient for him to do himself, he always thought it would be good for her. Still, this time she hadn't minded. She did want to attend the funeral, and she wasn't busy. She had just finished a year as a music teacher at a private school. The year was over, she was out of work and the next months were empty unless she found a summer job.

There weren't a lot of positions available for failed concert pianists. She was—had been—one of the best pianists in America, and that meant one of the best in the world, give or take a few ten thousand. She knew it, and her teachers knew it, and one of them had finally said to her, "It's no use, you don't have the stage presence, you'll never make it as a performer, I don't care how good you get. You're wasting my time and yours."

"But I could learn presence, couldn't I?" she had asked pitifully. She hated to remember it.

The reply had been brutal. "You're not eccentric; you're not good looking. You're obese. You haven't a chance."

That had been Hans Bertholdi. As he had finished speaking, shuffling sheet music together to avoid looking at her, and shrugging bony shoulders beneath his too-long gray locks, she had begun to play, unthinkingly, to hide her embarrassment, a piece from the first movement of Beethoven's *Appassionata*, where the climax built on the diminished seventh chord recedes. He had stopped for a second, arrested; then he had given a despairing shake of his head, and left the room with rapid steps. It was the last she had seen of him.

"Wiktor wants you to come. And Ania. They haven't seen you for so long. They're inviting you to stay for a month or two, for the summer." So her father had said. She had been willing enough to fall in with his ideas, eager almost at the thought of spending some time in Warsaw again.

Still, now that she was here, she was beginning to have doubts. The third full landing. This was the door surely. She felt for the bell and pushed it. Her heart was pounding but that was surely from the climb. Nothing happened and now her heart was really beating. She put down her bags and calmed herself, stilling her breathing and her pulse. In a moment the door would open and someone would say, "Hania, come in, come in, welcome." The bell was probably broken. She knocked softly and waited, listening. Nothing happened, no sound came from within. That's what was different—the thing that had bothered her as she came up the stairs. Always, at every moment of her childhood until her parents had emigrated, and on each of her subsequent visits, there had been music in the building, drifting down the stair-case and wafting out the windows. She had awoken to the racket of someone's scales and slept to the whisper of a Chopin nocturne. Now there was silence.

She knocked harder, but nothing happened. Well, suppose they weren't home? she thought with a sinking feeling. What should she do? Go to a hotel for the night? Someone was coming up the stairs; she could hear a man's step. A neighbor, no doubt, perhaps someone she would recognize, could ask for information. There was no reason at all to look around in fright and seek a place to hide. Should she go up to the next floor? Nonsense, she told herself, she'd obviously been living in New York too long. Here was the man. She took a step towards him. "Excuse me, sir."

He moved to the side and held down a light switch. He was a tall man in his mid-thirties, very clean cut, with a serious face. He seemed rather surprised to see anyone there.

She didn't recognize him. "Excuse me. I wonder if you live here? If you know my uncle?"

"With whom have I the honor...?"

"Hania Lanska."

The man seemed even more surprised.

"Do you remember me, *pani*?"

He used the formal expression: '*pani*'—ma'am, *madame*. She was unaccustomed to it. The last time she had been in Poland she had been too young—everyone was still addressing her as '*ty*'—the just plain 'you' for children, family members, or close friends. His look of solidity, the slight incline of his head as he bent courte-ously toward her, made her feel rather elevated. Did she remember him? She searched her mind vigorously, hop-ing for a spark of enlightenment.

"Konstanty Radzimoyski. I live in the apartment above."

It was, it was—the very boy—now a man in his thirties, but still the same. Oh, no. Please not him.

Yes, she remembered her grandmother taking her to tea at *Pani* Radzimoyska's when she had been what—five, six? It had been something of an occasion. The Lanski family, in the centuries before it turned to music, had only been occasional standard-bearers; their 18th-century estates had encompassed scarcely a few villages. The Radzimoyski family had been really grand: Russian titles and inheritances larger than a small country. "Now you mind your manners, we're going to *Pani* Radzimoyska"—as one might say "we're going to visit the queen today." And then there had been a great deal of sitting about being abominably bored while the conversation of the group of adults, like loud radio static, went on over her head, and no one brought the refreshments. At some time she had slipped away, while her grandmother and all the ladies had been laughing inexplicable laughter, and found the kitchen. There had been no one there. The window was open and some flies had come in and were swarming over a platter of cheesecakes. She crossed to the counter and waved the insects away. The flies had been on that one. It couldn't be served. That wouldn't be right. She would eat it. It would be very noble of her. She ate it. Then she ate another. The talk went on in the other room. The platter was empty now and she felt a little ill. She leaned against the sink and looked at the other plate. This one had little cakes with meringue frosting. The frosting looked like crusted snow. If she pushed her finger into it would the crust break? She tried it. The meringue popped with a little crackling noise. She licked her finger and pushed it into the next piece. She didn't notice the teenager until he was standing over her. He was very tall. She jumped guiltily and looked around at the shambles she had made of the refreshments. What would her grandmother say? She wished she were dead. She couldn't say a word—she just stared at the boy with her cheeks flaming red and her finger in her mouth. They looked at each other for a long moment.

"Were you hungry?" he asked. She shook her head, and mumbled something, tears starting to her eyes.

"The refreshments are always too long in coming, aren't they?" he said.

He put down the book he was holding and chopped the meringues into pieces to disguise the holes she had made. He took the platter into the other room and she heard him apologizing to his mother. He was very sorry—he'd dropped the cheesecake on the floor. So clumsy of him.

She had run from the kitchen, found the door to the apartment, heaved it open with difficulty, and fled downstairs to her grandmother's apartment.

Horrible. It had been horrible. A memory that always brought an inward cringe. Please don't let him remember.

"You came to tea once, I think, when you were quite small."

"Yes."

Now she was blushing. Thank goodness it was fairly dark on the landing. And here she was so fat. He was probably thinking she hadn't changed, was still so greedy. Oh, why was she so overweight? There was no dignity in it. However, one did what one could. She pulled herself together.

"You saved me, I remember. I had eaten all the cakes and you covered for me. I ran away and never thanked you. Please accept my sincere thanks now—even if twenty years late." Her slow speech and outward poise gave her a certain majesty.

He smiled very slightly. "That I only vaguely recollect." ("Were you hungry?" he had asked. He had liked her straightforward answer: "No, I just felt like it.") "I believe you were wearing a pinkish dress with ruffley things and had sugar on your face."

Horrible.

He changed his tone, as if suddenly remembering why she must be there. "I'm sorry about your grandmother. I'm afraid I couldn't make it to the funeral—I had a shift at the hospital."

A doctor then. He would be, of course.

"I missed it too," Hania said wearily. "The plane was delayed. And now no one seems to be home."

"Did they know you were coming?" He leaned over and knocked hard on the door. "I ask, because I saw your aunt and uncle getting into their car earlier with luggage. But perhaps they came back...Anyway, the children should be here." He knocked again, harder yet, with the natural air of someone accustomed to helping others out of difficulties.

From within a high female voice called "coming!" in a rather irritated tone.

"There you are, then." Konstanty Radzimoyski gave Hania another slight and distant smile, his eyes already looking somewhere over her head, (problem solved—goodbye, *pani*) and had reached the next landing before the door opened.

With a sinking heart, Hania waited for her aunt to open the door. Instead, it was pulled back only to the length of the chain and a shank of dishwater hair and a pair of eyes, one above the other, appeared in the crack. There was no light in the apartment, and the light had gone out on the stairs again, but she thought the eyes must belong to her cousin.

"Kalina?" she questioned.

"Who are you?"

"Hania. Your cousin, Hania."

There was a long pause, and the sound of whispering behind the door. Then:

"Prove it."

Hania was so taken aback for a second she didn't know whether to laugh or cry. But this was ridiculous.

"Kalina, is your mother or father at home?"

"Why do you ask?"

A second, younger voice added, "We're not supposed to talk to strangers." There seemed to be a bit of a scuffle inside and then the door was slammed shut.

She knocked and it opened the six inches again.

"I can show you my passport. Is that proof?"

She heard the younger voice saying, "No, no, don't let her in yet," but the elder said "okay," in a dull tone, and she handed the document through the crack. A while later the light came on, the door opened wide, and Hania found herself looking at a stony-faced girl of around fifteen, dressed in low-cut jeans and a tight, cropped top. Her hair was pulled back and she was wearing makeup that looked like it had just been hastily applied.

"Okay, you can come in." She held out a limp hand to shake Hania's.

Konstanty washed his hands, as he always did after being out, but he neither loosened his tie nor took off his blazer. If he was no longer a prince in anything but family memory, it pleased him still to keep up a certain standard. He stood for a moment in the center of the room considering: to watch television or work on his history project? He was tired, but the intellectual exercise drew him more. He sat down at his large desk. It was a very fine desk, made of Gdansk oak—the kind of wood that is seasoned for twenty years in a bog hole before being used for furniture. This one was carved all over with scenes of Sarmatia and was one of his grandfather's few salvages from the estate in Radzimość. At the moment the wood was almost hidden under a load of books and notepads. He sifted through a stack of neatly arranged papers. Strange, he thought, as he read the headings on the papers, strange that he should have remembered that incident when he was a teenager with Hania Lanska. The brain was an odd repository. What had made that stick when so many other things were irretrievably flown? Her childish face had come back so clearly. He supposed it was that his own behavior that day had pleased him. He had felt quite good about himself afterwards. Yes, that must have been it. It was always self in the end, he noted with a touch of wryness, but glad to have solved the minor puzzle. He liked to have his own motives clear and he had no illusions about himself. Here was what he was looking for:

The Neolithic people in the area of today's Poland, like the later Slavonic tribes, are known to have practiced trepanation, the drilling of holes in the skull of a live person. He began to type, pecking slowly with two fingers. *In this, the early Poles showed their common humanity: trepanation would seem to have been a world-wide practice, encountered from Polynesia to*

Alsace. Is this where the phrase 'a hole in the head,' originates? Well, no. He erased the two sentences, and began again.

Poland was then a vast wilderness of primeval forest, of dune and meadow, cut across by the wide-flowing Vistula and dotted with lakes. By the 6th century B.C. the local inhabitants were already the target for raiding Scythians and Sarmatians, Germanic and Celtic tribes. A century later Roman traders were coming too, travelling to the Baltic and beyond in search of amber. Like loose change in a parking lot, the Amber Route today is peppered with Roman coins.

The pause in the hallway was growing embarrassing. The girl neither invited Hania in nor made any explanations.

"Er...so your parents aren't home?"

"No."

"When do you expect them back? Didn't they tell you I was coming?"

"I don't expect them back." Kalina still spoke in that dull voice. "I don't expect anything from them anymore." She turned abruptly and, leaving the entry way, passed through a door into a small sitting room, where she threw herself on a sofa, and picking up the remote, clicked on the television. It was rather loud, so that Hania would have nearly had to shout to be heard above it. She stood indecisively in the doorway, looking at the girl, who pretended to be engrossed in a commercial.

Should she just turn around, walk out of the apartment, and go to some nice, sane, ordinary hotel? Even if it did mean crossing town on foot at a late hour? Yes, that's what she should do.

The problem was, she thought, she never gave up as easily as she should. With a sigh, she walked over to the television and turned it down, then, puffing a little, she straightened and said, "Excuse me. I suppose you're very unhappy because of Babcia"—she saw Kalina widen her eyes and look up startled—so it wasn't that then—"and I'm sorry to intrude, but I really need to talk to your parents. I mean, I thought I was invited to stay here—obviously I made a mistake. Perhaps I should go to a hotel?"

"Yes, I think you made a mistake," said Kalina. "You'd better go."

The phone rang. Kalina stared at it as if trying to make up her mind, while Hania waited in dismay and suspense. Kalina let it ring five times and then picked it up.

"What?" she growled into the receiver, listened a moment with her eyes rolled towards the ceiling, then at last handed it languidly to Hania. "It's them."

With a sense of enormous relief, Hania put the receiver up to her ear.

Wiktor's warm voice resounded down the line. "Hania! How wonderful that you're here. We're so sorry that we missed you at the airport, but things have been so hectic! You wouldn't believe! But tell us about you first! Are you all right? Did you have a good flight? What a way to treat you! Fourteen-hours delay. I would write and complain to somebody…"

The charm was turned on full. Hania recognized it—wasn't it the same charm her grandmother had had, and her father had?—she recognized it and couldn't resist giving way to it, to finding herself wrapped in the warmth of suddenly being cared for, liked, met more than halfway…she gave in, and yet a part of herself steeled for the follow up.

"Listen, Haniu, *kochanie*, it is so fortunate that you are there. We've had to come here overnight—"

"Where?" Hania tried to squeeze in, but Wiktor swept on.

"Absolutely unavoidable. You wouldn't believe the problems we've had."

She sensed the self-pity. "Yes, but…" she tried to stop him but he kept talking.

"So it's very fortunate that you're there, and we'll be back on Thursday, Friday at the latest…"

"But..." Thursday—that was three days away.

"The children will be good. They won't be a problem for you. You've been teaching right? Yes, yes, of course, I've always kept track of what you're doing..."

She felt a little glow and stifled it, trying to get a word in edgewise. "But where are you?"

He didn't answer that. "So you'll be fine with the children. Excellent then, that's all settled then, thank you so much for everything you're doing…" and in the middle of her questions the line went dead, and she was left staring at Kalina.

Kalina didn't lift her eyes, but just observed in her monotone voice, "That's my dad."

"Yes," said Hania wearily, "I have the same sort." Kalina actually turned her head then and gave her a quick upward glance before returning to the television. But after a second some better feeling perhaps prompted her to say, "I'll show you your bed."

"Thank you," said Hania, and then, "Where's your brother? I remember meeting you when you were small, but I've never met your brother—he wasn't born yet the last time I was in Poland."

"He's asleep," said Kalina brusquely, "I wouldn't wake him. He bites."

2

Childhood burns with an inborn heat;
there is no need to add fire to fire.
– Andrzej Frycz Modrzewski on diet, 1551

Hania woke early and stared at the high ceiling of her room, not certain at once where she was but aware of a feeling of stiffness and discomfort. Things came back to her in a moment. Warsaw, she was in Warsaw, in her grandmother's apartment. She had met Konstanty Radzimoyski on the stairs. She had missed the funeral. Her aunt and uncle had disappeared and left her in charge of their children. She turned over and looked at her wristwatch and as she did so the sofa bed creaked and a support banged against the floor. It sagged at all points. It was a miserable bed but it was hunger that had woken her. Extreme hunger. Later she would re-member to resent her uncle's actions, later she would wonder what was wrong with Kalina—at the moment she just wanted something to eat. Only five o'clock. Of course, there was the time difference.

She lay in bed and looked around. The room was small and higher than wide, with tall, tall windows and a plaster medallion around the light fixture. This had been her grandmother's room, the smallest room in an enormous apartment, an apartment that for forty years had been the envy of all their acquaintances, an apartment Babcia had received from the Communist authorities in exchange for staying in Poland, for proving that Natalia Lanska approved of the true socialist way. Natalia Lanska had cared nothing for ideology but had known a good opportunity when she saw one. When, after stunning successes abroad in the late forties and fifties, her career had begun to falter—was it because her once Valkyrie-like figure had begun to take on unbecoming rondeurs? Because she quarreled with too many impresarios, concert managers, and conductors? Or just bad luck?—she had abandoned Paris and returned to Warsaw, where she had remained at the top of her teaching profession, treated with humble—even abject—respect by her students and catered to by the authorities. She had had a maid and trips abroad and tutors for her children. For a long time her concert earnings and master classes had allowed her to lead a life of luxury, and with the end of the Communist era she had begun to make money again from lessons in Warsaw too. She had done well. Still, she hadn't ever thought about much besides music, and her room was decorated in a mix of inherited 19th-century furniture and the ugliest of central-planning-era pieces. This sofa bed had held more weight than it could bear for thirty years at least, thought Hania. Time to get out of it.

The room had already begun to collect Ania's paintings. Ten or so large canvases were leaning against a wooden wardrobe. Hania had hung her clothes over them last night in the hopes that some of the wrinkles would be gone in the morning. Now she looked at the top painting as she got dressed. It had a background of thick black impasto and a red figure that might have been a cubist nude in the center. Somehow the nude had become detached from its (realistic) eyes, which floated in the upper-right corner. She found it rather unpleasant and wondered if there was anything she could put over it again.

It was light out, but even the local grocery stores wouldn't open for another hour or so. Still, there must be something to eat in the kitchen, if only an end of dry bread.

She dressed quietly, hoping not to wake her cousins. If Maksymilian were anything like his sister she didn't really feel she could face meeting him before breakfast.

The kitchen was rather small, divided as it was by the *służbówka*, the four-foot-wide, walled-off space that all pre-war apartments with pretensions to dignity provided for the maid. One looked at the *służbówka* and felt a sudden sympathy for communism. There would have been just room for a cot in it.

She opened the refrigerator. It was empty except for a bottle of Heinz ketchup and some mold. She opened the cupboards, but they only held dishes, glasses, pots, and vodka bottles. There was not a scrap of anything to eat. She found some tea in a canister, but there was no sugar, no coffee, no milk, no bread. She opened the door to the *służbówka*, and saw stacks of boxes and a pair of someone's dusty old shoes. She had a moment's impulse to fall upon them and chew the leather.

"What are you doing?" said a firm but squeaky voice.

Hania turned quickly. A small boy was standing in the doorway. He had his sister's dishwater hair, with a round head, round eyes, and round glasses. He looked like a pale little owl, except that he was wearing only blue briefs with a space-ship design.

"Are you trying to steal something?" he asked suspiciously.

Obviously he was a pair with his sister, thought Hania.

"No," she answered deadpan, "I'm wondering whether I could eat that shoe."

The boy considered this for a moment. "Can I watch?"

"No."

"Why not?"

"I can't eat it. There's no oil for frying. I only eat fried shoes."

"You could go to the store," the boy suggested eagerly.

"Mmm. Yes. But it's too early—that's the problem. By the way—I'm Hania. You must be Maksymilian." She held out her hand and he shook it politely. Then he stepped back and, holding his glasses against his nose, regarded her for a long moment.

"You look like Babcia."

"Do I?"

"Yes. She's dead."

"I know. I'm sorry about that."

"She wasn't here. She hasn't been here for a long time. She was in the hospital." A long pause. "I don't remember her face, really. Only she was fat like you."

"Yes."

"Will she get thin now? Since she's not eating, I mean?"

"Maks," said Hania with sudden decision, "How about you get dressed and by that time maybe the stores will be open and we can go together and buy something, okay?"

Maks disappeared obediently and Hania left the kitchen, hesitating before the tall double doors to the right. Beyond those doors had been her grandmother's territory. She put a hand on the brass door handle, pushed gently, and walked in. It was a large room, perhaps forty meters square, with tall windows along one wall and three grand pianos filling the space. Nothing had changed. Only there was a fine layer of dust coating the heaps and heaps of music scores that covered every available surface: Mozart, Brahms, Scarlatti, Clementi—everything from solo pieces to orchestral scores to the most advanced études for virtuosos. Only her grandmother had known where everything was. The pages spilled over one another and threatened to topple from the piano lids. The Bechstein and the Bösendorfer were her grandmother's. The Steinway over there was Wiktor's. It had fewer scores on it and a heap of dirty coffee cups, un-emptied ashtrays, pencils, and electronic equipment. Wiktor composed atonal music.

Wiktor, in Babcia's opinion, which she had expressed to whomever cared to listen, had been a traitor, a turncoat, and a serpent of a son. There had been no possibility, however, that he would move out, find his own apartment, lead his own life, and play his own music at a distance from his disapproving relative. And perhaps the emotion generated by a friction of artistic ideas had been stimulating. Wiktor had turned up the volume. Babcia had played louder, been driven to new heights of musical dexterity, had taken Rachmaninoff and the Goldberg Variations to technical perfection. Public opinion, moreover, had been on her side; the neighbors had only banged on the floor when Wiktor sat at the piano. Or perhaps they were afraid to do so when Babcia was about.

And it wasn't Wiktor Hania was thinking of now, but of Babcia. She had stood here, sat here, played at this piano. Hania sat down at the Bösendorfer, put her hands forward and then drew them back abruptly. Anyway, people were sleeping.

Maks was back.

"I can't get dressed."

"Why not?"

"All my clothes are dirty."

"So wear whatever's least dirty."

"Well," she thought with a shudder when he reappeared a little later, "at least he's not my child."

They descended the cool, dim stairs together in companionable silence and went out into the morning. There were a surprising number of people about, walking with the quick determined step of Polish people—not the frantic rush of New York, where everyone was always behind-time and scurrying to catch up—but the step of people unaccustomed to dallying; people getting in cars, climbing off buses with shopping sacks—where had they been shopping at this hour?—people heading to the grocery store for the morning bread. Young women in clicking high heels, mothers with small children in strollers, elderly men in neat, pressed shirts. Hania drank in the sights and sounds: the city was clean and calm, had order without rigidity. Or so it pleased her to imagine as she walked along looking right and left.

"Why do you keep looking about like that?" said Maks.

"I just want to take in the city. I haven't been here for so long."

"I don't like to walk."

"Just to the store?"

"We passed it way back there."
"Oh."

There was already a line at the grocery. They stood behind three blonde older women in skirts, and waited their turn. The lady in front was in no hurry as she gave her order item by item. "And half a kilo of the Maasdamer cheese, or no, make it the Edamski, and some slices of pastrami, or do you suggest the *karkówka*—we had some of that other last night—and…" Hania and Maks waited patiently, jammed between a counter of cold cuts, a rack of rye bread and rolls, a rather fly-infested platter of sweet pastries, and a barrel of garlicky pickles.

Hania looked up as someone joined the line.

"Good morning, *pani*, morning, Maks."

"Good morning, *pan*."

Konstanty Radzimoyski, being polite to a neighbor.

"You're up early. Are they putting you to work already?"

"They aren't home." No need to explain who "they" were. "I guess they'll be back on Thursday or Friday." Why had she said that? He wouldn't be interested, anyway. Probably she just wanted to reassure herself that "they" really would be back.

"Are you planning a long visit?"

The line was hardly moving.

"I was intending to stay the summer."

"Then you will have lots of time for sight-seeing."

It was the merest small talk. No need at all for her to confide in him.

"I'd like to see if I can find work."

A pause. "What sort of work, if I might ask?" They couldn't stand there side by side without making conversation.

"It should be as a piano teacher, of course…"

Hmm, he thought, his mind half on something else, why did that ring a vague bell?

"…but I know it would be difficult to find students during the vacation period, so…I don't know…it seems there's a glut of translators, or I'd do something like that...I'll have to see…"

It was his air of actually listening that was so flattering, she thought, as she heard herself go on talking. Even though she knew it was only, after all, a mannerism.

The person in front gathered her bags from the counter and the shopkeeper was rather impatiently requesting the next order. A bit flustered, Hania turned back to the counter and asked for bread, sugar, eggs, potato chips, two—no, three please—packages of cookies—as quickly as possible so as not to keep Konstanty waiting—handed over her money, and was stuffing her purchases into bags when Maks raised his voice.

"You forgot the oil."

"I don't think we need it now."

"But you said you were going to fry the shoe in it. You said!" His voice held a tone of disappointed outrage.

How embarrassing. There was Konstanty listening with interest.

"Maks, it was a joke."

Maks wailed so loudly that everyone in the vicinity turned to stare. "You're just like everybody else! You don't keep your promises! I dooon't liiiike yoou aaafter aaall!"

He turned and ran from the shop and she hurried after him—"Maks! Wait!"

The day didn't get any better from there. Maks sulked and refused to eat breakfast. Kalina got up around noon. When she came into the room Maks jerked his head in Hania's direction. "I don't like her."

"If you have a problem, you fix it." Kalina answered in a high, false voice, obviously quoting. Hania recognized Ania's insouciant optimism. "You paint over it and start anew. Every day is a fresh canvas." And then in her own dull voice, "Leave me alone, Maks, you told me you'd take care of it."

And after that she lay on the sofa in front of the television, claiming she felt ill and answering questions only in growls.

"I will take care of her," muttered Maks, folding his arms and narrowing his eyes. Not the knife though. He had a different idea to try first.

Hania realized she couldn't leave the apartment without taking Maks, and as he made it clear he wanted nothing to do with her, she was stuck there. The apartment grew hot as the day passed. She decided to do some housework. On the one hand it wasn't her job, on the other she was living there and it needed to be done. She would start with the laundry, she decided. The bathroom was heaped with dirty clothes. She did a triage, sorted out what she assumed were Maks's things and began a wash. Then she retreated to her grandmother's piano room and started on a bag of cookies as she flipped over the music. By the time she'd finished the second bag, the laundry was done, she'd dusted the tops of the music sheets, cleaned up the dirty dishes, and it was time to make lunch. She put some effort into it, since she knew the children hadn't had breakfast, but by the time she'd finished and called her cousins to eat, Kalina had disappeared—had left the apartment without saying a word—and Maks said he hated *pierogis*, he never touched *pierogis*, he was sure she was trying to poison him, and she should order a pizza or he'd starve, and it would be *all her fault.*

She sat down and ate lunch herself, her own portion and Kalina's as well, and then went back to the piano room and subsided onto the Bösendorfer's bench. The day would pass somehow, she told herself. Bad moments always passed, and she'd been through far worse than this. She placed the potato-chip bag within reach and turned automatically to the keyboard, hands hovering over the keys, hearing the music already in her mind. And stopped. She looked down at her round hands—agile hands, strong hands, but padded. She put them down in her lap. Babcia had not looked like this until later, much later…after various triumphs. She looked around the room; the walls were full of photographs. There was her grandfather, a small man in a small photo, who had given up the race early, overwhelmed, no doubt, by the size of his wife's personality. The other photos were larger: Babcia playing at the Met, Babcia with conductors Karl Bohm and Ernest Ansermet, Eugene Ormandy, and Bruno Walter. A handsome woman wearing an evening dress and all her charisma. She, Hania, had no charisma, and for a year now every time she tried to play she heard her teacher's voice telling her so. She gave herself a little shake.

One got on as well as one could in the world anyway. She took a potato chip and began to play scales. She could make scales sound like music, but now she didn't want to. Like this they were just mechanical, not music at all, just physical exercise and relaxation.

From the apartment below an anguished howl arose. "Noooooo! *Pani* Natalia's come back!"

And there was the sound of windows being slammed shut.

Konstanty, coming up the stairs in the evening, heard the sound of scales being played. That was what he'd almost remembered this morning, he thought with sudden enlightenment: his mother, leaning toward a folded newspaper as she drank tea from a thin blue cup in their London apartment. "Kostku," she was saying, "do you remember Natalia's granddaughter, Hania? Oh, no, I don't suppose you would, Norbert and Elka moved to America when she was still quite small, a year or two before we left for France. It says in the *Tribune* that she's just won an international piano competition." She waved the paper at him. "It says the judges were 'very impressed' but she wasn't a 'crowd pleaser' so there's some dispute about the award. The sponsors aren't happy." That had been, what, three-four years ago now? A concert pianist—well.

He went on up to his apartment, crossed the spacious room containing his desk and opened a window. Below, almost within touching distance, the crowns of lime trees obscured the sidewalk and a part of the street. Beyond was a row of Secession-style buildings and beyond that, early summer Warsaw, green and gray and sandstone beige in the afternoon sun, a horizon marked by church crosses and small towers, elements of past centuries and, further out, the harsh, raw, upstruck fists of the high rises. He brought his gaze back to the more mellow foreground. He was very fond of the city. The scent of lime blossom enveloped him. From the apartment beneath came perfect, fluid flights and cascades of notes, repeating, repeating. He listened for a time, wishing she would play something. Some strong but indefinable emotion came on tiptoe. He greeted it gravely, and with only a little of his customary irony. Was it happiness, longing, nostalgia, or a little of all those? But nostalgia for what? For that moment as a youth when he had met a small girl in the kitchen and they had shared a few seconds of complicity, of understanding? Was that really the closest he had ever got to another human being? He paused before this idea, almost shy of staring at it with too intent a gaze. Here he was, a respected professional, with an exalted background, from a happy family; how could there be anything missing that only that one brief episode had supplied? What utter nonsense, he thought, closing the window in spite of the lift of his heart, and turning away—as people so often turn away just on the edge of discovery, corralled within the limits of convention or their own expectations.

He got out, as usual, his history project. Sometimes, though, he found himself thinking, quite impersonally now, of the girl downstairs. The thought would recur: the girl was a concert pianist. He appreciated the discipline, the dedication necessary to get anywhere near that good. It must be rather like going to medical school from early childhood, he thought. That kind of hard work. Still, presumably she liked her profession—not like himself, he almost caught himself thinking. A pleasant-spoken girl, he considered, but how could anyone let themselves get into that shape? The poor thing was nearly round. Very bad for the heart, too.

'*...they carry cytars since they are not accustomed to clothe themselves in armour, they are unacquainted with iron and this allows them to live in peace; without dissensions, playing on lyres...and for people who have never heard of war a sterner type of music is obviously unnecessary*'—so wrote the Byzantine historian Theofylaktos Simokattes about the Slavs in the 7th century.

*Unfortunately, one doesn't know of which Slavs he was writing. Slavonic tribes had arrived in the territory of today's Poland in the 6th century. The people they must have met were certainly not unacquainted with iron, as it was being produced...*He paused in his laborious typing.

...in the vicinity of Warsaw and the Holy Cross Mountains from the 1st century B.C. to the 4th century A.D., in thousands of ovens, on a scale unequalled elsewhere in Europe, which could be called the mass production of weapons.

That sentence didn't seem right. Presumably, though, the girl's career hadn't taken off or she wouldn't be considering teaching, or even worse, translating. Did she know how to write, he wondered? That was something else he remembered hearing over the years—that she was very clever, good at school. (He could almost hear *Pani* Natalia telling his mother, in that curious tone in which pride mingled with surprise, that Hania was doing well. *Pani* Natalia, he remembered his mother saying, always expected the worst from her descendents.) The girl had said, that morning in the grocery, that some of the English she'd seen in Poland on previous visits was rather funny, like "beaten-up cream" on a menu, or "officers to rent" on a building. He wouldn't make mistakes like that, but he knew how quickly even small errors detracted from a text. Well, perhaps he'd have a job for her. Or was it too trivial a thing to offer?

It was some half hour after dark, when Kalina still hadn't come back, that Hania became fully aware that she had no way of contacting Wiktor and Ania, that she didn't even know where they were, and she didn't know when was an appropriate time to get really worried, call the police, etc.

"Maks," she tried, "is it usual for Kalina to stay out this late?"

"I don't have to answer your questions." He was watching television and he didn't turn his head in her direction.

She stepped in front of the set, blocking his view very effectively. "Is it usual for Kalina to stay out at this hour?"

A sound like a tea kettle boiling over. Then, "Yes."

She moved away from the television, breathing a sigh of relief. If it was usual she'd probably come back.

Maks had his chin on his fist and kept his eyes glued on the set. He added, "Course, I can't tell time."

Fortunately, it was only a short while later that Kalina came back. Hania considered speaking to her—"it would have been polite to inform me of your intended absence, etc."—but decided against it. To what end? She'd just get through the next two days, and then her uncle would come back and she would—what? Go back to America, or move to a hotel, or look for an apartment? One of those things, anyway. She wouldn't stay here with these…these children from hell. And now she'd just have something to eat and go to bed. The idea of sleep sounded extremely inviting. By the time she'd finished off the leftover *pierogis* and the leftover bread and was ready for bed, the children had retreated to their rooms and were asleep. Well, that was one good thing. They seemed very self-sufficient.

She slipped on her nightgown and turned out her own light. The room was enveloped in soft blackness and the floor was warm beneath her feet. It would be so nice to lie down. She crossed from the wardrobe to the bed in the dark, pulled back the cover, and made a sort of wallowing dive for the center of the sofa bed in the hopes it wouldn't collapse with her. It didn't collapse, but what was that horrible, that viscous, slimy stuff all over the sheet? Feeling revulsion in every fibre she tried to escape, but it stuck to her. She rolled from the bed and the sheet came with her, clinging to her nightgown. Stifling a scream, she pulled at the cloth with panicked fingers and a beating heart and flung it from her. She stampeded to the light and snapped it on.

Butter. It was butter. Someone had spread butter all over the bed.

Maks!!! She felt like shrieking. Come here and clean this up!!! She controlled her rage with difficulty. It occurred to her that that was exactly the sort of scene he wanted. Well, he wasn't going to get it.

Inwardly fuming, she lay down again on top of the covers.

So, all right, she realized as she began to calm down, there wasn't really anything personal in it. Maks was angry with the world and he was taking it out on her. Maybe Maks had good reason to be angry, she didn't know, but why, oh why, had she come here? How foolish she had been. Her father hadn't had much of a job to persuade her to come. She remembered now, when he had called about Babcia, what she had felt. There had been a little sorrow for her grandmother, a little chagrin at the passing of a stage in life that would never return, but more, there had been the desire to return to Poland, to meet what she had always thought

of as "the other half of the family," to see if she could-
n't in some way make them her own, let them fill up the
emptiness of her own social existence, to flee for a
moment from the boundlessness of her American life
back to the rootedness of her earliest years. Ania and
Wiktor—they'd always been kind enough to her on previous visits. A little condescending perhaps—no, actually,
very condescending—but she had tried not to remember that, and anyway, wasn't it normal enough, in adults
toward a teenager? Now, she had thought, maybe there
would be contact, mutual ground, liking, acceptance.
She would meet her cousins; they would feel the bond
of blood, of family.

Obviously not. The future was an empty void,
and she had nothing, not the piano or any person, to
furnish it with purpose. She tossed and turned on her
uncomfortable bed and eventually slept.

3

Konstanty, his tie dangling over his computer keyboard, was thinking a number of thoughts at once. Should he include that bit by the Roman geographer, Pomponius Mela, describing the women of Sarmatia who accompanied their men in raids on Byzantium? These were the people from whom the Poles once liked to think they were descended:

As the country's climate is severe, so the character of the people is wild. The people are belligerent, freedom loving, indomitable, and so wild and cruel that even women take part in wars at the side of men...Every grown girl is required to kill an enemy. If she does not, she is covered in shame and as a punishment is unable to marry.

Ah, Polish women.

Actually, he quite liked Polish women. No—correction—he really liked Polish women. He liked their femininity, their competence, their self-assured flirtatiousness. He'd been surprised, coming back to Poland after years in London, at the beauty of Polish women. He'd forgotten that. The only thing they lacked was the responsiveness of English women, those pleasant, pear-shaped women in their long cardigans. He liked the way English women actually listened, took what one said and gave it back to one with a new twist. He'd come to appreciate that sort of wit in the years he'd spent at medical school in London. Of course, it had taken him awhile. He hadn't realized at first that not everything was to be taken literally. There had been the time, for instance—no, he wouldn't remember that. There were memories that had to be bashed down into the subconscious the second they stuck their heads up. Still, he had got used to a certain humorous way of looking at the world and now he rather missed it.

The pianist girl had it. He'd met her again today. She'd quite enlivened his day with her strange tale of Maks and a practical joke. It wasn't so much the story itself but the way she told it that was amusing. He'd repeated it to a rather depressed patient and got a laugh out of him.

Still, the boy had problems, he thought. The girl had dealt with it well. He could sense her weariness but she had told him with a certain gusto that when Maks got up in the morning she had met him with a big hug––he had writhed out of her grasp—and every appearance of great pleasure: "Oh Maks, thank you so much for the nice surprise. That's just what I like best—how did you know? It makes my skin feel so smooth in the morning. It's better than a beauty treatment." And then, at breakfast, regretfully, "I'm afraid we'll have to eat bread without butter, because I can't afford to buy any more."

No, Maks definitely had problems, and his sister too. And the pianist girl presumably also or she wouldn't be that shape. But she wasn't a warrior-type and that was a mark in her favor.

His fingers paused, poised, over the keyboard. Thinking of shapes had brought his mind around to his occasional date Agata, whose very shapely, perfect, curvy body was certainly in no danger of ever suffering from heart problems, either physical or metaphorical.

Why did he continue to see her, he wondered? The motives were, let's see, physical attraction…how did women get into clothing that tight? That white tee shirt molded to her round bosom—the image hovered before him, hampering for a moment his ability of consecutive thought—okay, very nice, but those tight jeans? Strange the way women thought the corsets of yore so appalling. Surely jeans like those Agata had been wearing on Sunday were worse, grabbed and squeezed in more uncomfortable places? He'd certainly hate to wear them. He stifled a slight shudder. If research were done would it show that the narrow hips of Polish women were due, like the narrowed ribs of Victorian women, to continual wearing from an early age of very tight miniskirts and hip-huggers? So that the body mass was shot, like toothpaste from a tube, upwards into the breast area, giving Polish women those very good figures. Of course, their long legs were natural from birth.

So let's see, motives: physical attraction…and she was rather lively, talkative…like the pianist girl; that one was talkative too. She babbled away at him and he was close to a complete stranger. Konstanty rarely laughed, but a corner of his lip lifted as he remembered some of her expressions.

He tucked his tie back and went on with his typing.

In the apartment below, the day was waning. Hania was counting the hours till she could sleep. The previous hours had passed somehow. Maks had brooded. Kalina had again woken late and again claimed to feel unwell. Hania hoped she wasn't going to fall ill for real and need to be taken to a doctor or anything like that. There was Konstanty Radzimoyski upstairs, of course, but somehow she doubted that he was a pediatrician. Or was Kalina too old for a pediatrician? Here she'd been a teenager just a short while ago and already she felt as if she knew nothing about them. This one was a closed book anyway.

"Kalina, do you know where your parents went?" She didn't like prying for information from the children, or letting on how helpless she was, but she was beginning to be a little desperate. Somehow, she had this feeling that Wiktor and Ania might not be back on Thursday—or Friday. Nothing definite. Just twenty-some years as a member of the Lanski family.

"To the sea, I think," Kalina spoke in that dead voice. Really, the girl looked very unhappy. Or maybe she really was unwell.

"Where on the sea?"

"I dunno. Sometimes they go to this posh hotel in Gdansk or Sopot or someplace. It's called the Neptune or the Royal or something. It's where all the rich people go."

"What do they do there?"

"Well, what do you think a man and a woman do in a hotel?"

She should have had an answer to that, Hania thought later. She shouldn't have let herself be put off so easily. There should have been some way of getting around it without discussing Kalina's parents' sex life with her. Still, she hadn't been able to think of any at once. All that had come to mind was "Oh, not Wiktor, surely," and she could hardly have said that.

And then later Kalina had disappeared again and she'd had no one to question at all. Maks certainly wasn't going to tell her anything. So she cooked, and cleaned, and played scales, and ran through, in her mind, one piece of music after another. She was very gifted this way; she could turn on the music like switching on a radio, and it accompanied her through the hours, when her only other comfort was food. So Tuesday had passed.

Wednesday had started as a repeat of the day before. Some time in the afternoon Kalina got up off the sofa, put on a skirt that was an eight-inch band of cloth, a halter that didn't begin to reach the band, and four-inch platform sandals, and headed for the door. She wasn't pretty enough to make such exposure attractive or anything but a lurid come-on.

"Where are you going?" Hania asked anxiously, surging out of a chair as if to stop her, as she saw her pass.

"Just out." Kalina was already at the door, already through and banging it a little behind her.

She could hardly run after the girl and stop her, Hania thought with exasperation, but what if Kalina didn't come back till late, what if she got into trouble? She stood still in the middle of the room.

Maks was watching. He said, "She's going to church."

"To church?"

"To see someone."

"Oh." Hania was taken aback. Was that really what one wore to church in Poland? "Oh, that's all right then."

"No, it's not all right. It's a sin."

"A sin?" How could going to church be a sin?

"That's what Kalina says. Kalina's a sinner." Maks went back to his lego blocks, his face inscrutable.

I want out of here, thought Hania.

Ten minutes later Hania left the apartment with Maks trailing reluctant and resentful to the rear. On the stairs down they came across a middle-aged man stumbling up, a bottle clutched in one hand. He raised the bottle at them in salute. "I wish you…your very good …very healthy…healthy…health." And staggered past. "Thank you," thought Hania, rather pleased, every good wish helps.

Then they were out in the street, blinking in the sunlight after the dim interior. "Where are we going," Maks whined. "I don't want to go anywhere."

"We're going to sit on a park bench and eat ice cream."

She saw him open his mouth to say, "I don't like ice cream," but then he shut it again and began to walk. Aha.

The trees of Ujazdowski Park were cool and overarching and green. The water of the shallow lake was a dark mirror surface broken by the flickering movement of golden carp. A small waterfall trickled over boulders. Wide gravel paths stretched away in calm serenity. How good it is here, thought Hania, closing her eyes. I could sit in this spot unmoving for hours; I could imagine myself in tune with nature and the humming humanity beyond.

Maks scrambled over the rocks of the waterfall, lost his shoe in the stream, and shrieked. Hania tried to help him and got her skirt wet. A gray-haired woman left her own tidy and obedient grandchildren and came to scold them both loudly.

Tomorrow Wiktor and Ania will come back, Hania thought, as she made dinner later and Maks ignored her. Tomorrow, tomorrow, tomorrow, she thought, mangling Shakespeare, or I'll light someone the way to dusty death. Only she wouldn't, of course. And poor children. What was it that made them the way they were? Most Polish children were so polite and sane. Destined, perhaps, to grow rather narrow, but that was the average lot in every country. These kids were... emotionally disturbed wasn't exactly the word for Maks, or was it? And what was eating Kalina? Why did they both repudiate her so aggressively? Okay, so she was a bit repulsive with her great bulges and tent of a dress, not the kind to appeal instantly to a teenage girl or a small boy, but still—you'd think they'd be glad of any sort of support in their situation. Only, as she well knew, neither children nor adults could be expected to behave rationally. So it was no surprise to her when Kalina didn't reappear at once.

But nine o'clock came, and then ten, and no Kalina. Maks refused to go to bed and Hania didn't feel like insisting. She was drooping with weariness. The effort of keeping her eyes open seemed superhuman and prompted images of propping the lids apart with toothpicks. If only Kalina would come back, then she'd just have Thursday to get through. She wouldn't expect Wiktor and Ania tomorrow, but they'd come on Friday. Please, please, please.

And maybe she'd meet Konstanty Radzimoyski again at the grocery. At seven. He'd been there at seven twice. A small voice told her that it would be wiser to go at seven fifteen and avoid him—that it wouldn't do at all to develop a crush on him—and although that is the sort of small voice that young women almost always ignore, she had a strong desire not to be ridiculous. The crush, though, she admitted to herself—the crush was already firmly in place. It had been in place since she was six, since that day in the Radzimoyskis' kitchen when Konstanty had saved her. It had remained there all through those years abroad, through her teens and early twenties, through music and studies. She had always had the incident at the back of her mind, always thought that if someone else came along she would measure him by that standard. Would he be capable of behaving like that?

Of course, no one had come along. She had had her yardstick ready and not a single taker had come by to be measured. There had been no need for her to turn anyone down. No one had even asked her for a date. And yet she was of a very romantic and loving nature. Had anyone shown a little interest or a little kindness she would have flung Konstanty's image aside like a used rag.

Somewhere, in the midst of these thoughts, her head dropped onto her chest and she fell asleep.

It was the click of the door shutting that woke her. She raised her head, thinking through her sleep, "Good, Kalina's come back, I can go to bed." But when she opened her eyes the apartment was strangely empty. Maks wasn't sitting in front of the television anymore; the television wasn't even on. She stood up abruptly and looked about. No one was there. "Maks!" she called. "Maksiu!" No answer. Well, he wouldn't answer. Quickly, rubbing the sleep away, growing momentarily more awake and worried, she scurried through the apartment looking for him. No Maksymilian. The truth dawning on her, she ran back through the apartment, bumping awkwardly into corners and doorframes as she went, until she reached the front door and tried to open it. It was locked on the outside.

She pounded on it. No response. "Maks!" She hissed through the crack. "Maks! Open the door!" There was no response, only silence. She put her ear to the door and listened hard, holding her breath. No sound, no movement reached her. She straightened, panting.

So there she was, locked in. And Maks, her six-year-old charge, Maks whom she was supposed to be taking care of, was gone. She had a moment of furious anger at Wiktor and Ania. Stupid, irresponsible parents! And of anguish—what if something happened to him? And of remorse—she'd be responsible.

And there was nothing to do about it. A moment's reflection convinced her that even if she could scream loudly enough to be heard by the neighbors, they still wouldn't be able to get her out and they wouldn't find Maks unless he wanted to be found. Hopefully he was with Kalina. Please let him be with Kalina. She paced back and forth.

The minutes passed, then half an hour. She went periodically to the window—to each window in the apartment—to see if she could spot Maks or Kalina in the street. She saw her friendly drunkard of the other day; he was leaning against a building with one hand, and as she was wondering whether to call to him, "have you seen a small boy?" he subsided onto the sidewalk and lay inert. An occasional passer-by walked with quick steps along the pavement and disappeared, and an occasional dark cat flitted across the street, but her relatives didn't reappear. She suspected—hoped—they were sitting on the bottom step of the building. And she hoped that Maks was very tired. But she couldn't be sure.

She picked up the telephone and dialled a number in the States. "Hallo, Tato?" Her father had gotten her into this; maybe he'd have some idea how to get her out. No, she didn't really believe that, she just had no one else to turn to. "Tato, Wiktor and Ania went off and left me with their children and now Kalina has disappeared and Maks has locked me in the apartment."

"So how was the funeral? Were there lots of people?"

"I missed the funeral. The plane was delayed. Maks has locked me in the apartment."

"Good, good. So how's Wiktor? How's Ania? Is everyone healthy?"

Hania took a deep breath.

"Tato, Maks has locked me in the apartment and disappeared. It's eleven o'clock at night."

"Eleven o'clock? Yes, I always forget about the time difference. So how's Warsaw?"

Hania stifled a desire to scream. Why would he never listen?

"Tato! Wiktor and Ania left me with their children and now they've disappeared. What should I do?"

"Whoooo's disappeared?"

"Wiktor. Ania. Kalina. And worst of all—Maks."

"What are you saying?"

Hania could see him shaking his head, unwilling to understand, to get involved, to have to make decisions. She could hear the note of self-pity creeping into his voice.

"You know, I don't understand what you're saying. I don't know why you always have these problems.

I thought you'd be a help to Wiktor, you know, Babcia just died and—"

"I know. Should I call the police?"

"About Babcia?"

Why had she called? She'd known how it would be. Between a theoretical physicist and a composer of weird music there wasn't much to choose. She said good-bye quickly and put down the phone.

She went into the kitchen. She should have been ready for an emergency. She should have stocked up on chocolate.

After making herself a cup of tea, she ate four slices of toast with sugar, and then because Maks still hadn't come back, she ate four more, and then she went into the piano room, sat down by the Beckstein, and leaned her head on the rim. On consideration, she didn't think Maks was running around the streets. Maks slept with the light on in his room. He was hiding in the building or he was with Kalina. There was nothing she could do but wait. Sometime, in the early hours of the morning, she lifted her head for a moment and watched as two figures tiptoed into the apartment.

Konstanty, seeing Hania at the grocery store in the morning, considered that she looked like a heart patient after an unsuccessful operation. Not one of his, of course.

"Good morning *pani*, any luck with the job hunting?"

"No, I think I'm stuck as a babysitter for the moment. Unless I can get something to do at home."

On a sudden impulse he thought he'd probably regret later, he said, "I may have a job for you—of course, I don't know if you'd be interested…it's not much, a little typing and editing really…"

"I'm sure I'd be…" don't sound so eager, she told herself, and ended the sentence on an entirely lower key—"interested."

So, thought Konstanty on his way to work, maybe that was a mistake, but probably not. He wondered what she'd make of his writing, felt almost a little anxious about it—not very, just that tiniest little uneasiness. He had asked her some question; he forgot what, something about her reading habits, to see if she actually had any literary interests. He'd got more of a reply than he expected.

Pianists, she said, were supposed to know literature. There were so many links between literature and music. The themes of novels, she continued, went by nations. English novels were about requited love, she said. (Any other Polish woman would have batted her eyes at him at that point. She didn't even blink. There was no need for him to let a twinkle show in his eye, to smile his three-quarter Mona Lisa smile. Had he missed it?) French novels, she said, were about love, disillusionment, and self-knowledge—and more love, and more self-knowledge. American novels were all about struggle—for money, position, survival, something. In American novels it was always a battle. In Russian novels it was all suffer, sin, and suffer. Polish novels, whatever their ostensible subject, were only about Poland, always and *toujours* Poland. And then he'd had to admit that indeed, he was writing about Poland, but it wasn't a novel…

So, okay, maybe he, like other Poles, had his country a bit too much on his mind, but really, where else in the world would one find a prince and a pianist discussing literature while standing over a barrel of pickles? Or was that just his romanticizing view? If one looked at them differently, weren't they just two perfectly ordinary people chatting as they waited in line? Or—an unintentional illustration of Jack Sprat and his wife?

Although Konstanty could be charming when he wished, his general austerity of manner was such that few people realized he had a sense of humor.

He walked into the gray-floored hall of the hospital, down the corridor toward his examining room in the cardiology department. His colleague Jacek, middle-aged, round, and jolly, was ushering in a patient while humming a tune—something about a "heart beating to the rhythm of the cha-cha." Jacek was always singing, and he told his patients off-color jokes in a way that rather scandalized Konstanty, trained in a different tradition. Jacek's patients adored him, spoke easily to him as to a friend, left him with smiles on their faces; Konstanty's patients treated him with deference and reserve and left him with grateful little bows. One accepted the limitations of one's character and did the best one could. So, all right, his best wasn't at the level of Jacek's, but he knew he was doing good and that was tremendously important to him.

It had surprised him, a little, when he had come back to Poland, that there were so many other doctors——and nurses—in the country who had not taken the opportunity to go elsewhere, who were also willing to work for a pittance, for the disinterested reason of helping their fellow humans. Not, certainly, that he had wished to consider himself unique in any way, only it had struck him, coming from abroad, where his position was so clearly linked with economic advantage. Well, yes, there were a few doctors in the hospital, he knew, who took bribes, a few even whose avarice might be described as extortion, but that there were such numbers of the others gave him hope, whenever he was inclined to feel discouraged about his country's future.

Hania, with the prospect of the job from Konstanty to sustain her, found the day almost bearable. She didn't say anything to the children about the previous night, she just hoped, hoped, hoped, that their parents would come back. She also found the house keys and put them in her pocket. She had brought a newspaper from the kiosk, and had marked several possible apartments for rent. Tonight, she would get the work from Konstanty, and tomorrow Wiktor and Ania would come back, and as soon as she could she would move out. It would be awkward, of course, but she would do it. She could afford to spend two months in a small, rented apartment, if she had work. She would enjoy a child-free summer and maybe sometimes she would talk to Konstanty about his writing. It would be lonely but anything was better than her pariah status here.

The telephone rang in the middle of the afternoon. She dived for it, almost choking on a bit of sandwich.

"Hania," it was Wiktor's voice.

"Waaugh."

"Hania, listen."

She hated sentences that began that way; they always ended badly for her.

"We can't get back for a while."

She'd known it—she'd been sure that's what would happen—she'd steeled herself for what to say. She took a deep breath in order to blast Wiktor with "No! You get back here and take care of your children! You can't use me this way!"

But he was saying, "Haniu, *kochanie*, you're a life-saver, we're so grateful, how could we manage without you? I'm mentioning you to everyone I'm meeting here —I think I've got a concert arranged—"

"No! I don't want anything arranged for me!" and there she was, arguing about concerts and completely derailed and then unable to get a word in. But this is ridiculous, she thought, I have to tell him to come home. She took her deep breath again.

"Wiktor, listen!"

"Haniu, *kochanie*, I have to end now." And the line went dead in the middle of her shriek of "Nooo!"

She listened to the silence for a moment and then slammed the receiver down, fuming. Kalina and Maks were watching.

"Are they coming back?" asked Kalina in a rather sneering tone.

"I don't know. I suspect you're stuck with me for a while."

Kalina shrugged; then she reached under one of the sofa pillows, pulled out a small plastic object, stuck it in her mouth, and began to suck on it. Hania stared, unable to see at first what the object was. Then she realized. Kalina was sucking on a pacifier. Somehow this upset her more than anything that had happened before.

"It's mine," whined Maks, "I want it."

"It isn't yours," said Kalina, taking the pacifier out for a second. "I found it in the park." She put it back in her mouth and sucked as she watched the television.

"I want one too." Maks' lip was trembling.

Hania said, "Maks, if you really want one, I'll buy you one tomorrow."

"I don't want anything from you! Why don't you go away?" he shouted and flung out of the room.

Hania felt for the children, since they'd clearly been abandoned, and because, more clearly, they were accustomed to it. But as they appeared to want none of her, there was not much she could do for them.

She took her laptop out and considered the paper beside her with Konstanty's handwriting. Those first words might be 'the neolithic peoples' or 'till narcolepsy prevails.' He had walked back to the apartment with her from the grocery store and handed her a large stack of papers. The handwriting was appalling—a series of mountain peaks peppered with stray accent marks. "I'm writing something on the order of a brief history for foreigners," he had said, "nothing scholarly, you understand, just a sort of hopefully readable, rough outline to fit into a guide with a lot of economic information. It's for my sister's PR company—she thought it would amuse me to choose what goes in and what stays out, since I've always loved history. And it has afforded me some pleasure, I admit. But I type at the speed of—well, let's just say, any bird hunting and pecking at that speed would die of hunger"—there had been that flash of amusement, so quickly disappearing—"and I have doubts about my English…" His English was quite good, actually, thought Hania, rather British-accented. "We weren't required to write a lot in medical school." That slight, deprecating smile again. "Then, too, I'd like another opinion about what to leave in and out—this is intended, you see, for people whose knowledge of the country, even though they may be considering investing here, will probably be very limited." The choices were good, she thought, but the writing was rather convoluted. Some—no, a lot—of the sentences needed rewriting. They were fairly grammatical, but not constructed in the way a native English-speaker would speak or write.

There was an email. Konstanty had written to her. She stared at the heading for a moment before clicking on it: *Respected Madam, I am eager to know whether in your opinion the text that I gave you is in need of much work?*

She hesitated. It wouldn't do to be fulsome or gushing, to say 'oh thank you for writing to me, I feel so much less lonely now.' And besides it did need work. She had a curious image of her grandmother standing beside a piano student.

Respected Sir—that was how one began letters in Polish—*Yes.*

She clicked send, and very quickly received an answer.

Respected Madam, I am obliged for your prompt and laconic reply. I was not aware that it was as unacceptable as your answer leads me to believe. I wonder if you could elaborate?

Respected Sir, In English, one says and writes, 'I'm going for a walk.' Polish people say 'I'm going for a walk,' and write 'I intend to fulfil the concept of performing the action of going for a walk.'

Respected Madam, I retire, carrying my wounded pride on a stretcher.

Oh dear. Was he joking? Had she hurt his feelings? *Respected Sir, It's very interesting. You are joking about the stretcher?*

Respected Madam, Yes.

By evening she had corrected several pages of text. Maks had disappeared after his outburst, which should have put her on her guard, but she was wrapped up in her reading.

The Slavonian tribes, Procopius writes, governed themselves in democratic fashion, without a leader, 'and therefore they are all concerned with what is successful and what detrimental…and agree on everything together…' The Slavs agreed so well that they often, curiously, turned to outsiders for leadership…

Konstanty had added in the margin: *Would it be better to write—'a jealous guardianship of their equality persisted through the centuries…'?* Of course, she realized that he must have written the words for himself, before he had any idea that she would be working on the text, but for a moment she had the pleasing illusion that he was asking her opinion.

Mieszko, a 10th century duke with whom the beginnings of the Polish state are connected, may have been of a Danish royal family. He had two wives: the first was a Christian noblewoman from the Czech lands; the second was a German nun, whom he abducted from the monastery of Kalbe.

Hania smiled at this, but besides the occasional images of prosperity and developing culture, of a land rich in *'grain, meat, honey, and fish'* with stone palaces and cathedrals going up, some of it, of course, made her blood run rather cold:

Mieszko also engaged in marriage-making. He had 3,000 men in armour and paid for their children's marriages, says the chronicler Ibn Jakub. His own daughter, Sigrid the Haughty, married the kings of Sweden and Denmark respectively, was famed for her 'exuberant lifestyle' (she burned two of her suitors alive), and became the mother of King Canute. Another daughter—or sister, the chronicles aren't certain—one Adelaida, was mother of the first king of Hungary, who became Saint Stephen.

Adelaida, however, 'drank excessively and rode on horseback like a knight. Once she even killed, in an access of furious rage, one of her husbands...'

Mieszko's son Bolesław behaved better with his unwanted wives; he simply sent them back to their parents. With his political opponents, however, he was harsher, ordering their eyes to be put out. Such were the times, and such ferocities common across Europe.

Konstanty had written at the bottom of the page, and then crossed out: *Think, for instance, of the 15,000 Bulgarian soldiers taken prisoner by the Byzantine Emperor Basil II in 1016, all blinded and sent home with a one-eyed guide, or of Richard I of England setting up a grandstand to watch the cold-blooded execution of 3,000 Muslim prisoners in the succeeding century.*

Hania sat for a moment, contemplating. One could skim over things like this in history books. Not let them really sink in. These things had to be left padded by the layers of years in between or the sense of revulsion became too strong. Shuddering away the images of pain and gore, she turned back to the text, and began to rearrange a sentence.

Maks appeared at her side. That was unusual. He actually looked like he'd gotten over his anger, like he wanted something from her. She felt a little surge of warmth towards him. She had an impulse to click off the text before he saw it, but then remembered he couldn't read English. Actually, she didn't know if he could read at all.

"Maks, can you read?"

"Of course." He pushed his glasses up and regarded her with his disdainful, owlish eyes. "But why should I read when there's the television? It says on the news that there's a murderer around."

She should pay attention to what he watched, she realized. Children shouldn't watch the news.

"Yes. A murderer of children. He chops them up with a knife."

What did one say to that? Oh, surely not? Not here in Warsaw. Hardly ever anywhere? Err…

"Well, I'm sure you're quite safe, Maks. There are a couple billion children in the world and the murder statistics among them are miniscule. Um…There aren't any murderers here, I'm sure." So why did she have that creepy feeling down her spine now? Drat Maks. He gave her a long look and turned on his heel. "I'm going to bed," he called over his shoulder.

Hania went on typing for a while, then rose, made sure the apartment door was locked, made sure the chain was in place, and prepared to take a shower. Both children appeared to be asleep. She wandered from room to room, peering into each; she didn't know why. She had an urge to lift the curtains, to look behind them before she turned her back.

The apartment was large and eerily empty-seeming. Steamy in the hot weather. In the bathroom she piled her heavy brown hair on top of her head, and paused for a moment to look over her shoulder. The door was closed. It was difficult to get over the sides of the high tub. She pulled the curtain, let the water run. In the shower one heard nothing. Somehow she didn't like that. She turned the water off a time or two and listened, but no sounds reached her. Why did she have that strange feeling? Almost gooseflesh in spite of the heat.

She got out of the tub, dried herself, and let down her hair, feeling all the time that she should hurry, hurry, and telling herself that that was ridiculous, what could have happened? She would come out and the children would be in bed sleeping, horrid as ever, but safe. She put on her nightdress and robe and opened the door. No sound. The light was on in the hall.

But what was that on the floor? Her heart gave a painful thud. A long smear of blood. And another down the hall. Dear God, no. Her mind sent her racing toward Maks. Her legs kept her rooted to the spot, shaking. She forced herself to move, to follow the red stains to Maks' room. The light was out. She batted at the wall wildly, mouth dry and hands almost powerless for trembling. Somehow she kept jerking her head over her shoulder to see if someone were there, were waiting. "Maks," she rasped, "Maks." The light sprang on. And her heart stopped. Maks lay in a heap on the bed. His arm was flung across his face and blood ran over it and around his neck, blood soaked his shirt, and a knife lay beside him in the bed.

The world reeled, time stood still—no, thought Hania, this can't be happening. No, no, no. And then: first aid measures. Was he still alive? Go to him. And ice in the veins freezing movement.

Then the world righted itself. Still shaking, she crossed the room, reached for the bottle lying half under the bed covers, turned about, and left the room, snapping out the light as she went. She stalked into the kitchen, threw the ketchup into the garbage bin, and returned to her room. She lay down on her bed and stared at the ceiling, relief and rage and shock washing over her in turns. It was such an old trick but who would have thought a six-year-old could make it so real?

A loud wail arose from down the hall. It was Maks. "Heeeelllppp! I'm afraid of the daaaaark!!! Kaliiii-ina!!!" And louder: "Kaaaaliiiina!!!"

Sometime later Hania rose and went into the pi-ano room. Holding down the soft pedal to muffle the sound, she began to play scales. Up and down, up and down. The noise was just enough to take the edge off Maks' sobs. This way she could think. Something had to be done about these children. They needed help and she didn't think a psychologist would fit the bill—even if she had the authority to take them to one, which she didn't. So she had to be the help. At least she had to do what she could while she was here. Maks needed atten-tion and Kalina needed comfort. Actually, she thought Kalina was a harder case than Maks, but she'd have to try for her too. She looked across the piano top at the photo of Babcia with the singer…You did this Babcia, she felt like saying, you had no time for your children, you left them with nannies, you wouldn't listen to them, you were unkind and authoritative and denigrating; you made sure they'd grow up to behave the same to their children. Had Babcia been treated that way herself? Each generation was responsible for the next, and eve-ryone was required to help out where possible. She hadn't intended to come to Warsaw to be a surrogate mother, but that's what had been handed her. She'd bet-ter put her mind to doing it well, at least for the short time she would be here.

Maks was still crying in his bedroom. Why didn't Kalina go to him? She left the piano, peeked into the girl's room and found her sleeping, curled in a ball with a pillow over her head. She went to Maks, turned on the light, and sat down on his bed.

"Truce, Maksiu.

4

She was up early, working at her laptop. She wrote an email to Konstanty: *Respected Sir, I'm sending back the parts I've done:*

By Mieszko's time, the slave trade had existed for over a millennium, first as the prisoners of inter-tribal warfare were sold to Roman traders, later from raids of the Vikings and Slavs living along the Baltic. Sometimes also, impoverished parents sold their children.

Sell Maks? Hmm, there was an idea.

...The adoption of Christianity did nothing to stop the practice. Bolesław the Wrymouth, a 12th century king of Poland, supposedly took 8,000 maidens and children to sell after he conquered Pomerania. Czechs, Danes, and Poles sold one another back and forth. Prague, too close to Poland for comfort, joined Dublin and Marseille as a European center of the export trade to Muslim and Byzantine markets.

Isn't it appalling, Hania added as a postscript, *that the slave trade still goes on in our day?...At least old women are now safer. The numbers you give of those executed in Poland over the centuries for witchcraft are also bloodcurdling—even if they were less than in the Holy Roman Empire or France. Still, it's rather intriguing what you say about the end of the pagan rites on Mt. Łysogóra and Mt. Ślęża, and how witches were later said to come there riding on broomsticks. It's like the Walpurgis Night celebrations on the Brocken mentioned in Goethe, isn't it?*

'…the whole length of the mountain side,
The witch-song streams in a crazy tide.'
Do you suppose women really did gather on the moun-
tains?

Hania added a word or two about the number of
marriages recounted in the text, and sent the message
off. Then she sat thinking about women who were
witches and warriors. She rose and went to a bookshelf
that covered one wall to head height. It was way too
early to wake the children yet. It was the time change
that had pulled her out of bed at this hour. She stood
before the books. They were practically lost under
sheaves of music that had been stuffed in over the tops
of the bindings, but by lifting the papers she could see
beneath. There were the usual books of music theory, a
number of lives of great composers and pianists, corre-
spondence between musicians, and the usual array of
Polish classics: Reymont, Żeromski, Orzeszkowa, Dąb-
rowska, the Nobel Prize winner Sienkiewicz. She paused
before his *Deluge*. There, that was exactly what she was
thinking of: what a revolting passage that was where the
patriotic young woman thinks her fiancé has joined the
wrong side during the Swedish invasion and sternly
consents to his execution. What a strain of iron in the
soul. Like the young woman insurgent of the Warsaw
Uprising in 1944, who composed the song '*hey boys, get
your bayonets out.*' Brrr. Hania shivered. She'd posed for
the mermaid statue too, that one; it's holding a sword,
of course.

Well, thought Hania, she was glad none of the
Polish women she knew displayed those martial capaci-
ties, and as for herself, she was just a young musician,
whose life had revolved around piano practice, who had
lived rather too long in America, and who was begin-

ning to doubt her ability to cope with practical matters. Perhaps if she ate something, then dealing with the children wouldn't seem so bad. Determination always carried one through, she thought, as she finished off four eggs.

She prepared breakfast for the children, and then sat at a piano and played reveille fortissimo with the sustain pedal down, and when that didn't rouse them, she marched down the hall, banging on their doors: Kalino! Maksiu! Get up! We have important things to discuss!

"What? What's so important?" Kalina growled as she sat beside Maks at the kitchen table. "Why'd you wake us up like this?"

Hania could see that curiosity was gnawing them, keeping their rudeness just slightly in check.

"I'll tell you when you've eaten." A pause. "And it might be your last meal for a long time, so eat up. Go on." She folded her hands on the table and waited, her face calm.

Maks looked at her with interest, Kalina gave her a half glance under the lids and a small sneering lift of the lip, but both started to eat.

She waited until they were finished.

"So the deal is this. Your parents didn't leave any money. No money equals no food. I have a little, but, if I'm going to spend it, I'm going to need some cooperation. Look, we're all in this together, aren't we?

"I hate them." Said Kalina with vehemence. "They make me sick."

"Okay," said Hania, recruiting her ideas. "Okay. But what we need here are some positive ideas. Hating people won't help."

"It's fun, though," said Maks positively.

"No, no. It doesn't do any good. The point is—we're stuck here together, we don't know when your parents are coming back, and we have to get along. We can make life miserable for each other, or we can help each other out. Which do you think would be best?"

"I thought you were here to take care of us," said Kalina angrily. "Why should we help you?"

"I didn't come here to take care of you. You're old enough to take care of yourself, aren't you?"

"Yes."

"And old enough to take care of Maks."

No answer.

"So since we're two adults living here, I suggest we treat each other with courtesy—like saying if we're going out somewhere—and we divide up the chores, and divide up looking after Maks—you could watch him for, say, two hours in the afternoon, and then, probably I won't mind spending my money—my own hard-earned money—on food. Otherwise..." She let a long silence follow. "Maks can help out too."

"What can I help out with?" Maks looked alarmed.

"You could take your plate to the sink, things like that."

Kalina got up from the table without saying anything and left the room.

After this, Hania didn't know if she'd scored a total failure or only a partial one. Her brief period of enthusiasm waned sharply. How could she think she could help? She could only hope the situation wouldn't last long. Maks played with his toy cars and she worked on the history. She had an email. She opened it in excitement: it didn't matter that it was only about the work, it made her feel she wasn't alone. Konstanty had addressed each of her comments.

Respected Madam,…Do you really think I spend too much time on marriages? I think they're rather important, but perhaps I was brought up to pay over much attention to genealogical matters. Still, just think: Charlemagne was making arrangements to marry Irene, Empress of Byzantium. If the marriage had gone through how differently history might have unrolled— both for the world, if the empires were united, and for Charlemagne personally (she is thought to have done away with her son, the Emperor Constantine, and why should she have stopped there?) …

Respected Sir,…was the murdered son the Byzantine ruler who sent Charlemagne a fabulous organ?

Hania looked up. Here was Maks again at her side. He probably had some horror for her. He wouldn't talk to her otherwise. He sat down beside her, not looking at her, kicking his feet. "You promised you'd eat a shoe and you didn't."

"Maks, I never promised. I never said 'I promise.' You can't twist things people say to you." On the other hand, did she remember exactly what she'd said? Maybe she'd given that impression. And he was clearly holding out an—so to speak—olive branch.

Respected Sir, May I ask a medical question? Will I be harmed by eating a small piece of leather?

Respected Madam, Re: the small piece of leather. I presume we are considering a very small piece here. I am not a gastroenterologist but my guess is that the tannins, etc. are unlikely to be of sufficient quantity to cause lasting damage. The possibility of choking should, however, be considered, and the portion to be consumed should be suitably reduced and masticated. In regards to the necessity itself, I think it comes down to the following: if there was a promise, then there's no question, if it kills you, you have to perform it. If there was no promise, then why ever?

Respected Sir, There was no promise, but I'm trying to win him over.

Respected Madam, Bon appétit.

The next days passed without incident. She had no need to put her threat into action. The children regarded her warily, but were tolerably polite and helpful. Still, she had a feeling they were waiting for something.

"You really don't know where your parents went?" she said one morning to Kalina, when the prospect of the week ahead seemed too daunting. Kalina took her pacifier out of her mouth and after considering a moment, deigned an answer.

"They went to meet some people to talk about a film. Tata is making the music for it."

Goodness. What kind of film could that be?

"They were going to Gdansk and then to Berlin——someplace in Germany anyway."

Germany!

"You really don't know when they'll come back?"

"I don't want them to come back." She burst into tears. Hania stared at her, distressed. The tears ran down the girl's childish face. What on earth was the matter with her? She put out a tentative hand in sympathy but Kalina brushed it away.

Here was Maks, sitting on the other side of her. "I'm bored." That was his latest method for making her uncomfortable. He followed her around saying "I'm bored" like a broken record and refusing any of her suggestions for entertainment.

"Maks, can't you see your sister's unhappy?"

"Kalina's...."

Kalina tried to hit him around Hania, and got Hania instead.

"Kalina's....what?" thought Hania, as she sat at the piano, touching the keys slowly. C, C sharp, D. Involved in drugs? Kalina and Maks didn't usually fight. What was it that she had had to keep him from saying?

Here was Maks again. "I'm bored." Maybe it was better when he was ostracizing her. "I'm bored."

"Maks, can you play the piano?"

"No." A fierce look, very reminiscent of his grandmother. "Babcia said I have no talent."

"Mm. She said that about me, too. And then everyone thought I was brilliant."

"So why do you just play da-di-dum-da"—he sang a very good approximation of a scale—"like that?"

"Well, it's a long story. Come, sit here on the piano bench. Sit up straight, hands like so…"

He tried a key or two and began to bang hard on A flat. "Tata makes music like this."

"Er. Yes. But I think we'll start with something else."

"I saw the most enormous young woman going into the Lanskis'," said Pelagia to Konstanty, as he let her into the apartment. "A piano student pressed into babysitting, I suppose. You'd think she'd break the bench. Really, she was like this." Her hands gestured widely around her own slim hips as she dropped her designer handbag on a sofa and sank down beside it with gracefully crossed ankles.

Konstanty regarded his sister. For facial features, Pelagia might have been Queen Jadwiga come to life.

Really, why had he never thought of it before? The picture of Jadwiga's tomb effigy came to mind. Only Pelagia, slim in a straw-colored linen suit, had none of Jadwiga's inner demureness.

"So how's the history coming?"

"It's coming. I gave it to the"—his hands imitated her gesture of roundness—"to type and correct. She's Natalia Lanska's granddaughter. She's being very helpful."

Pelagia raised her eyebrows, made a little moue. "Oh, okay." She forgot the subject immediately, moved on to other topics. She was very different from her brother. She spoke whatever came into her mind, moved impulsively and joyously from one activity to another, and threw herself into the organization of gala balls and charity events with a clear sense of mission to advertise the family and keep it in history, or at least in the illustrated journals. That she belonged to an expanding public relations firm and was married to a wealthy German banker both made her task easier. (Actually, the German banker, however estimable, was a bit of a come-down, but no appropriate member of royalty, even minor, had had the sense to notice her by the time she turned thirty-three, and she was one to make the best of things.)

"So are you coming to my house-warming party tonight or have you got a shift?"

Pelagia had just bought a large villa in Konstancin.

"I haven't got a shift. But I invited the girl downstairs out for a drink."

Pelagia looked her surprise. He could see her hastily wondering if she had said something she shouldn't.

"Oh. A business meeting, I suppose."

"Of course."

Actually, he'd thought that Hania needed to get out; that it was hard on her, being locked up with the children. He'd felt sorry for her—as another human being—that was all. But he didn't say any of this to his sister. Unlike Pelagia, he was reserved, complex, capable of seeing two sides to every question, of seeing himself from a distance. Anyone he met at the café would assume it was a business meeting.

"I find her rather interesting."

Pelagia looked doubtful. As if even friendship might find it difficult to get past the extra layers.

Pelagia, Konstanty considered, had this in common with every Pole—that appearances were tremendously important. But he was very fond of his sister, and knew he had faults too. She probably thought he was stiff and a little dull, if nothing worse. Good family relations depended on not pointing out a sibling's defects.

"I'll stop in later," he promised.

Hania stood before a mirror, trying her hair this way and that. Kalina appeared behind her.

"I like it up like that."

Hania turned in surprise, blushing a little. Kalina was regarding her critically.

"I could give you a clip to hold it."

"Thank you." She considered a moment then shook her head, "But I don't want to look like I tried to make an improvement."

"Do you have a date?" Kalina asked curiously. She almost sounded friendly.

"No. Just—I'm going out to have a coffee or something with Mr. Radzimoyski from upstairs. To talk about this work you know I've been doing for him."

"Well, maybe something will come of it," Kalina suggested hopefully.

That was nice of her, thought Hania as she shook her head; I know she thinks I'm a totally hopeless case.

The telephone rang and Kalina went to answer it. No, Hania thought, looking at herself in the mirror again and letting her hair fall down onto her shoulders, there was nothing she could do to get ready for her first date. Only why should she imagine it was that? Don't be silly, don't be ridiculous. It was a business meeting. Well, not business exactly, but something like that. There was no need at all for those butterflies in the stomach. She felt the way she felt before a major piano competition. She took some deep breaths.

Every dress she had looked exactly as shapeless as the next. It was a choice between black shapeless sack or brown shapeless bag. She flipped through the hangers in the closet: Blue sack, black sack, beige sack. All she could do was brush her hair and polish her shoes. She tended to forget about her shoes, she couldn't see them unless she took them off. She held one up and rubbed the toe. Anyway, it was all just her imagining. But what did it hurt if she imagined a little? He would never know it wasn't a 'business meeting' for her. It would be like a piano competition. One was nervous beforehand, and then one would walk out to perform and it would be all right.

She emerged from the bedroom and found the children in front of the television. They'd be fine together for a couple of hours, Kalina had said. Kalina had been almost pleasant about it.

"Mama just called," she barely lifted her head, sounding uninterested. "She's coming back to pick up some paintings. She says she'll be here in an hour."

In an hour? No! thought Hania. "But I have to speak to her," she exclaimed in dismay. "And I have to go out!"

Kalina just pulled on a strand of hair and didn't look at her.

But, but, but…thought Hania. The first date of my life and she picks tonight to come back?

"I should be leaving right now."

Konstanty had said he'd meet her at the café. Calm, be calm, she told herself. She had to make a choice. Okay. She wasn't staying in, no matter what it cost—even if it meant spending the whole summer with the children.

"Please will you ask your mother to call me later? Tell her it's important. Tell her I had to go out. Will you do that?"

"If I remember." Kalina spoke in a tone of total detachment.

"Maks, will you help Kalina remember?"

"I'm trying to watch this," he waved her impatiently away.

Late that evening, Hania sat in bed with the laptop propped before her, opened the email program, hesitated a moment and typed. *Respected Sir, Thank you for the lovely evening…* And then erased it. She had walked down Nowy Świat Street. There had been the two lines of 18th-century façades, arched doorways, decorated window piers, curlicued balconies, stucco swags and intricate cornices; a mass of fashionable women sweeping past—less lacquered than Manhattanites, but less haggard too—they were slim and light and natural. (And just occasionally, one with something unusual in her costume—that one, for instance, with the snakes on her fishnet stockings, winding round her legs.) And the luxury goods in the shop windows—that hat with the fluffy feathers—but what had that to do with her? She could not wear any of those things, and she had her meeting ahead. Konstanty was standing waiting for her outside the café. She saw him almost every other day or so at the grocery; there was no reason for her heart to skip a beat. Only he was so distinguished looking, so exquisitely polite as he held the door open. And then the café—a memory of plush chairs and columns and people who looked like they'd never had anything to do with communist Poland. That middle-aged woman over there with the wild hair and the brocade shawl could only belong to the theatre, but the white-headed, humorous-looking man in an expensive jean jacket, or the young woman in pearls, embroidered skirt, and pointy sandals, carrying a briefcase, what were they? The café was probably the only place she'd yet been in Poland where people weren't instantly identifiable as construction worker, government clerk, humanities teacher, nouveau-riche businessman, thug…And then they had begun to talk and she hadn't noticed her surroundings anymore at all…

Respected Sir, I really enjoyed…

Should she be writing to him on a personal note? In spite of numerous friendly conversations, she certainly couldn't consider him a friend. She didn't want to sound pathetic.

…discussing work…

She erased the message. *Dear Konstanty…*She blushed at the very words. Erase. Why couldn't she just write to him in a breezy American fashion? *Hi Kostek, Nice talking to you tonight…* She erased the words, closed the email program and went back to typing. But this part too was about a marriage. What had he thought in writing this, she wondered?

...In 1384, the grandniece of the last Piast ruler was crowned king—not queen—of Poland. Jadwiga was beautiful, multilingual, educated, refined, and ten years old. Much to her horror, within a year or two her marriage was arranged to Jagiello, Grand Duke of Lithuania, a pagan, and much her senior. Before the wedding a former fiancé came to attempt her rescue from Wawel Castle, but he was discovered and departed through a window, by a rope, while Jadwiga hewed desperately at the door with an axe. To no avail. Perhaps she gave in to pressure then, or perhaps—the official Catholic view—being very pious, she was moved by the idea of bringing Lithuania into the Christian fold. After assurances that Jagiello was not a wild animal—the chronicles mention a discreet inspection in a bath-house by a messenger——she agreed to marry him and the result was the personal union of Poland and Lithuania in 1385. Although Jadwiga continued to take part in running the country, she mostly engaged in philanthropy, and before her death from childbirth complications in 1399, sold her jewellery and clothes to finance the future University of Cracow. She was canonized in 1997 and is the patron saint of queens and of a United Europe.

Konstanty thought marriages important. Of course, a man of his background would, she knew; the marriages of his ancestors hadn't been about mutual attraction, but about alliances or wealth, and if today the wealth was no longer such an issue, she suspected there was still a definite ideal of the type of 'girl from a good family' that would be suitable. She blushed again, not liking her own thoughts.

In spite of Jadwiga's earlier, and successful, peace-making efforts, it came to bloodshed with the Teutonic Order. The battle of Grunwald in 1410, which the Order lost, was one of the largest battles in medieval Europe...(Konstanty, she saw, had scribbled in the margin, *'We love superlatives for our country, here's one')...Tens of thousands of foot soldiers were killed on both sides; 209 knights of the Teutonic Order died, and 12 Polish knights...*Twelve? Only twelve? Were the others hiding to the rear?

Although the Teutonic Order continued to be a problem for some time, and the Grand Duchy of Moscow was rising, which would be a problem for the next 500 years, and Hungary was later to be lost to the Turks, who ruled it for the next 200 years...

Was there any evidence, Hania wondered, pausing, that the inhabitants were worse off for the fact? She would have to ask Konstanty. Or did she dare? There were qualities she could be certain, from his background, he would possess: he would be honest and civic-minded, for instance. She had had experience of his kindness. Beyond that, she wasn't quite sure yet: she didn't think, from his conversation or what she had read of his writing so far, that it was the case, but there was always the possibility that he saw the past in terms of Matejko's overwrought historical paintings, saw Poland in terms of '*agonia.*' He might have exclusive metaphysical certainties; perhaps he would be offended by the suggestion that Muslim Turks could rule as well as Catholic Poles.

Here was a happier note:

...Poland-Lithuania consisted of one of the vastest territories in Europe. For the top 10% of the population, there were legal gains: Poland had an early Habeas Corpus act and one of the first parliaments in Europe; the king could make no new laws single-handedly, and any deputy could cast a vote annulling the work of the entire legislative session. This system of consensus worked well for over a century and a half.

During the two centuries of the Jagiellon period, learning, and then the Renaissance, flourished in these parts. The University of Cracow became famous for mathematics; Polish literature took off as poetry was written in the vernacular ('Poles are not geese,' wrote the poet Mikołaj Rej, 'they have their own language'); the court was full of scholars, and Copernicus, by holding that the planets moved about the sun, began a scientific revolution....

Hania noticed there was a note in the margin: *Was the rise of the vernacular a good thing? It's always mentioned as an achievement, but I'm inclined to wonder. A common language, such as Latin was, makes a universal culture, transcending borders, possible...Few things divide people as much as language. Copernicus, for instance, born in Torun of German or Polish or mixed parents, educated in Poland and Italy, speaking German and writing in Latin, was typical of the age...*

Well, these comments were quite encouraging, thought Hania, and she wasn't thinking of Polish history at all.

5

It's safer, beneath a green canopy, with a girl,
Playing on a charming lute, to lie under the eiderdown,
Than to wear a shield and kicking spur,
Or to flatten one's scalp with heavy headgear.
— Hieronim Morsztyn (c.1581-1623),
'Pleasant Advice'

Hania, opening her eyes in the morning, thought that something had changed in the room, but she couldn't think what at once. She blinked several times and looked around. The bed was still holding together, sort of; the wooden armoire was there. That chair with the ripped upholstery and the lion's-head armrests—she remembered that from her childhood. She hadn't noticed it before. Oh no, it must have been behind the stack of paintings. The paintings! The paintings were gone. She'd forgotten all about Ania coming. How could she have forgotten? She sat up abruptly. And the children wouldn't even be up. She'd have to wait to find out what Ania had said.

She dressed and went into the piano room. To her surprise Maks was already there. He was intent on the keys, pressing them very lightly so as not to make a sound. He was practicing, she realized, and was touched. He seemed to be applying the same concentrated energy to the piano that he applied to thinking up mischief. He looked up guiltily and saw her standing there.

"I didn't make noise, did I? I can't reach that pedal over there."

"No, no, it's fine. That's good that you're practicing. What did your mother say last night?"

"I don't know. I wasn't here."

"You weren't here?"

"No."

"Maksiu!" Hania had great self-control, but she came near to exploding. "How could you not have been here?"

"We went out. Kalina and I." Maks returned to his playing.

Hania strode down the hallway to Kalina's room. "Kalino! Wake up, please, Kalina. Kalino!" Kalina moaned and turned over in bed and opened one eye under her hair.

"Whaat?"

"You were supposed to tell your mother to call me last night. Maks says you went out."

"Leave me alone. I feel sick."

"But I really needed to talk to your mother. Now…"

Kalina sat up in bed, and almost shouted, "Why do you want to talk to her? To tell her to come back and take care of us? Well, she won't. We learned that a long time ago. Tata says she should go with him so she goes. And she calls up and says 'oh, my dear little children, I love you so much'"—she mimicked her mother's fluting voice—"and it's all *gówno warte*." She saw Hania wince at the vulgarity, dropped back in bed, and pulled the pillow over her head.

Then, as Hania still stood uncomfortably in the doorway, Kalina raised herself up again and said, "she leaves us with one person after another. Maks hardly even knows what she looks like. I'm his mother. Me." She jabbed a finger into her chest. "And I have been since he was three. If you don't want to stay, you can go. That's fine with us. We don't like people coming and going. We wish they'd just go." She put the pillow back over her head.

Great, thought Hania, just great. Maybe I should just pack my bags and go like Kalina says. But of course then if anything happened she'd be responsible for having abandoned them.

She needed breakfast. Lots of bread and butter, lots of sugar in her coffee and then she'd feel better. Something was lying on the table. She pounced on it. There was a stack of photos of Ania and Wiktor—Ania and Wiktor seated at a restaurant table, Ania and Wiktor beside the sea—she pushed them aside. There was a brochure for a music festival and a note. She snatched at the note. It was in two parts. *Kochanie*—My Dears— said the first part, *I'm sorry to miss you. Didn't you realize I was coming? I thought I said on the phone. Tata is having a great success.* Where? wondered Hania.

The salt air is so good for our health, we both feel so much better. We don't know when we'll be able to get back though. Tata is getting inspiration from the waves and Herr Bonner and Pan Słominski are here too. We love you so much. Be good and we'll see you before long. Hugs and kisses. Mama

The second part, below, said:

Kochana Haniu, We don't know when we'll be able to get back. Wiktor is involved in a very important project. He's doing the work for the festival and the movie...I'm starting a new series of paintings in gradations of beige, whole canvasses of beige. I'm going to call it 'Ecce Sando' and I really think it's the most significant work I've done yet. But we couldn't do it without you and we're so grateful that you offered to stay with the children this summer. Wiktor suggests that you all go to our country house in Żabia Wola for a week or two. It would be good for you all to get out of Warsaw. Hugs and kisses. Ania.

P.S. Kalina knows how to get there and the neighbors have the keys.

P.P.S. I've just sold two paintings, isn't that wonderful?

Poor, batty woman, thought Hania. She flipped through the photos, picked up the brochure and opened it. It listed the events of the festival, with biographies of some of the musicians. There was an interview with Wiktor: *...it is the single sustained chord, the minor chord, that reveals the innate sorrow and sublime beauty of our universal reality. I am definitely a minimalist, and what I am trying to do through festivals like this one is to initiate a wider audience into the potentialities immanent in this type of music. This is why my piece 'Penetration,' which we are playing for audiences here, consists in the rich interplay between a single sustained note and a single note repeated in staccato... 'Penetration' lasts for forty-three minutes....I want listeners to be moved, I want them to come out of the concert hall feeling shell-shocked. The idea came to me one night, when I was listening to a jackhammer...*

Maks came into the kitchen. Hania put down the brochure and rose to get his breakfast.

"There's a letter from your mother there," she gestured toward the paper.

He picked it up and put it down. "I can't read."

"What? You told me you could."

He shrugged. "I lied." The fact didn't seem to bother him.

"What grade are you in at school?" Polish children started later than American ones, she knew.

"I finished kindergarten last year." He added proudly, "I went to a private school."

"Oh. Was it a good school?"

"I guess." He shrugged again, adjusted his glasses. "Mama read me the advertisement. It said 'you can tell what sort of school we are by looking at all the BMWs and Mercedes in the parking lot.' I'd like to have a BMW."

"It didn't really?" Hania asked him, scandalized at his nod. *Boże*, the quantity of human folly in the world.

"Do you have friends there?"

"Ye-ny." He made an inarticulate sound that might have been either yes or no. "Next year I have to go to the school here. It's on the street over there." He jerked his head. "Like Kalina."

"Oh. Are you looking forward to that?"

"It's okay, I guess. Everyone says it's really hard but it doesn't matter because Kalina's going to teach me how to cheat."

"What?"

"Yes. Only it's harder for boys, because girls—they can put the cheat sheet under their stockings, on top of their leg here." He patted his thigh. "And wear a skirt." Obviously the idea appealed to him. "But boys can't. I'll think of a good trick though."

I'm sure you will, Maks, thought Hania. And then, as in duty bound, "You know, it's not right to cheat." Or lie, either, she thought, but we'll get to that later.

"Why not? Everybody does it."

"Oh, not everybody, surely."

"Yes. Everybody." Maks was very definite. "Everybody, everybody, everybody. Only some kids have to do it on their own and some their parents help them."

Kalina came into the kitchen in her nightdress, looking pale and puffy-eyed. She seemed to have forgotten her earlier rudeness, and spoke to Hania in a friendly-enough, if rather morose, manner.

"Maks isn't going to the private school anymore because Mama and Tata forgot to register him or pay for him or something. They'd forget we existed if they could."

What was there to answer to that? "Oh, no, I'm sure they care about you very much."

Kalina and Maks just regarded her with expressionless faces. She squirmed under their gazes.

"Okay," she agreed, putting bread and jam on the table, "okay, so maybe they only care about you a little bit."

"A tiny little bit," added Kalina forcefully.

"A weensy bit," insisted Maks. It seemed to matter to them that she agree.

"No. I don't agree. I think that if push came to shove, you'd find they showed up."

"Like for Babcia?"

Someone was knocking on the door. A heavy impatient knock.

Glad to get away from the conversation, Hania went unsuspecting to open it. She found two men standing there, with clipboards. "We're from the electricity company," they said. "The bill hasn't been paid"––one of the men shuffled through a stack of papers— "for over three months. That's nine hundred seventy-six *złoty* and forty-eight *groszy*. You can pay now or we'll turn off the electricity." He rested his hand on the clipboard and both men gazed at her expectantly.

Hania stared back and at last managed, "I expect they—the owners—just forgot. I'm sure they'll pay when they get back."

"Can't wait, I'm afraid."

"But I don't have nine hundred *złoty*. I don't even live here."

The men shrugged. "Okay. You can tell the owners that if they want the electricity turned back on they should come to the electricity company with proof of payment."

"But you can't just turn it off..."

A woman paused on the landing below, gazed upwards over the railing, and then came on up the stairs. She was a shapely young woman with dyed black hair and a sturdy tall boy of seven or eight in tow.

"Hania?" she asked, "Hania, do you remember me? Aneta? We live in the apartment below. I remember you from when you were little."

"Aneta." Hania tore herself away from the electricity problem. The two men ignored the interruption and were already dealing efficiently with a fuse box on the landing.

"And this is my son, Kuba, and I have a daughter too."

"I'm so glad to see you again," Hania managed faintly. Yes, she remembered—a sweet girl, the youngest in a family that drank. So that must have been her father, the man who'd wished her good health the other day. Let's see, twenty years times 365 days times two bottles of hard liquor made how many bottles since she'd last seen him? He was holding up very well, and Aneta seemed to be flourishing too.

The electricity men were putting their clipboards under their arms and descending the stairs.

"Don't worry about them," Aneta said with a deprecating wave of her hand, "I'll show you how to deal with these little problems. You've been abroad so you probably don't know."

"What do you mean?"

"You have to stick a needle under the meter cover so the bill doesn't run up. It's easy once you know how."

"I'm afraid I couldn't do that," said Hania. A slight noise made her look up and she found she was looking into Konstanty's eyes. He nodded 'good morning' to them both and went on down the stairs.

So, thought Konstanty, as he descended the stairs with his unhurried step, there was no need to be quite so chummy with the girl. Why had he just smiled at her in such a friendly way? He could have put a little more distance into it. After all, he'd been kind and that was enough; he wouldn't want to carry it too far, make her into a close friend. He thought these thoughts and then felt ashamed of himself. The problem was...was what? He liked her, he thought she was very entertaining, why shouldn't he enjoy her company? Because...Well, there it was: He'd actually been rather uncomfortable being seen with her in town last night. So all right, he had to admit it to himself. He was as concerned with 'how things look' as Pelagia, as everyone else in Poland. It was an uncomfortable admission but there it was. He had thought he could escape the iron hand of—of what? Not tradition exactly, but of doing what was expected, that was it—he was in the grip of the expected. It was not expected that aristocratic young men dated obese young women. Discreetly buxom, maybe. Not blush-for-her obese.

His car keys jingled as he took them out of his pocket. She had told him that the human ear could hear 20,000 vibrations a second and that the Nazi war propagandist Goebbels had organized a conference in London to try to set the pitch for C in 1939. In 1939! Who attended the conference? He would have to ask her, he thought. And then he remembered that no, he had been kind enough already.

*Respected Sir,…*Oh, how mortifying. What was she going to do? She'd have to pay the bill…*The battery on my laptop will only last two hours so I'm sending you this email to tell you that I won't be able to do any work for the next* …Delete. He had gone on down the stairs with the curtest of nods. His 'good morning' had been frosty. There was nothing to do but have some more breakfast and go on typing.

Like Copernicus, many luminaries of the Polish Renaissance went abroad for a time: There was Jan Łaski (John a Lasco), for instance, who brought East Frisia into the Protestant fold, became superintendent of foreign Protestants in England, and had an influence on the English Book of Common Prayer. Erasmus considered Lasco to be 'a man of such parts that I wish for no greater happiness than his single friendship.'

And I wish for no greater happiness than…Hania tried to stifle the thought, but the words '*his single friendship*' kept repeating in her mind.

King Edward was so charmed that he donated part of an Augustinian monastery to Lasco for a church. Oxford was less happy, however, when he took up quarters in Christ Church with his wife, the first woman to have, as one historian says, 'invaded the sanctity of College life.' After her death, which occurred not long after, 'she was buried by the shrine of St Friewide in Christ Church Cathedral, but on the accession of Queen Mary the Celi-

bates had their revenge, for her body was thrown out in scorn and buried in a dunghill without the precincts of the College.' Her bones were restored to the saint's tomb itself, though, in Elizabeth's time.

There was a scrawl at the side of the page. Hania struggled to make it out: *Is this just trivia or is it symbolic of the variable fate of those who go against tradition?*

Then there was Andrzej Frycz Modrzewski (Modrevius), a pioneer of modern political thought...

Another person who went against established ideas, Hania noted.

...He advocated an equitable welfare system and the idea that the law should be the same for everyone. If anyone, persons in privileged positions should be more severely punished than other people for any crimes committed, and wealthy young men should be better educated so they would stop spending their time playing lutes, singing indecent songs, and thinking of nothing but feasting and pomp; they should learn common sense and how to listen before giving orders themselves.

Really? thought Hania, was poor listening a problem even then?

He desired the freeing of the serfs —'Their bread, he wrote, lasts them scarcely half the year, they spend the rest in utter poverty, they are helpless before the law, and they are oppressed by the service and tithes forced from them by both lord and parish. 'A peasant is not your slave, he is your neighbor.'

Modrevius did not become popular for these views. His book On the Reform of the Commonwealth was banned by Pope Paul V, and King Zygmunt August had to issue a mandate to protect him from persecution.

...The lot of the peasants, though, Konstanty had added, *which grew progressively worse as the centuries passed, has to be seen against the background of the slave economies of America, England, France, and other European countries; even Sweden*

*kept a slave colony into the mid-19ᵗʰ century...*Hania paused, considering how to reword this. There was another note in the margin: *Is this really a mitigating factor, or am I made uncomfortable by the fact that my ancestors no doubt also objected to Modrevius and grew rich on the basis of such a system? Still, life for the peasant was fairly brutal all over; Lafayette, when told that the peasants on his French estates were starving, took five days off—only five—from his activities on behalf of revolutionary America.*

Hania sat with the laptop before her, staring at the screen, considering how to respond to these various points without offending Konstanty's sensitivities. Kalina, having finished breakfast, appeared beside her.

"The lights are out."

"Hey! There's no television!" said Maks in dismay.

"The electricity company just turned the electricity off."

"Oh." Kalina just nodded; obviously she knew what that meant.

"What do you usually do in such a situation?"

"You mean, when they turn the electricity or the phone off because they"—she said it as if in quotation marks, 'they'—"didn't pay? We go buy candles."

"No!" whined Maks, "Candles are scary! I don't like the dark! I want the lights back on."

"How long does it take to get the electricity back once one's paid?"

"Depends. Maybe a couple days, maybe a week."

"A week!"

Reading ahead in Konstanty's history she had found that it was a Pole, a certain Łukaszewicz, whose inventions had started the oil industry—and also produced oil lanterns. They could have used oil lanterns now.

"We could go to the country like they suggest."

"No!" shrieked Maks, "Kalino! You know we can't! We can't go!" He made expressive eyes at Kalina and meaning jerks of his head toward the ceiling. Hania observed him in surprise. Whatever did he mean? He couldn't have understood her romance with Konstanty. But that was all in her mind! He couldn't have guessed––or had her little conversation with Kalina before the mirror given rise to ideas on the part of the children? Oh, how embarrassing. But how touching that they wanted to help things along. Only, of course, it was completely hopeless. Oh, how very, very embarrassing.

Maks was still fussing, "We can't go! Kalina!"

"Hush, Maks, I'll arrange it."

Maks was saying "You're the one who didn't want to leave town! You refused to go to camp. And I know why. Because you wanted to keep meeting…"

"*Quiet*, Maks!" Kalina aimed a blow at her little brother, while hissing, "There are such things as vacations. Vacations, get it? Some people go on vacations..." tears sprang to her eyes, "with their families."

"Oh." He looked unconvinced and whined again, "but our secret upstairs."

Our secret upstairs? So they weren't talking about Konstanty?

"What secret?" she asked. No, of course they weren't thinking of her and Konstanty—that was all in her mind, just as she'd thought. And the way he'd smiled this morning, so distant, and he must have heard about the electricity as he was coming down the stairs—what would he think? It would be more dignified not to be too friendly. She felt like running away.

"Oh, Maks thinks everything's a secret. There aren't any secrets." And to Maks:

"I'll ask Paulina."

"Oh." He brightened.

Kalina was saying "Please. You'd like it there, really."

"I thought you wanted me to 'just go'," Hania said, "and now you want me to go somewhere in the country with you? I don't understand."

"I'm sorry about that. Actually, you're not like the others."

The other babysitters? Hania wasn't sure what she meant, but she was pleased anyway, even though she suspected the apology was made out of expediency.

Maks was bouncing beside her on the sofa. "Please, let's go to the country. It's great there. There's a frog pond…"

A frog pond and Maks, thought Hania, horrors—

"…and a river."

Worse and worse, thought Hania.

"There's electricity in the house," said Kalina. "And the internet."

"Let's go," said Hania.

There was fruit on the trees, said the children, and vegetables in the garden; the air was clean, said the children, and we leave from Central Station.

The air in Central Station was not clean. Or maybe it only gave that impression. They had not crossed the busy expanse of high-rise construction and cars and buses under the looming crenellations of the Palace of Culture and Science, but had dived into extensive underground passages, come out near their destination, and rushed along the street and into the building. Central Station looked like a war zone, thought Hania, as they picked their way down to the platform to wait for their train. Homelessness was rare in Poland. Even drunkards, who might spend a night or two on a bus-stop bench, were sooner or later usually hauled home by their relatives. Families didn't live in cars or tents as in America, she knew, but all the deranged old women and unclaimed addicts of Warsaw did congregate in tattered heaps about the station. Hania shuddered and turned her eyes away from unwashed limbs even as she dug in her purse for a coin.

Still, constrained as their hearts were for various reasons, the three had something of a holiday feeling as they rushed down a staircase with an assortment of bags and packs. Only Kalina edged away from Hania on the platform, leaving a wide-enough gap between them so that other passengers might not think they were together. Maks dropped a soda bottle and it rolled across the platform and over the edge onto the rails. Hania screamed at Maks to leave it as he headed after in hot pursuit. And then the train came in with a rush and whoosh.

She couldn't see the step. She always hated that moment of stepping from the platform over an unseen chasm, onto the narrow confines of the railcar ladder. Would she stick? No, there, puffing and pulling her bags after her, she followed Maks down the aisle to their compartment. Only the compartment was crowded with a family of a type she recognized instantly in spite of her intermittent association with Poland: church-going, godly, moving up from the lower to the middle class, disapproving, uncompassionate. The type who kept a hawk's eye on their neighbors for signs of degeneracy and envied them bitterly—to the point of hatred––for any acquisitions or attainments. They never looked directly at her; they put their noses in the air and didn't like how much room she took up on the bench.

She went out to stand in the corridor by an open window. A young soldier, trying to pass, was momentarily nonplussed, politely apologetic. She squeezed back into the compartment to let him by and extracted a package of cookies from her luggage. Someday she was going to lose weight, she thought, as she returned to the corridor. She would go on a diet. Someday she was going to get on the scale and be able to see it. Someday she would feel happy enough not to need comfort.

They were leaving Warsaw. In the distance she could see the roofs and spires and domes of the Old Town; somewhere over there, she had read in a book called *Warsaw Triptych*, was what had once been 'Crown Warsaw,' the area around the later residence of kings, the castle built up by successive generations on the fort of a medieval duke named Trojden. Beyond, in the Middle Ages, there had been the little agricultural and trading communities belonging to individual nobles and clergymen: Areas clustered around Warsaw that were entities unto themselves in the kingdom, even sometimes having their own measurements and monetary systems. Warsaw, the author said, had once been a sea of orchards surrounding manor houses.

Now they were crossing the river, its broad gray, empty water spread below them. The Vistula was the last large river left unregulated in Europe.

And now they were out of Warsaw, into the countryside, and there were fields and trees and farmhouses, bicyclists waiting at railway crossings, combines mowing here and there, and troops of men and women lying under trees at the edge of hay fields, resting from their work in the midst of the day.

She wasn't really leaving Konstanty behind, she thought as the train picked up speed; she could get an internet connection over the phone, Kalina had said.

They had been travelling a long time through forests. The sign Żabia Wola passed before the windows as the train came briefly to a stop, let them off, and departed again. Hania watched it leave, feeling there must be some mistake. The station was a slab of cracked cement beside a dirt road. Pines rose all around, their narrow brown-orange trunks reaching straight for the sky, there to burst into a profusion of branches that obscured the light. The air was clear and heavy with pine scent and very quiet.

Hania looked around, "Here?" she asked doubtfully. "But we're in the middle of nowhere."

"Isn't it great?" asked Maks happily.

"We have to walk a ways," said Kalina, shouldering some of the lighter luggage. "This way." And she set off at a brisk and swinging walk. Maks trotted happily after her.

"Wait!" cried Hania, as she slung a bag over one shoulder, a backpack over the other, picked up a grocery sack and the remaining soda bottle and staggered after her charges.

There followed a period in which she was aware only of the awkwardness of her bundles, the sunlight flickering through the woods, and the passing of the tree trunks against an infinite green underworld.

"Stop!" she panted to her companions after a time, and sank down onto the pitchy soft needles at the side of the trail.

"No, we're almost there, come on," they urged her.

The walk was difficult, but worth it. Hania, seated at the edge of the forest with Kalina and Maks, leaned back against a tree and thought, "this is heaven." Before them stretched a pale-green field of grain, in the distance a heavy dun horse was pulling a wagon, and under them the moss was soft and springy. It was neither hot nor cold and the sky was blue and wide and full of birds.

"Oh, look. A stork," pointed Maks, as a big white bird rose from the grain and glided, all legs and long beak, past them.

The village was a string of houses along two sides of a narrow, paved road: houses ranging from cabins of vertical wood slats, with windows sagging at odd angles, inhabited by the elderly, to spruce stucco blocks belonging to persons who owned cars and commuted to work in nearby towns, to old, Germanic-looking structures of patinated red brick fronting identical-looking barns. The yards opened onto meadows, the meadows onto fields. There were grape vines scrambling over doorways, and fruit trees, and hens, and after the city, an amazing absence of noise.

The house, when they reached it, was a small brick building with low beams and rooms that opened inconveniently one off the other, with big white tile stoves in each corner. The kitchen facilities were rather charming but antiquated—a brass faucet and a large gas stove of dangerous aspect. The bathroom, however, had been renovated in an un-aesthetic Leroy Merlin style that left nothing to be desired in the way of hygiene.

Kalina and Maks struggled with the wooden shutters and flung open the back windows. They did indeed look onto a frog pond and a bit of the neighbor's barn-yard. Somewhere a cow was lowing and a large rooster, with a speckled neck and mad jumble of tail feathers, strolled superciliously about the grass. It would be fine here for awhile, thought Hania, pleased at the children's pleasure. Even Kalina's face had lost its sullen and in-jured air; she looked almost happy and carefree for a moment.

Hania hooked up her laptop, feeling an immense sense of relief when the screen lit up and the internet appeared. Konstanty was within reach. Now he seemed even more accessible than when she had known him to be living above her head in Warsaw. She was barricaded by distance from any hint that she might be pursuing him, and yet she had a perfect excuse for writing to him. Happily, she began to type:

As Catholics and Protestants were burning each other elsewhere in the 16th century, Poland remained 'a country without stakes,' full of differing ethnicities and faiths: There were Poles, Lithuanians, Germans, Ruthenians, Tatars, Jews, and smaller Armenian, Dutch, Italian, French, Greek and Scots minorities; the population was not only Catholic, but also Muslim, Jewish, Karaite, Orthodox Christian, Uniate, and Protestant. Jews had had far-reaching protection since Bolesław the Pious's Charter of Kalisz in 1264: if a Christian fought with a Jew, the matter was to be judged by the Jews, if a Christian injured a Jew 'with a bloody wound' he was required to give him half his possessions; anyone jeering at a synagogue was to be fined in pepper. Muslims, like Jews, were also left to pursue their religion unimpeded; nor was either Islam or Judaism a barrier to ennoblement.

The prevalent attitude was tolerance. King Zygmunt the Elder declined to get involved in religious matters; 'permit me to rule over the goats as well as the sheep,' he said, and his son Zyg-

munt August was similarly broadminded. 'I am not the king of your consciences,' he told the parliament.

6

Konstanty, seated at a restaurant table, was regarding Agata with a serious look. She was very prettily dressed today; he couldn't have recounted the exact details, but he had a general impression of elegance. However, she wasn't listening to him, or she wasn't responding anyway. He said that he would like to see the Land of the Falling Lakes.

She said, giving a passing woman the once over, that she'd never heard of the Lake of a Thousand Fishes.

He said it was a wildlife reserve in Croatia that had been much disturbed by war.

She said she got tired of people talking about Iraq.

He said he'd read an interesting article on linguistics.

She said linguini always had too much garlic and what did he think of *The Da Vinci Code*?

Still, when he mentioned President Kaczyński and she said she didn't care for potatoes, he thought it was mildly encouraging.

Konstanty, reading his email that evening, was disconcerted. Left town? Without saying anything to him? Well, why shouldn't she have done, and what business was it of his?

He opened 'new mail' and typed:

Respected Madam...Somehow writing emails always made a person more uninhibited. He wrote in a way he would not have spoken, a way he would not—quite— have written had he been holding a pen, seeing the words form on paper. The computer added an element of impersonality to the whole exchange. The fact that she was at a distance also freed him somewhat. He didn't think much about what he was writing; his thoughts just came out his fingertips.

Thank you for sending the next section. I've had a less than entertaining day. Lunch with a woman who made me feel the existential isolation of every individual and of myself in particular—if I weren't so imperviously conceited already, I'd have come away feeling I hadn't a thought worth sharing. We might have been two robots knocking with programmed fingers on each other's plated aluminum casing—and getting, of course, no answer. Dinner with a colleague whom I used to think tolerably intelligent. Perhaps my luncheon date had made me incautious. A propos of a discussion on town planning I told him—why?—that I wonder at the number and size of Warsaw's statues to soldiers. I got carried away: I suggested that perhaps some negotiators— however futile their efforts—should be looked up out of history, even very minor ones—some little clerk, maybe, who heroically lifted his hand and said 'Wait. I think we should talk about this first,' or 'I doubt this is really worth it?'—and put upon a pedestal. His best response was to smile patronizingly at me and say 'don't tell me anyone could have behaved more gloriously than the heroes of the Warsaw Uprising.' The heroes of the Warsaw Uprising! 150,000 civilians died!

...I'm cataloguing all the obstacles ideas encounter: there's the mental turn off, the attitude of mental superiority, the anger, the lack of imagination. The worst is that I find such mechanisms in myself as well.

I'm very obliged to you—if you're still reading—for allow-ing me to unburden myself. I didn't know you were leaving. When will you be back? I hope you enjoy yourself.

He got a rapid reply.

Respected Sir, I don't know when I'll be back. I'm sorry you had such a day. I agree with you about the statues. A few days ago I passed the one by the parliament buildings that says 'God, Honor, Fatherland,' and I thought—why not 'Peace, Charity, Brotherly Love'?—I'm sure God would like that better, at least the God of the New Testament.

No really, he thought, she goes too far.

It does seem that too many of the ideals we hold up for fu-ture generations are belligerent. How about statues to men of the medical profession instead? I don't mean to flatter you but surely they've done more for humanity than soldiers? When one considers that in medieval and early modern Europe two-thirds of all chil-dren died before their teens—I'd put up statues to Pasteur, Flem-ing, the smallpox man, the Japanese fellow who experimented with anaesthesia, etc. It would be a very international group, too, and that would be good.

Speaking of which, I've rewritten these sentences about poor Queen Bona—who was brought from Italy to Poland, then retired again to Italy, only to be poisoned at the Spanish king's bequest, by her...doctor.

Why couldn't Agata write to me like this? won-dered Konstanty, as he mused over Hania's letter. Why is it that the first person with a kindred-seeming mind that I meet in a long time should be the size, the size of...—Tsk, unkind, unkind, he chided himself; why did you write to her if you intend to insult her, even in your imagination? But some part of his intellect wasn't listen-ing, some part was already formulating a reply: '*...the research of the Nobel laureates North and Fogel indicate that it* *was better nutrition not medicine that caused the drop in mortality...shall we put up statues to cooks?*

The next days passed pleasantly. Kalina and Maks had been instantly claimed by a gang of neighborhood children—girls in pink sandals and boys in football tees—with whom they spent the whole day. Kalina had made efforts to disassociate herself, considering herself too old, but had been quickly drawn in. Curiously to Hania, who was accustomed to the strict age and gender divisions of childhood friendships in America, the group was comprised of all ages and sexes, from five-year-old Kuba up through his thirteen-year-old sister Patricia. Hania had trouble distinguishing some of the middle members, but Patricia stood out as a live wire, a leader. Patricia was slim and long-legged and going to be beautiful. She was also untruthful, unreliable, and self-centered. So if life were like a chick-lit novel, thought Hania, watching the children out the window, Patricia would grow up to marry a rich, sensitive, humorous, perfect man and live happily ever after. On the other hand, her cousin Yola, pale and quiet and sweetly mothering all the younger children, was obviously destined for hard work and a husband who beat her.

In the meantime, the children were having fun. They never seemed to be at a loss for ideas, but if all else failed there was always the unending game of *berek*––tag—to be played. And when it rained one day, the game of *berek* was played through the rooms of the house, while Hania sat typing.

"Don't you mind them?" said Kalina, who had not joined in the chase, but was sitting on the sofa beside her. "Mama won't let them in the house. That is, she didn't, the time she came here."

Hania shook her head, "No, I don't mind. Children have to do something." She was pleased Kalina spoke to her; the girl had been doing so more and more often, usually only to voice some dissatisfaction, but still—it was a start.

"Anyway, it lets me work. I'm typing this nice bit about Zygmunt August and Barbara. Well, I don't know if 'nice' is the word for it. This romantic bit, I should say. Could I read it to you?" And, not waiting for an answer, she began:

"The habits of Zygmunt August, the last Jagiellonian king, were refined and ascetic. He dressed habitually in black, woke and slept early, was served by one personal servant. His disposition, wrote a papal nuncio, 'is very pleasant and engaging, his character far from stern, but he is constant and unshakeable in his decisions.' He remained unshakably attached to Barbara Radziwiłł, a beautiful young noblewoman whom he had married against convention and whom he refused to abandon when parliament demanded he get a divorce. When she died, only five months after her coronation in 1550, the heartbroken king walked or rode behind her funeral cortege for a month, from Cracow to Vilnius, where she had desired to be buried."

"Yes," said Kalina dubiously. "I know all that. There's that famous painting too, that's in all the history books. I forget by whom. Where Zygmunt is sitting by Barbara's bed at her last illness, looking so sad. I used to like that when I was younger."

'When you were younger,' thought Hania in amusement, but she didn't say anything and Kalina was continuing:

"Now I don't believe in all that stuff anymore."

"You mean you don't believe in romance?" Hania had a little difficulty keeping a straight face. Kalina's tone was so worldly-wise and weary sounding.

"No. I don't believe in it. Do you?"

Hania was taken aback. "Well...of course, not for me, maybe. But I like to think that love exists, yes." What else was there of any value in the world? Even music was only a consolation for people without, or an enrichment for those who had—but that was a sacrilegious thought, and she suppressed it.

"Well it doesn't." Kalina's tone was very flat, and Hania was looking at her with concern, but she suddenly jumped up and ran after the other children. What was wrong with her? Hania wondered, feeling that there was something about Kalina she should understand but that, like a word on the tip of her tongue, just eluded her.

Konstanty had sent an email attachment with a miniature thought to be Barbara, showing a blonde young woman in an amber velvet doublet, large slashed sleeves, and a cap with a swirling plume. She had a delicate narrow face and a lively, almost impish expression. Hania looked at the picture for a moment.

Love didn't exist? For Barbara it had. Hania went to the window and stood looking out at the fields. The rain had almost ceased, only here and there an occasional drop still spread a ring on the green water of the frog pond. Beyond the grain the pines were dark and wet. Just so the countryside must have looked to Barbara when she stood in a doorway in Vilnius.

The damp had brought the snails out. Big and small they littered every bare surface, leaving sticky trails of slime. "Look *pani*," said Patricia with a giggle, pushing Maks into the room, "Look at Maks." Hania looked and shuddered. "Maks! Take that snail off your nose at once! Oh, yuck."

Respected Madam,…Some of your questions rather startle me. They're perfectly legitimate, but I never heard them asked before. You wonder if the country would have been worse off if conquered by the Turks? It's too large a question. Does anyone like foreign rule? But offhand, I suppose for the serfs not much would have changed, and the nobles—would have moved to Paris.

I'm glad you like Zygmunt August. He's rather a favorite of mine.

Respected Sir,…Any ruler of Poland has my sympathies. When I look around the neighborhood it seems incredible that a system based on consensus could have worked and even more incredible that Poland had reached a civilizational level allowing it to pass so mildly through a period where opinions differed so much on matters of such weight. No—I don't quite mean that as harshly as it sounds. I'm always very admiring when people can manage to be tolerant, to compromise.

7

I could happily stay here for a long time, thought Hania, sitting on her bed one late evening. From here she could listen to the sound of the night outside her open window and see a pale moon rise over the pines. Here, when she got up in the morning and found an email from Konstanty, she could almost believe her imaginary romance was real. Not that she let her dreaming go very far. Some sense of self preservation stopped her from that—only she could imagine, a little, that he liked her, that he enjoyed their exchange of ideas, that some feeling of empathy reached out toward her. It was that feeling that was her romance—nothing more. She would set it to music as she sat there. So much music was night music. There were Berlioz's *Les Nuits d'été*, John Field's nocturnes, Chopin's—she ran through *Opus 9, no. 2*, the one in E flat major, in her mind, feeling her hands move on the keyboard; then Debussy's *Clair de Lune*; and afterwards the romanza from Mozart's *Eine Kleine Nachtmusic*. She lay down, and with her eyes closed, she began to play the *Moonlight Sonata* in her mind—dum da da, dum da da—and as she dropped off to sleep it was intersected by the croaking of frogs. Dum da da ker-oak.

When she woke in the morning it was to all the farmyard sounds: the crowing of roosters, the clanking of feed buckets, the ring of a wrench striking the pavement, the curses of *Pan* Gieniek as he tinkered endlessly with his tractor, the voices of the women as they moved off to work in the potato patch or to find a neighbor to gossip with.

And yet, she became aware that the neighbors quarrelled too, passionately at times and hopelessly, since circumstances forced them to continue meeting constantly, forced side-taking amongst their relatives and acquaintances, and spread angry ripples of long-lasting dissent through village politics. Patricia's parents, she learned, did not speak to Yola's, and had not done so for sixteen years. "You don't want to have anything to do with those Kruczaks," *Pan* Wieboda had said, shaking his head righteously. "They'll take advantage of you—you're from Warsaw, you aren't on the look-out for their tricks. Those are very primitive people."

"But *Pani* Ola keeps the house beautifully—and the garden," Hania had tried to defend her neighbor.

"You wait," the man had said, "she's just biding her time. She's like a fox that one." Hania said nothing and also listened in silence when *Pani* Ola brought over the present of a head of lettuce and a warning against the Wiebodas.

"Don't have anything to do with them. Those are low, mean, sly, despicable people—every one of them. It's a bad family. Stay away from them."

"It's like this," explained her neighbor from across the road, a large bald man with a walrus moustache who had waylaid her early in her stay to set her straight on all the village intrigue. *Pan* Piotrek always left off tying dahlia stalks or sweeping a walkway to chat with her when she came out of the house. "*Pani* Ola and *Pan* Wojtek are cousins—the same grandparents. And there was a dispute about the inheritance. You see that fence line on *Pan* Wojtek's? According to *Pani* Ola it's supposed to run not to that tree but to the next post over there—oh, that one there." He pointed. "For a year after the grandfather—God rest his soul—passed on we lived in daily anticipation of a massacre. One day *Pani* Ola was chasing *Pan* Wojtek with a kitchen knife, the next he was hollering below their windows that he was going to burn the house down. Ah," he waved a hand with a slight air of disappointment, "they've calmed down a lot since then."

"But," said Hania, looking at the markers he'd pointed out, "the difference isn't half a meter's worth—and there's all this space about…"

Pan Piotrek gave her an intent look. "It's the principle of the thing, *pani*—the principle. You have to defend what's yours. You can't just lie down and let someone walk all over you. Why I—when there was an inheritance in my family…My brother-in-law—may lightning strike him! tried….*God's wounds*…" Suddenly his eyes were dilating and he was beginning to swipe angrily at the flower beds with his broom. She quickly changed the subject.

A curious flaw, she thought as she walked back to the other house, in many Poles' characters; they were usually argumentative but not physically aggressive—until one touched them in certain ways, and then everything flared up, unreasonably, and boiled over.

Respected Madam,…It's not only in the village that people get so unreasonable over things that don't matter. Some of my colleagues at the hospital had their scalpels out the other day over the way their titles were listed on a board. It's rather surprising here how the instant someone disagrees with someone else that other becomes 'uncultured' and 'uncivilized.' It's quite true, as you say, that we have only to open the newspapers to see how the spirit of spite and envy can overrule the ability to see the larger picture or to value issues at their true worth.

Have you got to the Socinians yet? I don't mean to hurry you, only I had an idea in connection with the Museum of Polish History. Sorry, my thoughts are jumping about but I know you'll be able to follow. (Hania read this line ten times). *I think I'll suggest a room dedicated to alternative solutions. Perhaps my sister could get involved in the funding; she's good at that sort of thing.*

Hania wrote to Konstanty again that evening. Here in the village there was no lack of material; something was always happening that seemed to her strange, worthy of comment, or illustrative of some quality already revealed in Konstanty's writing. That morning, for instance, a police car had taken up its station at one end of the village, hidden in a ditch, with waiting radar. As the neighborhood had been much bothered by the speed with which tourist cars zipped along the paved road between the houses, it was viewed with mild approval. But when elderly, very elderly Pan Józek hobbled to the other end of the village on his cane, and sat down on a bench there, lifting a slow bony hand to each passing driver in warning of the police car ahead, his public spirit was even more strongly approbated.

Respected Madam,…,yes, we like our rebels. My heart warms to Pan Józek, I admit. In Poland we're allowed to defy any authority but convention…Do I talk too much about 'in Poland?'—it's only that coming from some years spent abroad, I am struck by certain facets of my own country, and think perhaps the situation is the same for you…And speaking of rebels, how is Maks?

Hania made a quick check. Maks was playing some game in the dirt with the other children, so that was all right then. Kalina was sleeping in a chaise longue. She went back to her typing. The disaster was to come later in the day.

…One group which was eventually subjected to persecution and chased out of Poland in the 17th century were the Socinians, later called Arians, who became forerunners of the Unitarians in America. Although their total numbers were not large, one historian lists over forty of the major Lithuanian magnatic families who were followers, and they also found converts amongst the gentry. They were anti-trinitarians and pacifists: they did not believe in eternal damnation or original sin; they objected to spilling blood, to war, to capital punishment, to carrying weapons (some nobles wore symbolic wooden swords); they believed in equality before the law, and, as some members became more radical, the return of the land to the peasants. They believed in applying reason to the Bible and attempting to live by the teachings of the Evangelists, and even their enemies had to admit that the Socinians were 'characterized by virtue, devoutness, and scholarship.' According to a contemporary, Archbishop Tillotson, 'they could be taken as a model of the manner for honest disputation and

touching on religious questions without excitement and indecorous slander of their opponents…'

Maks came into the house looking disgusted. "What's wrong, Maksiu?" said Hania, guessing that he had quarrelled with his friends. This happened fairly frequently; words would fly, maybe a slight blow or push or two, noses would go up in the air, there would be a cooling-off period, and then everything would be forgotten and everyone would be best friends again. It puzzled Hania a little, accustomed as she was to the permanent falling-outs and lasting animosities of American childhood. Maks flung himself into a chair and crossed his arms, "They're all a bunch of rooster eggs."

"Maks, roosters…" Hania began and then stopped, not certain how to proceed.

"They're pond scum."

"Okay, well, why don't you just cool off a little. I want to finish what I'm doing here, all right?"

He shrugged and took himself off angrily.

…'They ordinarily argue with moderation and seriousness, without excitement and temper…clearly and precisely, carefully, skilfully, and decently, sometimes with a subtle emphasis or moderate enthusiasm, but without rude or cutting comments…Some Protestant writers, all Catholic polemicists, and particularly Jesuit writers…are bunglers in comparison with them.'

Hania came to the end of the section and paused, feeling uplifted and encouraged. Yes. There were people in the world—even back then—who were capable of behaving like rational beings.

Her pleasant reverie was shattered by an ear piercing shriek. Aaaaaaeeee! Heeeeellpp! And sobs. She surged from her chair, the laptop flew off and hit the floor with a crash, and she tore in the direction of the shrieks. Aeeeeeiiii!

She reached the kitchen. Water was spraying everywhere. Maks was leaning across the sink on his stomach and had his finger in the faucet. Aaeeeeiiiii!!! The
spray soaked her as she pushed through it to the sink.

"My finger. My finger's stuck!"

Hania grabbed for the knob and turned it but nothing happened; the water continued to gush and spray.
She tried to reach for Maks' finger and got such a quantity of water in her face that she was momentarily
blinded.

"Pull it out!" she gasped.

"Aaiiiii!" Maks sobbed, "I can't."

She caught his finger and tried to wiggle it out,
but Maks screamed louder. "Stop! It hurts! It hurts!"

Water shot to the ceiling, hit the floor, spattered
like machine gun fire along the wall. She was soaking
wet and so was Maks.

A gaggle of children's faces appeared in the open
window, then ducked in unison with loud screeches as
the water flew in their direction.

"Run!" Hania said to the group collectively, trying
to hold Maks so he wouldn't slide off the sink, "someone call someone to help!"

A moment later and the room was full of people,
Pan Gienek, *Pan* Piotrek, *Pan* Wieboda, *Pani* Ola, and
many others, each one giving advice, cursing and dodg-
ing the water. "Where's the shut off valve, *kurcze blade*?"
No one knew.

Someone said it was under the sink, *cholera jasna*.
Pan Gienek dived under the sink and in a moment
emerged with a piece of pipe in his hands.

"Idiot!" shrieked someone, "that's the catch-basin,
what'd you take that off for?"

"*Kurcze*, the knob won't work," said someone.

"It's a faulty washer, *cholera*," said someone.

"Get a hacksaw," said someone.

"Noooooo!!!!" screamed Maks in a panic.

"Blllaaagh!" said Hania as the water caught her full in the mouth.

"Cholera take the washer!" said *Pan* Gienek, applying his wrench to the base of the faucet. A second later and the top of the faucet came loose, and Hania could pull Maks away from the sink. He still had the spout stuck on his finger, and from the decapitated water inlet the water now pumped into the sink, down through the dismembered run-off pipe, and onto the floor.

Maks waved the pipe around and cried. Someone said to pour soap on it. They poured dishwashing liquid on it and pulled till Maks screamed. No luck.

"Try oil," said someone, as they all stood about Maks in a quarter-inch of running water.

Someone found the oil. Pop! His finger came out.

"*Kurde*, it was I, I who said to use oil," said someone in a pleased voice.

"Oh thank you, thank you," said Hania in relief, as the participants began to depart. "Thank you so much."

"Thank you, thank you."

And then, as the last one went out the door. "But, but…wait, wait a moment! Please!"

Pan Piotrek turned. "Yes?"

Hania gestured towards the faucet, where the water was still pumping vigorously over the floor. It made a flood out the back door and was creating a pool in the yard.

"The water…"

Pan Piotrek shrugged. "Have to call a plumber, I guess."

"Do you know a plumber?"

"No. We do all our own, here in the village."

"But..." Hania clung to him as her last hope, "where will I find a plumber?"

"I can't help you." He shrugged, then, as if touched a bit by her despair, he added, "You can walk to the grocery at the crossroads; they might be able to tell you. But around here..." He shook his head and took himself off.

Late that evening Hania sank exhausted into a chair and closed her eyes. She was too tired even to get undressed and go to bed.

After *Pan* Piotrek disappeared, she had left a reluctant Kalina minding a bucket placed under the sink and had trudged along the road to the end of the village and along the highway to the grocery store. It had been hot, the sun had beat down on them, Maks had whined about the heat and complained about his finger, and dawdled so that she had to catch his hand and practically drag him along with her.

They'd passed the two policemen by the radar car. "Could use her as a roadblock," she'd heard one of them snigger behind her back. Of course, he hadn't meant her to hear.

When she had come in through the door of the grocery the plump fiftyish woman behind the counter had looked up and asked where she'd come from and told her she shouldn't have walked there at that time of day, it was very bad for the health to go out in the noonday sun, and "*pani* being so fat and all" it wasn't a good idea at all, and what could she do for her? A plumber? She had looked doubtful, taken a step or two into the room behind, and had a loud, shouted conver-

sation with someone in the back purlieus. "Kowal-
czyk?" and the reply, "*Niiiee*, he's a rascal, that one."

The woman's voice again. "Stąpek?" and the reply, "*Nie*, he's a cad, that one."

"How about Zbyszek?"

An explosion of anger from the man: "That *skur-
wysyn*! He still owes me ten *złoty*." A pause, then, "There's
Włodek might be willing, but I wouldn't trust him…"

A moment later the woman reappeared and handed Hania a piece of paper on which a name was written
in ill-formed block letters. "STĄPEK." The cad. Great,
Hania thought.

A phone number? No, the woman didn't have it,
but she could tell Hania where he lived. It was the next
village over—only a matter of two kilometers or so.

The cad, however, when they'd arrived panting at
his gate, had got up out of a lawn chair and said he
couldn't come that day. "But the water is pouring all
over the floor," said Hania.

The cad had rubbed his head, and looked into the
distance, and said that it was hardly worth his while, but
if she wanted to pay emergency rates he could come the
next day.

Maks had made the walk back so miserable that
she had felt several times like leaving him along the side
of the road in the hopes he'd be picked up like a stray
dog by some kind and unsuspecting passer-by.

And then there'd been an afternoon of emptying
buckets and of mopping and mopping the floor. It was
only some time in the evening that Yola had put her
head around the open door and spoken to Hania as she
rose from her knees with a wet towel.

"Excuse me, *pani*." She pulled forward a little brother. "Hubert says he thinks he knows how to turn the water off."

Hania just stared, unbelieving. "If he does, please tell him to do so."

"We have to go in the bathroom."

They all proceeded to the bathroom. Hubert pointed to the wall. Yola said, "He says he watched our uncle when he renovated the bathroom last year. The turn-off-thing's behind the tiles. Nice, isn't it?" She smoothed the tiles with a hand, "It doesn't show at all."

"Which tile? Hubert, are you sure?"

"This one." He said, pointing, "Or this one or this one." He touched three tiles.

The tiles were sealed with cement grout. They did make a hollow noise when tapped.

"How do I get them off, I wonder?"

"You have to break them," said Hubert. "With a hammer. Pow!"

Great, thought Hania, and if I break them and find nothing? Then I pay for the redoing of Wiktor's bathroom? But the bucket in the kitchen would be overflowing soon, she remembered, so she couldn't dither too long.

No. She had an idea. She rushed to get her nail file, and applied it with vigour to the grout. The children watched in silence as she worked and worked; she could feel her whole body shaking up and down as she filed. After fifteen minutes she had made a small scratch and she was panting and gasping for breath.

"Okay," she said to Hubert and to Maks too, who had been watching excitedly but were beginning to get bored, "let's find a hammer and bash away."

The children scampered to find the tool. And lo and behold, when they'd demolished six tiles the water pipes were revealed and a shut-off valve.

Well, thought Hania, as she rewarded Hubert lavishly and he went off a hero, I will write about my adventures to Konstanty. Then of course, she had picked her laptop up from where it lay on the floor and found it wouldn't work.

It is only because I'm so tired that I feel such anguish about the laptop, said Hania to herself as she sat still with her eyes closed. It doesn't really matter so much that I can't email Konstanty. It was just in my mind, a crush that I was indulging because there seemed no harm in imagining. I will find a way to let him know that I can't work for a while, or we will go back to Warsaw. But no, we should stay because the children are happier here. She tried to concentrate on that thought: The children were happier here.

If she needed to talk to someone she could pick up the phone, of course. Whom would she call? Not Konstanty. To write an email in the vague context of a common project was one thing, actually to talk to him on the telephone about her own problems quite another. He seemed immensely unreachable. She felt quite hollow and shaky at the thought.

Her mother? Her parents had divorced when she was fourteen. When her mother remarried and moved to Montana, Hania had stayed in New York for the sake of her piano studies. It had all been agreed amongst them; it had all been for the best. But her mother, married now to a rancher in Montana, seemed often to be living on a different planet. She had no patience at all with the Lanskis, she hated Poland—it was a primitive, uncivilized place, she said—and she was always in a hurry to go feed the cattle or clean the barn. There were many things Hania couldn't talk to her about. She dialled a number and heard her father's voice.

"Hallo, Tato?"

"Haniu, *kochanie*, where are you? I've just been talking to Wiktor."

"I'm in Żabia Wola. Where *is* Wiktor?"

"Żelazowa Wola? You're giving a concert?"

"Tato, I don't play anymore. Not Chopin's birthplace. Żabia Wola."

"Never heard of it. What on earth are you doing there?"

"Looking after Wiktor's children. Tato, I really need to have a phone number to Wiktor or some way of getting in touch with him."

"Well, why don't you call him?"

"Where?"

"It's like I was telling you, he's in Berlin." A pause. "Or Bern? You know he's taking part in this festival. That's why you're looking after the children, isn't it?"

"You knew about all this?"

"All what? Hania, you don't speak clearly."

"You knew I'd end up taking care of the children?"

"That's what you went to Warsaw for, isn't it?"

She held the phone for a moment in her hand, away from her ear. So he had arranged it all. She could see it clearly. Wiktor had called about Babcia and mentioned he needed someone to look after the children. Her father, with his love of arranging things, of setting events in motion, had sent her off. He had probably not meant to deceive her; it had just seemed better to him to present the situation in a light that would appeal to her—a vacation in Warsaw. Wiktor needed help, Hania wasn't busy, why not?

She said goodbye quickly and hung up the phone.

She sat down and stared into space, feeling very tired and alone. Kalina appeared in the doorway. Hania closed her eyes; she really didn't think she could deal with Kalina's freaks tonight.

"Are you all right?"

Hania opened her eyes. Kalina was regarding her with a look almost of concern on her face.

"You look really tired. You should go to bed."

Hania was so touched she almost felt like crying. "My laptop's broken," she said. "I can't…do my work."

Kalina picked up the laptop, turned it in her hands, shook it, shrugged her shoulders.

"I know someone who might be able to fix it."

But in the morning Kalina didn't want to get out of bed. It must be psychological, thought Hania; so often in the morning she said she wasn't feeling well, and then in the afternoon she was just fine and chasing around with the other kids. At least Kalina hadn't brought the pacifier to the country, she thought, as she waited more or less patiently for the girl to bestir herself.

"Okay," said Kalina around noon, "let's go find *Śrubokręt*."

Śrubokręt. "The Screwdriver?"

"That's what everyone calls him."

They traipsed, Kalina with Hania clutching the laptop, to the end of the row of village houses. They came to a fence where a vicious-looking dog lunged at them with bared teeth until they passed through the gate, when it subsided onto its back with waving paws and wagging tail and every appearance of friendliness. They gave it a pat and passed on through a yard into a murky barn that contained a pen of young pigs with twitching noses, bobbing ears, and backs pale against the dirt. A lean, long-faced young man in dirty overalls was shovelling manure in the obscurity but paused to lean on his shovel when they came in.

"Can you fix this laptop?" said Kalina without preamble.

The young man came towards them, reaching for a rag on which he wiped his blackish hands. He didn't say anything, but took the laptop from Hania, held it up to his ear, and shook it. Hania was not encouraged.

They followed him out of the barn and into the house in silence.

He gestured to them to sit on a blue plush sofa. "Mamo! Bring tea!" he shouted.

Then, as they sipped tea and made small talk with a thin and weather-beaten woman, he proceeded to take the laptop apart into little pieces. It will never go back together again, thought Hania as she watched his dark work-worn hands twiddling with something inside the computer—never, never. And it will be very embarrassing. Kalina will be unhappy and the young man will be unhappy, and I won't be able to write to Konstanty.

"There," said the young man, "Look. Works fine now." He turned the screen so they could see it, then unplugged it, shut the lid, rose, and was heading out of the room, almost before Hania could close her dropped jaw.

"Wait! How much do I owe you?"

"It was nothing, you don't owe me anything." He waved a dismissive hand and was gone in the midst of her thanks. He would never know, she thought, how much it meant to her to have the internet back. She tried to phrase it that way in her mind, but what she really thought was 'to have Konstanty back.'

There was an email awaiting her:
Respected Madam, I've had an absurd evening...

Having informed his sister that he had decided he and Agata were not suited, she had promptly invited him to Konstancin. It had not surprised him to find a young woman had been summoned as well. Not exactly a beautiful young woman, but slender, tall, good-looking, with that stiff upper-body posture he found familiar. He didn't recognize the name, Kalpurnia something-or-other, but he was sure it would turn out that her grandmother was a Potocka or some such thing. Pelagia was careful about these matters. Pelagia knew, although he had never said so, that he had reached an age where he wanted a wife. He kissed Kalpurnia's hand, smiled his half-smile, inclined slightly towards her. Her answering half smile and incline had been so much a mirror of his own mannerism that he had actually laughed, startling himself, his sister, and the guest. He had had to exert himself to be very charming all evening to make up for the gaffe. It had been hard work, Kalpurnia's ideas and statements being all so exactly what one would expect. As they had politely discussed London and Corpus Christi celebrations, he had thought– –I will marry a woman like this one, and we will have children whom we will educate carefully and teach to behave formally. They will grow up in accordance with the model, and be well-mannered, believing, and follow tradition and that's what I want.
...I'm sure you will feel for me.

Hania read this message over many times. He had never written so familiarly before.

Respected Sir,…How do I feel about tradition? It entirely depends on which ones, doesn't it? The traditions of a cannibal tribe may be very long, but not worth perpetuating. If the future is going to be better, each generation has to be an improvement on its elders; if our children are only as good as we are, then we've failed, don't you think? They have to discard some of what we believe in or there's stagnation.

Anyway, a lot of Western culture could be discarded as pernicious: Almost all folk tales, all cruel painting and sculpture, large parts of our literature, a number of kinds of patriotism, so many unjust habits…Did I answer your question, or get way off the track?

She got way off the track, Konstanty thought, reading this email, but that's all right. It's not how Kalpurnia would have answered me, or Agata either. He did not stop to wonder why he was making comparisons, or to consider that he would not have made any had he received such a message from a male acquaintance. He read the rest of the message.

I don't know if absurd is the right word for the last twenty-four hours, but I know they were entirely different from anything in my previous experience…Between your history and real life I feel I am learning a great deal about Poland…

Konstanty, as he finished reading her account, was both amused and bemused. What he found most appealing, he thought, was her lack of resentment toward Maks or disdain for the villagers, her charitable attitude in a trying situation.

8

The neighbors continued very friendly, even if they were inclined to tell Hania, after the fact, everything she should have done whenever anything went wrong. But she listened politely. They were well meaning, and very generous. In fact, she and the children had hardly more to do in the way of acquiring groceries than Elijah, fed by ravens. Someone was always stopping by with a basket of plums, or a bunch of carrots, or an enormous smooth, green cabbage. (If she only had the imagination, she thought once, to create dinner from a bundle of radishes and three brown eggs).

She experienced, too, that quintessentially Polish outing, a mushroom-picking expedition, little imagining how it would end. She walked in the forest with *Pani* Ola. There was not much underbrush and the needles of the pines were thick under their feet. The light was diffused and soft. Somehow, it was the melody of Debussy's *Prélude à l'après-midi d'un faune* that came to her, but perhaps, she considered, it should really be Kilar's *Polonaise*, or some other piece reminiscent of the mushroom gathering in Mickiewicz's *Pan Tadeusz*, the epic poem of country life in Napoleonic times:

> *Who would have guessed these figures, so serene*
> *And silent, were the people we have seen,*
> *The judge's guests, from noisy breakfasting*
> *Gone to the solemn rite of mushrooming?*

They moved into the mixed forest, where the paler leaves of the deciduous trees mixed with the dark evergreens, walking quietly, as in the poem, like shadows amongst the tree trunks. There were wild geraniums here, tidy three-foot-wide shrubs covered in magenta flowers. Bees hummed lazily in and out amongst the foliage. But Hania's mind, instead of anchoring itself in these surroundings and on the search for mushrooms, kept wandering off to her future. She made an effort to return to music. Music, now. It was a pity her job at the school consisted of teaching bored first graders to sing rounds—she had so much more to give. She'd like to have students like—well, like Maks. Somehow the idea of going back to this teaching job didn't seem appealing at all. At the back of her mind she knew that she'd had an idea of staying in Poland, of working at something or other. Only there were the financial reasons: she would make so much more money in New York. More by far, she supposed irrelevantly—oh, very irrelevantly—than Konstanty as a doctor in Warsaw.

"This one," said *Pani* Ola, bending and picking and straightening, "is a *rydz*. See? It has this cap like a dish? It's very good fried, with lots of butter." They walked on, *Pani* Ola instructing: "These here are *maślaki*, they grow in little clumps, see? These are good for pickles. I'll give you a jar when I'm finished and teach you how to prepare them."

They went on, talking a little and collecting. At the edge of a meadow *Pani* Ola dropped an ordinary-looking mushroom into her basket. "This one's good," she said, "and that one over there"—she pointed to an identical-looking mushroom—"is poisonous."

"And you've never made a mistake?" Hania asked nervously, wondering if she would dare to eat *Pani* Ola's mushroom pickles.

"*Nie*. Look, there's a big difference." *Pani* Ola picked up another mushroom. "See, this one's edible—" She broke off, stared at the mushroom in her hand, turned it this way and that doubtfully. "Or maybe..." Then with sudden decision: "Ach, it's probably good." And she dropped it in her basket.

They crossed the meadow and a field and were at the end of the village. Hania saw that Maks was seated by the road with two of his friends. *Pani* Ola walked on toward her house, and Hania strolled over to Maks. Kalina had said that her brother had been allowed, for two years now, to run about the neighborhood unattended. Still, freedom for an almost seven-year-old was all very well, Hania thought, but they really shouldn't be this close to the road. She was going to speak rather severely, but when she got near she saw that the children had three small containers full of mushrooms. Maks jumped up when he saw her.

"We sold two containers already!" he shouted.

"You haven't been selling them?" said Hania with horror, taking in the scene. The Polish roads were full of mushroom pickers selling their gatherings, but Maks —Maks knew nothing of mushrooms. Or did he?

He looked up in surprise at her tone. He had obviously expected her to be pleased. "Yes. We sold two, like I said. We're going to split the money. Look." He pulled two crumpled *złoty* bills out of his pocket. "We have to sell one more so we can share it evenly." His two friends nodded, eyeing her warily, sensing her alarm and prepared to flee already. *Boże*, he couldn't do simple math and he was selling potentially fatal commodities. She looked at the mushrooms, lying in a heap. They looked like the last ones *Pani* Ola had hesitated over. Like the ordinary mushrooms found in grocery stores.

"We picked them in the woods," one of the boys offered. "They're good."

"Do you know?" Hania asked hopefully. Maybe, young as he was, he had some expertise. "Do you really know which ones to pick? Did someone teach you?"

"No. But I think they're good." He added, as if that clinched the matter. "The people who bought the other ones thought they were good."

"How many people have bought them?"

"Just one car stopped," said Maks with disgust, "and we've been sitting here a long time."

Hania fought down a moment of hysteria. What was she supposed to do in this situation? Somewhere there was a car full of people, who were going to eat mushrooms that might be poisonous. Did she call some health department and ask for a bulletin to be broadcast? "People in a blue Lancia who passed through Żabia Wola at approximately 3:00 p.m.—don't eat those mushrooms!" She quailed at the thought. But she had to know.

"Maks, were all the mushrooms like these? Just like? It's important. You have to be sure."

Maks and his friends both nodded. She compared them to the ones she had picked with *Pani* Ola. They looked the same. She would hurry home, she decided. She would eat them, and if nothing happened, well and good, she would assume that the purchasers were safe too. If not, then at the first twinge she would call the authorities.

She walked home fast, cooked at top speed and ate, forcing each bite down and thinking she was soon going to lose all interest in food of any kind. In the revolted wake of this hasty meal, she set about typing to take her mind off the consequences.

...When Zygmunt August died without an heir at the end of 1572, both Polish and Lithuanian, Protestant and Catholic parliamentarians gathered in Warsaw in January to ensure that the existing order of tolerance was not disturbed: They swore that although they were 'dissidentes de religione,' they would 'keep the peace...and not spill blood for the sake of our various faith and difference of churches.' A suitable king was sought, but the options were not encouraging: it was between Ivan the Terrible of Russia, a Habsburg prince, and the King of France's twenty-two-year-old brother, who had just helped orchestrate the Saint Bartholomew's Day massacre of Protestants. This French prince, Henri de Valois, was eventually elected by a gathering of 50,000 noblemen in Warsaw, and came reluctantly to Poland, where he was unimpressed by the noblemen's jewels, their clothing, their Latin speeches, their large, cold palaces, and their strange, quarrelsome politics. He was supposed to marry the late king's sister Anna, who was over fifty—and he was polite, but made no move to do so. He retired to his room and played sick until word came that his brother's death had left the French throne empty. Then he jumped on a horse and raced for the border, threatening to knife anyone who tried to stop him. (A few months later he was crowned King of France in Reims, and two days after he was married to a princess whom he had chosen for completely non-political reasons. They were hours late for their wedding because he was busy dressing her hair.)

More weddings, thought Hania. But at least this too had been a case, apparently, of inclination overcoming convention. Curious that Henri, who was a weak and not particularly worthy character, had managed it—

she would have to ask Konstanty if the marriage had been happy.

In his stead came Stefan Bathory, a Hungarian nobleman of no particular means, who had been in the diplomatic service of various rulers, and had once been imprisoned for three years on the pretext that he had lost his mind. In prison he spent his time reading Julius Caesar, and in 1575, at age 43, was elected to the Polish throne. Considered one of Poland's better kings, he duly wedded Anna, fought with Russia over Livonia, abided by the constitution, and died in 1586...As frequently then at a royal death, there was some thought that he might have been poisoned.

Probably just ate mushrooms, thought Hania, looking down at her empty plate beside the laptop, and wondering how she was going to feel shortly.

The next king was Zygmunt Vasa, son of a sister of Zygmunt August and the King of Sweden. A fervid Catholic, he spent his reign working against religious toleration and trying to reclaim the throne of Sweden, with the result that, having avoided the religious turmoil of the 16th century, from the next century on, Poland was constantly involved in warfare and internal troubles.

Of course, she reminded herself, she shouldn't giggle at the word 'internal troubles,' when what she was writing about was Poland's descent from its golden age into misery as a result of human narrowness. But a couple of hours had passed and nothing had happened. She thought she must be safe, so she sent the pages off to Konstanty, with a humorous account of her adventures, and got her reward in his reply:

Respected Madam,...Your conscientiousness is admirable, and your devotion to our project in such circumstances beyond the call of duty.

She read these words over and over: 'Admirable.' He had called her 'admirable.' And he had written 'our project.' Of course, she reasoned with herself, it was just politeness, a trained manner of being civil and charming, and he spoke in this fashion to many people. And yet, she didn't think he would say something he didn't mean at all; there must be some element of truth in it. Still, she couldn't really take it personally, so to speak. She knew this, and yet she opened the email repeatedly.

She kept a closer watch on Maks after this incident, but several days rolled by uneventfully. There were mornings when Hania woke early to the sound of church bells and rose to find mist hovering over the meadows. Afternoons when they walked through fields trimmed with blue chicory and red poppies, purple vetch and tall-growing cow parsley to the river, where the water ran shallow and cold over small, round boulders.

There was always, thought Hania later, in remembering this pleasant bucolic interlude, a lull before the storm. It broke one morning. The phone rang. Who would be calling? Maybe it's Wiktor or Ania, thought Hania, leaping for the receiver. It was a girl's voice, asking for Kalina. Hania looked about: no Kalina.

"Kalina's not here right now, could I take a message?"

The caller hesitated, and then said, "Please, *pani*, could you tell Kalina that I can't get into the building because they fixed the intercom?"

"I don't understand."

"It doesn't matter. Just please tell Kalina that Paulina says they fixed the intercom and she can't get into the building. Goodbye."

Maks was watching her. "Who was it?" he asked.

"How strange. Someone named Paulina says to tell Kalina she 'can't get into the building because they fixed the intercom.' Do you have any idea what it's about?"

But Maks was already gone; he was out the door crying, "Kalina! Kaliiinaaa!"

From the sounds of altercation that ensued, Hania guessed he hadn't had far to look. She followed Maks to the back door. Kalina was lying in the chaise longue with a blanket over her head, fending her brother off with moans and attempts to kick him with a languid leg.

"Leave me alone, Maks. Leave me alone. I feel sick."

"But Paulina says she can't get in. What about Bartek? He'll die." He shook his sister, "Kalina! He'll die!"

"She'll die," mumbled Kalina from under the covers, "Go away, Maks, I'm sick. I'll think of something later."

"We have to go back…," said Maks, breaking off when he saw Hania.

"Go away!" whined Kalina.

"Kalina," said Hania, coming to the girl, "are you worse?" Good heavens, the girl wasn't usually this prostrated. Suppose she had to get her to a doctor—and here they were so far from everything. She didn't know anything about illnesses, she realized with a sinking feeling. Not a thing.

Kalina appeared to make an effort to pull herself together. "I'm all right," she said wanly. "I just want to sleep." Hania felt her forehead. She didn't seem to have a fever. That was a good sign. If there weren't any symptoms it was probably psychological, as she had suspected before. So that was okay—well, not okay, but not a case for a physician.

"Where do you hurt, Kalina?"

"I'm all right, I said. Just leave me alone," Kalina snapped irritably.

Thus rebuffed, Hania went back into the house and turned on her laptop. Should she ask Konstanty's advice? But in spite of the fact that the tempo of their email exchanges had reached two or three a day, and covered topics as varied as the people they'd spoken to and their ideas on Prus, she still didn't feel she was on those terms with him. She put Kalina and Maks out of her mind.

Respected Sir,…we were discussing Wokulski. Have you ever noticed that there are no—or at least very few that I can think of—love stories written by men that end happily? She could write to him about love because she knew it had nothing to do with herself; it was just an abstract question, like the change from *ut* to *do* in musical notation. All she could hope for—rather desperately—was his friendship…*Actually, if one leaves aside the chevaleresque tradition of the Middle Ages, men rarely write love stories, do they?—It's almost always about something else, while the love element is just a vehicle—and if they do write about love, it usually ends with the woman being left or dying—Dido, Manon Lescaut, Anna Karenina, etc. I wonder what that says about men's relations with women? (This is a rhetorical question, I'm just throwing it out like that, you needn't answer.) I'm working on the…*

Respected Madam,…I don't know what to answer. I hope you're wrong, but I note in my own reluctance to touch the question that you may have a point…I have read that the part of the brain that is most unused is the part relating to emotions, which is strange because it always seems to me that emotions get too much play in directing human affairs, but perhaps it's the better kind that don't get enough use…

Hania, typing about one dreary episode after another, thought he was right:

...In 1648 there was a rebellion, called the Khmelnytsky Uprising, against Polish rule in the Ukraine. One of the catalysts was a personal injury. Bohdan Khmelnytsky was a Ruthenian officer of Cossacks who quarrelled with a Polish nobleman named Czaplinski and whose estate was then raided, his son injured, and his fiancé kidnapped. (Khmelnytsky got her back, had her marriage to Czaplinski annulled, and married her himself, only to have her executed later, some sources say, for unfaithfulness). Finding the Polish king unwilling to help him in the matter of Czaplinski's predations, Khmelnytsky turned the Cossacks— who were angry that peace treaties between the Polish-Lithuanian Commonwealth and the Ottoman Empire would prevent their usual raids on the Empire—against the Commonwealth and convinced the Tatars to join them. Although the Ruthenian nobility was Polonized, the mass of Ukrainians felt oppressed by the rule of the nobles, the harshness of the Jews whom the nobles used as middlemen, and by the effects of the Counter-Reformation in an Orthodox country. Khmelnytsky roused the peasants against Poles and Jews both...fifty thousand to several hundred thousand Jews died; Polish men, women, and children were put to the sword wherever they were found; and the Polish army committed atrocities in return. The Ukraine east of the Dnieper passed from Polish into Russian hands, while Poland suffered the Deluge, a string of invasions from all quarters.

Hania contemplated the passage. How horrible and stupid. Why were people so often horrible? With a vague feeling of the disquiet she always felt on reading about wars, she looked about, not able at once to revert to the everyday world where people were safe, and children played in the yard...And speaking of which, where was Maks?

As if on cue, Patricia and a group of her cohorts appeared at the open door. "Please, *pani*, where's Maks?"

"He was here..." A minute ago, she was going to say, and then realized it was longer. She rose quickly. If he wasn't with the other children, where was he? She walked quickly through the house. No Maks. How long had it been since she last saw him? Half an hour, an hour? She'd lost track of time. Her uneasiness growing, she hurried into the backyard and shook Kalina awake.

"Kalina have you seen Maks?"

"I was sleeping." She closed her eyes again.

Hania walked from one corner of the house to the other, and scanned the distance in every direction. A minute ago, she thought, I was typing. A few minutes ago perhaps a tragedy was happening and I wasn't paying attention. The frog pond was fifty meters away. Gooseflesh began to crawl up her arms. She ran over to the water. It was only a meter deep, perhaps, at its deepest, and he had promised to stay away from it...but still. She pushed through the reeds and stared at the stagnant pool. The water was motionless, the surface broken only by skittering water insects. If he was in there, it was too late, she thought, the beginnings of panic rising within her. A frog plopped off a lily pad and made a little splash. It was a frog. It wasn't Maks, making one last effort to rise to the surface. She had to be sure. She plunged into the water, waded to where the sound had come from, and felt about in the murk with hands and feet. No small submerged body met her fumbling limbs. She pushed the hair out of her eyes, and bent over the water, peering down, her wet dress clinging to her bosom. "Maks!" Nothing. The water cleared slowly. She couldn't see the bottom but she felt sure there was nothing there. Almost sure. She waded in a circle, bent over, felt around, straightened.

No, but no, he'd just disappeared for a moment––he'd be at the other end of the village. She ran, wet clothes clinging and flapping, back to the waiting children. "Where's Yola? Where's Hubert?"

"Yola's with her aunt."

"Maybe he's with Yola and Hubert. Let's go see." She speed-walked down the road, the children following behind, pleased with the excitement, picking up additional children as they went. "Maks has disappeared, Maks has disappeared." Oh, goody.

They rang at a gate. Yola appeared. "Maks?" She'd seen him heading in the direction of the railway station. He was following behind some people with backpacks. Some tourists, maybe, she didn't know them. She saw them go into the trail by the woods. When? She didn't know, quite a while ago now.

Hania remembered what he'd said to Kalina: "We have to go back…" She'd been thinking about the email she was writing; she hadn't been paying enough attention. Oh, why hadn't she paid attention? Could he have gone back to Warsaw on his own? There could be no other reason she could think of why he would take the trail through the woods. It wasn't at all like him to go off on his own. He had lurid imaginings, was afraid of the dark, afraid of the forest. He would only have gone if he could have followed someone. Oh, Maks. Certainty struck as she tried to reason with herself. He wouldn't. He would. She had to follow him fast. Did anyone know when the train for Warsaw passed, she asked, her throat dry. The children all shook their heads. Yola went to ask her aunt. One went at eleven-forty-five and the next at one-thirty. After that there wasn't another until evening. It was ten to one now. Hania ran back through the village, through the house, and shook Kalina awake. "Kalino, wake up! Wake up! I think Maks has taken the train to Warsaw! Is it possible? Would he go to Warsaw by himself?"

Kalina opened her eyes, sat up looking dazed, thought a minute, and nodded her head. "Yes. He would. Because…"

Hania didn't wait to hear the reason. "Are you sure? Because if you think so, I'm going to call the police."

Kalina nodded, looking scared. "Yes. You'd better call them."

Hania called the police station. The receiver was picked up and she could hear sounds in the background, a leisurely conversation being finished before a voice came on. "Hallo. Police."

"Hello. This is Hanna Lanska in Żabia Wola. I'd like to report a lost child."

"One moment please." A long pause. She stilled her breathing.

"A…lost…child…" She could imagine the police officer writing slowly, the slow cursive of the uneducated.

"Please, it's a matter of urgency. I think he took the train to Warsaw."

"Name," the voice was bored.

"Maksymilian Lanski."

"No. Your name."

"Hanna Lanska."

"How do you spell it?"

"Please. It's a matter of urgency. He's only seven and I think he's on the train by himself…"

"*Pani*, please. One thing at a time. Spell your name."

"L.A.N.S.K.A." The minutes were ticking by.

"Is that L like 'Ludwik' or R like 'Robert'?

"L like 'Ludwik.'"

"Hold on a moment." She could hear a conversation in the background. Krzyś was going for coffee, or did he want a coke? And did you see the soccer game last night? Super goal, wasn't it?...

Hania trilled nervous fingers on the phone. "Please sir!" she wailed into the receiver.

"L like 'Ludwik' or R like 'Robert?'"

"L. Ludwik. Ludwik-Ludwik-Ludwik!"

"*Pani*, please! Don't get impatient." A pause... "Now is this lost child a boy or a girl?"

"A boy. Age 7. He just turned 7."

She could hear him repeating as he wrote: "A...boy....age...seventeen..."

"Name?"

She slammed the phone down in a fury.

"Kalino! Kalino! We have to go after him at once. We have less than twenty-five minutes to get to the station!" She ran through the house, stuffing their most indispensable belongings into a bag. A minute later and she was back outside, pulling Kalina to her feet. "Come on! Run! Or we'll miss the train!"

They ran, Hania with the bag slamming against her thigh, Kalina clutching her stomach. They ran along the edge of the field and into the woods and Hania stopped and leaned against a tree and wondered if her lungs would burst. Thirteen more minutes. They ran, stopping periodically to catch their breath, running on. Hania's throat was like sand paper, her lungs felt like a squeezed sponge and the world swam before her eyes. There was the cement slab of the station.

"The train's coming!" gasped Kalina, "I can hear it. It won't stop unless we're there!" She dashed on ahead and jumped onto the platform, flagging to the train. Hania came up as the train slowed to a stop with a long blast of its whistle. They just had time to stumble up the ladder when it was in movement again, then picking up speed. Hania opened a compartment door and collapsed onto a bench, gasping for breath, her chest heaving. Someone handed her a small bottle of water. She drank, and eventually felt better. She found a towel in her bag, dried her face, and looked around. Kalina was sitting opposite, watching her.

"What," said Kalina, "if he didn't take the train, and he's still back there in Żabia Wola?"

They rode for many miles in silence, contemplating this idea.

"He'll go to the neighbor's," they decided. "Someone will look after him. We'll call when we get to Szczotki Dolne."

"Of course," said Hania, when she came back from purchasing their tickets, "maybe he'll be in Szczotki Dolne. He'll have to change trains. How will he do that? How will he know where to go?"

"I don't think he'd leave the station," said Kalina doubtingly, "I think if he couldn't figure out which train to get on, he'd stay there. At the station. I hope."

"Let's hope so."

"Unless he got on the wrong train."

The two hours passed very slowly. The train stopped at every tiny town, every cement slab, every trail through the woods. It barely got under way and it was grinding its brakes again.

They were coming into Szczotki Dolne. They were jumping down from the train, rushing along the platform looking right and left, into the shabby glass and metal station. No one was around. Hania rushed to a ticket window. "Excuse me," she said to the ticket lady, who looked up from her tea, "did you by any chance see a little boy pass through here? About this high, with glasses? Around a quarter to two?"

"Lots of children pass through here, I don't pay attention, I'm sorry."

Another woman entered the booth. "There was a little boy like that. With glasses. He was asking which platform for the Warsaw train. I didn't see his parents around. I thought he was goofing off while they were in the restrooms or something."

"Do you know where he went?"

"No. He went off and I didn't pay attention."

Kalina said, "Hania, the train will be coming." They turned and hurried towards an underground passage. No Maks.

A warning signal. Could that be the train? They quickened their pace, were almost running, then Kalina stopped and stood still.

Hania came back to her. "What is it? What's the matter?"

"I don't know. I feel strange."

Hania looked at her. She did look very odd, almost white. Maybe it was just the light of the underpass.

"I think I'm going to faint." She was swaying.

Hania caught her. "Here, sit down."

Kalina collapsed onto the ground. The train whistle blew. *Boże, Boże kochanie*, the train was coming in.

"Kalina," said Hania with forced calm, "You can not faint now. You can't. We have to find Maks. Get up!"

The loudspeaker announced. "Train for Warsaw leaves in three minutes."

"Kalina! Three minutes. Come on, I'll help you. You can faint on the train." She pulled the girl to her feet again and supported her as they staggered along the passage, up the stairs, along the platform. The whistle blew. The train was going to go. A station guard stopped the train with a signal, rushed towards them, caught Kalina's other arm, and helped Hania drag her up onto the train. They were off.

On the train Kalina revived. "I'm all right now," she said, leaning wanly and limply against the window and leaving Hania to fret on her own.

If only the police had been helpful, she thought, they could have called Warsaw and someone would have been looking for Maks at the station. If this had been America, the police would have been helpful and efficient; they would have found Maks…and then would have charged me and probably his parents with child neglect or abuse and after ruinous lawyer fees we'd be lucky to get off with just our smirched names and suspended sentences and Maks would go to a children's home. In America someone always has to be to blame …I am to blame.

Maybe the conductor will have caught Maks, she thought, as the compartment door opened and she handed over her ticket to be checked. When the conductor left she said to Kalina, "Do you think the conductor might have found Maks? He won't have had a ticket."

Kalina opened her eyes. "If Maks doesn't want to be found, no one will find him." She closed her eyes again.

True, thought Hania, leave it to Maks. But he would have to get out at Central Station, go through all the taxi stands and traffic, around the station, through the underpasses, along the city streets. What if he got run over?

"Will he take a bus?" she asked Kalina, "when he gets to Warsaw? Got. Or do you think he'll have walked?"

"He'll walk. He wouldn't know which bus," mumbled Kalina.

"Will he know his way?"

"Maybe. Probably. If he doesn't get lost in the underpasses."

Of course, maybe he was still back there in Szczotki Dolne. Or maybe he never left Żabia Wola. Maybe he was wandering, lost, through the woods.

A train employee came by, pulling a refreshments cart. "Anyone want potato chips, sandwiches?" he queried. Hania shook her head impatiently. She was too nervous to eat. How could one eat at a time like this?

Warsaw. At last, they were on the outskirts of Warsaw. The suburbs passed, one after the other, the train stopping occasionally. And then here they were, coming into Central Station. She roused Kalina, made her walk to the door so they could jump out the minute the train stopped. It was entering the tunnel, the platforms raced by, a shriek of brakes and they were there and getting down from the train.

"Do we search the station first or go straight home?"

"Go straight home. He wouldn't stay here, I'm sure. This close to his goal he'd go on."

"But Kalina," Hania asked, as they rushed up a staircase against a tide of travelers hurrying down. "What is his goal?"

"Just to get home, I guess."

"But why?"

"Here," said Kalina, without answering as they emerged from the building onto the sidewalk, "which way do you think he'll go? Do we split up and take different routes? Or what?"

"No. I think we'll take a taxi. If he isn't at home, I'll call the neighbors in Żabia Wola, and if no one's seen him, I'll have to call the police again." She headed for the front of the taxi stand.

"Even if he's there," Hania said to Kalina in the taxi, "he won't be able to get in. Not even into the building if the intercom's fixed."

"'Course he will. He's not stupid like that Paulina ..." she broke off abruptly. "He'll ring at the neighbors and ask them to let him in or he'll wait till someone comes in or out."

"Yes. He still won't be able to get into the apartment though, will he? Unless you have a key hidden somewhere?"

"He won't care about that."

"What do you mean?"

But Kalina had the look of someone who was biting her tongue, and wouldn't answer any more questions, but only stared out the taxi windows and shrugged.

9

While Hania was still paying the taxi driver, Kalina had already rushed over to the entry, pushed a button, and been let into the building. The door didn't close fully behind her and Hania was able to catch it before it locked. She stood for a moment in the entryway, hearing Kalina's footsteps running up the stairs. She followed more slowly. One landing, two. Surely if Kalina had found Maks waiting in front of the door, she would have called something down to her? The third landing, the fourth. Hania was panting now. There was the Lanskis' door. No Maks. Above was only Konstanty's apartment. Maks wasn't here. So where was he? *Boże. Boże.* And where was Kalina? Hania looked about. Had she gone to a neighbor? To Aneta's family?

Kalina was coming storming down from above. "He's not here and Bartek's gone too!" she shouted.

Bartek? Who's Bartek? And what do I do now? thought Hania, her heart sinking.

"He's our dog. She is, I mean." Kalina stopped several stairs above Hania, and tears began to roll down her face. "We were keeping her in the attic," she muttered between sniffles, "in the old laundry space. We've had her there for months."

Someone was on the stairs above them, slowly descending. Konstanty Radzimoyski. Hania's heart gave a painful slam in her chest. Not him. Anyone but him.

"Good evening, ladies. Are you looking for Maks?"

Oh, wonderful Konstanty.

"Is he with you?"

"Yes." A smile. "Why don't you come up?"

Maks with Konstanty. Horrors. "I hope he wasn't too much trouble," Hania ventured, hurrying up the stairs.

"Oh no. He was quite helpful. I'm setting up a website with medical information for people with no knowledge of medicine. It has to be in simple language. I tried each sentence on Maks and if he understood I figured I'd got it right."

Konstanty's apartment was identical in layout to the Lanskis'—but how different in atmosphere, thought Hania. Somehow it had an air of peace and order that was completely lacking below.

They passed through the hallway, into a large room. The first thing Hania noticed was the large carved desk. The next was Maks, almost lost amongst the tapestry cushions of a wide sofa, holding a small mongrel dog.

"Hello, Maks," said Hania, calmly. "We've been looking for you."

"Why did you let people know about Bartek, stupid?" said Kalina angrily.

"I'm not getting rid of her!" returned Maks belligerently.

"Mama will make you."

"I'll run away." He lifted his chin, adjusted his glasses. "I know how now." He tightened his grip around the dog's neck.

"Maks. Kalina. Please. We can discuss it later." Hania turned an inquiring eye on Konstanty.

He said, "When I came home this afternoon and saw that the intercom had been fixed, I was afraid the girl who was coming to care for the dog might not be able to get in. So I went upstairs to make sure it was all right—had food and water and all that. And I found Maks....I got the Lanskis' number in Żabia Wola from information, but no one answered, so I thought I'd better hang on to him. I left an email message for you too, but I suppose you've had other things to do than check your emails."

"When he disappeared, we thought he'd come here."

"You knew about the dog?" asked Kalina incredulously, staring at Konstanty.

"Yes. I suppose everyone in the building does." Except your parents, he added to himself. "It's been a couple of months now since I first noticed you and Maks going up there to the attic. Sometimes I hear it barking. And sometimes at night I hear toenails clicking on the stairs so I know you walk it. I was afraid it might not be very good for it to be shut up in a dark attic. But I kept an eye on it and since it appeared to improve in condition, I decided to hold my peace."

"Improve in condition! Did you see it when we found it? It was skin and bones and now look how fat it is..." said Kalina indignantly.

"Er, yes. In fact, I wonder..."

"And its hair was all matted and it had sore eyes!" Kalina went on.

"We put my eye medicine in," said Maks. "It worked real well."

Konstanty the doctor raised his eyebrows a little, "I'm not sure that's recommended," he began and then stopped abruptly. "Yes. You've taken very good care of her."

"I suppose you'll tell our parents now." Kalina's remark was sarcastic in tone and delivered to the air between Konstanty and Hania.

"It's not my business," said Konstanty politely, withdrawing a little.

"Maks, Kalina, let's not bother Mr. Radzimoyski anymore. Let's go home."

"Have a cup of tea before you go?" Konstanty asked Hania. She realized that he was looking at her dress. She glanced down at it and found that the green frog-pond water had dried in tie-dye rings across her front.

"I thought Maks fell in the pond. I was searching for him." She explained, embarrassed.

"You must have had quite a day. You look worn out."

The sympathy of his tone was almost too much. Behind the sofa, a parchment genealogical chart hung on the wall. Below it, Maks and Kalina were quarrelling about the dog. Hania realized how very, very tired she was. She just wanted to get away, to go someplace and hide.

"Thank you," she shook her head at him, "Thank you anyway. And for looking after Maks."

"Don't mention it." But the reserve was up again.

It was a weary troop that entered the Lanskis' apartment a floor below. The apartment had the musty smell of closed-up rooms and a good bit of dust had collected. Only the little dog seemed in good spirits and ran about sniffing everywhere and exploring. No one felt like talking. There was hardly anything to eat in the apartment, but they opened a can of green peas and mixed it with a ramen soup, and after this unappetizing meal, divided in three, they all went to bed.

As Maks dropped off to sleep, Hania heard him murmuring, "the inner kidney has fifteen collecting tubes …"

When Hania woke the next morning, it was to the consciousness of multiple sore muscles, of relief, and of a curious flat feeling. In all her life, it seemed to her, only two people had ever said, with concern, "you look tired." That the first should have been Kalina and the second Konstanty was one of those strange ironies of life. Neither really cared for her. Why was it? Was it because she was so overweight that no one had ever felt she needed care or protection? Her grandmother had cared only for those who might be of use to her, or would in some way increase her sense of worth. To them she had been charming, warm, and imperious. Her father? He was too lost in his abstractions ever to notice other people's feelings, and her mother had been so concerned with trying to illicit a response from her father that she had never had much time for her daughter as a person. And yet Hania knew that if she had been a sylph-like figure, she would not have been as easy to overlook. Why is there a point after which excess weight makes a person invisible? It had seemed to her sometimes, playing the piano, that her love for the music, for the doing of it, the making it, was connected with the fact that it made her real, made people pay attention, made them notice—if not her, at least something she had created…She rolled over in bed. Enough, she said to herself, with an attempt at an inner laugh. Soon you'll be like Kalina, with her pacifier. Get up and eat breakfast and you'll feel better. Or was breakfast her pacifier? Now there was a shocking idea. Somehow the thought of breakfast wasn't at all enticing anymore. And there was the dog problem to deal with, and the apartment to clean, and she wanted to get Maks back to playing the piano, and—and, in short, it was time to get up.

The dog was lying curled on a sofa, but raised its head and thumped its tail when it saw her. It really was the most hybrid-looking creature, she thought, as she bent to pet it. Perhaps it had had a Dalmatian in its ancestry, and possibly a Yorkshire terrier. Very small, it was mostly white, with a few ill-placed black spots, and tufts of hair growing at odd angles. In fact, the sofa was already covered in hair. She supposed it needed to go out. The children weren't likely to wake early today she thought, so she searched through the apartment till she found a piece of string, which she knotted round the dog's neck. The dog didn't seem to mind the knotting, but when she suggested it get off the sofa and accompany her, it dug in its feet, lowered itself flat and heavy against the sofa cushion, and gave every signal that it didn't intend to budge. Obviously a Lanski, she thought with chagrin.

She stopped tugging on the makeshift leash and straightened up. "Bartek!" she said very firmly, pointing to the floor, "Get off and come along!"

Bartek gave her a reproachful glance, slid off the sofa with a thud, and waddled towards the door.

As they strolled slowly to the grocery store, Hania tried to ignore the fact that she was sure all the passers-by were thinking 'like owner, like dog.'

She went into the store with the dog. The proprietor leaned over the counter to look at it, almost friendly for the first time since she had begun going there.

"What a breed." He clucked to the dog, "nice doggie," and tossed it a bit of sausage, which it caught and swallowed in a flash. "I see it's going to have puppies!"

"No!" exclaimed Hania in horror.

"Oh, yes," said the man, "I know about dogs. Not a doubt."

Hania looked at the dog, looked up. Konstanty had appeared behind her. "Good morning, *pani*."

"Ah, here's a doctor," said the proprietor, indelicately, Hania thought. "What does *pan* doctor think? Isn't it going to have puppies?"

Konstanty put his head on his side, regarded the dog, looked at Hania, and nodded his head regretfully.

"No..." said Hania, but this time it came out more as a wail.

They came out of the grocery store. "Are you going home?" said Konstanty, "I'm walking that way."

They began to walk. "I heard recently that the building administration has plans for the attic. It's going to be renovated—part as storage space and part as apartments," said Konstanty as they headed toward their building. "So the children wouldn't have been able to keep the dog there much longer anyway."

Hania was silent, taking this in.

"The puppies are an additional problem, I realize," said Konstanty as they walked along. "But I should think having the dog is good for Maks. Of course, it's none of my business, but I've been noticing him since I came back to Poland three-four years ago, and I think he has problems. Or rather, that he could easily develop into a child with problems. Perhaps if you explained to your aunt and uncle how important the dog is for him––that it's not just a whim—they would let him keep it."

Yes, thought Hania, that's how it would be with other parents. But not with Ania and Wiktor. Konstanty didn't know that they'd just dumped the children on her, unsuspecting, and been out of touch for—how long was it now?—over five weeks. Concerned parents they weren't. Somehow family loyalty prevented her from saying this.

"You can be very persuasive," he added with a smile.

She felt the compliment but turned the subject and began to tell him about the previous day's adventures. Somehow, in telling it began to seem very funny and Konstanty was even laughing.

They were approaching the building. "Are you going in now, or would you like to take a turn around the block?" he asked. They walked on. His phone rang and she listened to him talking to a patient, his tone calm, kind, concerned. He was so good, she thought. He excused himself, begged her to go on with her story.

She got to the part about Kalina's near faint in the underpass. "I hope nothing's seriously the matter with her," she said, adding that Kalina adamantly refused the idea of medical attention and she had no power to force her.

"There are many different causes for fainting," said Konstanty cautiously, "mostly they're not serious …it's sometimes thought to run in families. Do other members of your family faint easily?"

No, thought Hania, no, all the adult Lanskis I've known are unusually stouthearted and hardheaded.

But Konstanty had stopped and was standing as if struck by a thought. When she looked up at him questioningly though, he merely began to walk again, his measured stride beside hers.

Why did I tell him all that, thought Hania later, miserably, as she sat in front of her laptop waiting for the children to awake. Why? What a family he must think us. Rushing about like complete maniacs, diving into ponds, running away, children with problems, neglectful parents...he would know that even if she hadn't said anything. She had an image of his own family—not that she'd ever known them—but they would be like other educated Polish families, only more so: Parents very concerned for the children, watching their every behavior—correcting, correcting—encouraging, ensuring that they did their homework, learned to speak English, learned to speak French, stood up straight, spoke respectfully, wore clean clothes, sat still, went to church and really took in the commandments, never ever caused heads to turn, and developed a sense of civic duty and strong family bonds. She had an image of Kalina and Maks quarrelling on the sofa at Konstanty's. She remembered herself barging onto the train in her soiled dress, luggage jammed in the entryway...Enough. They lived in two different worlds and that was that. She could still be friends with him. "You can be persuasive..." he had said that with a smile. She felt a surge of warmth, but it didn't last long. She opened the lid of her computer and began to type:

Poland spent almost the entire 17ᵗʰ century engaged in battle. In addition to the Khmelnytsky rebellion, and wars with the Turks due to incursions in both directions of Cossacks subject to both sides, the main struggles were with Sweden and Russia. The war with Russia began when Ivan the Terrible invaded Livonia toward the end of the 16ᵗʰ century. After Ivan's death, some Polish noblemen helped an impostor, the 'False Dmitri,' usurp the Russian throne, and when he was murdered in 1609 (his remains were shot from a cannon back in the direction of Poland), the Poles took Moscow and ruled there until 1612. A settlement put the first of the Romanov dynasty on the throne, but Poland and Russia still seized every occasion to fight, and their wars continued on and off across the century, intersected by wars with Sweden, including the invasion called the Swedish Deluge, which was accompanied by great cruelty…

Hania made a note to email a question to Konstanty, glad that she had something besides various persons' physical and emotional ailments to discuss with him: 'Would the consequences really have been worse if Poland had not fought Sweden? Of course, I realize there were no easy answers. Only, I do wonder at the spilling-your-blood-for-the-country gusto with which these events are portrayed in Polish films and books…'

When the century was over Poland had lost a third of its population; its territory had been reduced; agriculture and trade were failing; poverty became widespread; toleration diminished; corruption spread, magnatic families gained in power, and Sarmatism, a frequently regressive and xenophobic world view, became prevalent.

And now, thought Hania, looking up from these images of past disaster, I can go to the window and look out at a stream of shiny cars and well-dressed people walking their dogs. My world seems peaceful and secure. But in Poland's golden age, how impossible all the future catastrophes must have seemed too. What was it one thought of in looking back to the 17th century? Baroque architecture, with its combined swirl and brio and sobriety of bell tower and pediment and buttress? Someone occupied such buildings and attended such churches. In that age too there must have been boys who played with small dogs—before the tides of destruction rolled over their homes, flattening dwellings and harvests; before they took up a sword and, listening not to reason but the spirit of the times, rode off to add their blows in the beastliness.

She shook off the mood. As she reread a line she had just typed from the diarist Jan Chrysostom Pasek, she imagined some of these 17th-century Sarmatian noblemen, with their shaven heads and long, sashed gowns, speaking Polish in a macaronic mix with Latin: *'In decursu Augusti we went to Denmark to help the Danish king, who made an aversionem in the Swedish war...not ex commiseratione for us, but because that nation was ab antiquo well-inclined to Poland…and feeling odium against the Swedes...'* She went on with her work. Here, anyway, was a lighter reference to horrors coming from abroad, by a contemporary poet with a home-grown taste in beverage:

> *In Melcieśmy, I remember, I tasted coffee:*
> *A drink for pashas, Murats, Mustafas,*
> *And other Turks, such an abominable*
> *Drink, such a horrid poison and venom,*
> *No saliva could carry it past the teeth,*
> *Christians shouldn't pollute their faces with it.*
> *–Jan Andrzej Morsztyn*

She decided to get up and make herself some of the anathematized drink, but here was Maks awake and jumping onto the sofa beside Bartek, who greeted him with sufficiently lavish affection that Hania, whose feelings for the mongrel had previously been tepid at best, warmed toward the dog.

"Isn't she beautiful?" Maks asked.

"Yes," Hania lied. "Why did you name her Bartek?" In Polish, a male name for a female creature made for oddities in declension.

"I like that name. It's like Batman. She was starving and so poor. I thought maybe she doesn't want to be starving; maybe she wants to be a hero. Besides, when I found her I didn't know she was a she. Kalina said." He was stroking the dog's head lovingly.

"It's definitely a she. It's going to have puppies."

"Really?" He looked at Hania with delight.

"Really?" said Kalina, appearing in the doorway in her too short nightshirt, and throwing herself toward the dog with effusions: "Sweet little doggie. Are we going to have puppies? Are we going to be a mommikins?"

Hania observed the group with distaste for a moment.

"Yes. And what do you think your parents are going to say?"

That froze them for a moment. "They'll never know," said Kalina, after consideration. "We'll put them all in the attic…I suppose we'll have to give the puppies away when they get old enough," she added to Maks. "We can take them to the dog market by the Łazienki."

"Maybe we can sell them!" said Maks eagerly, "I saw puppies there for 500 *złoty*. If she had four or five puppies that would be a million *złoty*! We'd be rich!"

"No, Maks. When are you going to learn to count? It would be 2,000 *złoty*. But that's only for pure-bred dogs."

"Bartek's better than a purebred dog! Her puppies…"

"Yes," said Hania, breaking in on these calculations, "one way or another—if you try hard enough—you can probably get rid of the puppies. But what about Bartek?" And she told them what Konstanty had said.

"There's no hope," said Kalina, looking serious. "Mama and Tata will never let us keep her. If Maks makes a fuss they'll say 'okay, you can keep her,' and then one day he'll come home from school and find she's gone. What are we going to do? They'll take her to the pound."

"No!" shrieked Maks, grabbing the dog around the neck and squeezing it so that it squirmed and whined.

Konstanty would think she'd failed toward the children if the dog was disposed of, Hania thought, but she had no doubt that Kalina was right.

"Perhaps you want to think about trying, yourselves, to see if you can find someone to adopt Bartek. Some nice person." But even as she said the words, she knew it was wishful thinking. By the time the puppies were old enough to wean, school would have started, Ania and Wiktor would be back, she would be gone …and a dog of uncertain age and pedigree would be hard to get rid of at any time. There were so many dogs about. Everywhere one went there were people with dogs—boxers, terriers, limping Alsatians, quantities of dachshunds, and every sort of half or quarter dachshund. So many people in Warsaw already had a dog.

"*You* could keep her!" said Kalina. "You could tell Mama and Tata it was your dog."

"Yes," cried Maks happily, as if the problem were solved. "That's a great idea. And she would really still be ours, but you would say she yours. Oh, that's great!"

"No, Maks, it won't work, I'm afraid," said Hania with regret. "I have a job in New York. I have to go back to it at the beginning of September. I can't stay here."

"You're going away?" Maks asked in disbelief.

Both children were silent for a long time.

Then, "I told you," said Kalina to Maks. And to Hania, "but you could take her with you. It would be better than what will happen to her here."

"I can't. The lease on my apartment in New York has a no-pets clause."

"You're going away and you're not going to help us?"

"Oh Maks, I wish I could help you, but I don't know how. I'll try to think..." But he didn't let her finish.

"I hate you!" he screamed, his face turning suddenly red. "I thought you were okay. But you're not. You're just a big, fat, stupid *turnip*!" He ran out of the room.

Then he thrust the door open again: "I'm going to make your life *miserable*!" He slammed the door.

"He doesn't mean it," said Kalina with averted face to the silence in the air.

"Yes, I think he does."

"Yeah, he probably does." Kalina agreed, watching the dog as it began to scratch the paint off the door in an attempt to follow Maks.

10

Libertas elementum meum
– motto from a political tract by King Stanisław
Leszczyński

Konstanty stood in his apartment, looking at the genealogical chart. It had been made by a talented miniaturist some time before the war, on a large parchment sheet, so that a good part of the wall was covered with the small, partly imaginary, heads of his ancestors, surrounded with tiny laurel leaves, in all their branching ramifications. Here was a lady—he peered at the inch-high portrait—reputed to have had Socinian views; did she give in, weighed down and overwhelmed by her surroundings, her background, or did she want to scream 'no!'? Her three sons went off to war and only one, his ancestor, came back. His eyes traced the line downwards. Intriguers, plotters, inciters to rebellion— oh, and here was a black sheep, the family gambler.

Konstanty had a glass of red wine in his hand, but he wasn't drinking it. The wine was a cosmopolitan habit he'd brought back from abroad; Polish men didn't drink wine alone in their apartments, or not, at any rate, from glasses. Occasionally he glanced down at the liquid and watched the red climb the glass when he tilted it, considering. He should take that down, that chart; he would have done so when he moved back from London, only it had seemed rather improper to change anything in the apartment, it being all the way his parents had arranged it. There was a crucifix over the door of nearly every room. Like the chart, the tapestry covering one wall, and the scattered oil paintings, they seemed a part of the décor to him.

He was thinking of the last email from Hania. 'Is it possible to reject the history of one's nation?' she had asked him, and while he knew it was a rhetorical question, he was framing an answer. He didn't think she quite had the intellectual upper hand, and yet she was always pushing him to think further; just slightly beyond that point where, previously, he would have been content to rest, for a year or two at least. Under her influence, he realized he was beginning to think rather differently about a number of things he'd always taken as givens.

She had written once that 'rejection' was easier for her as an outsider. It had been easier anyway, in regards to American history. The American Revolution, she had written—with a sort of flippancy that rather perturbed him, in some deep corner of his being—was wrong, throwing the tea overboard was stealing, and being taxed, however unjustly, was no reason for killing people. She had said so, she wrote, during a junior-high history class. The teacher had been embarrassed. The students, fortunately, weren't paying attention. What, he wondered, would happen to a Polish child who objected in class to one of the accepted symbols of Polish glory?

He had written to her: 'Are you talking about not venerating events that cost so many lives? Of course, it's axiomatic that historians are supposed to give a balanced picture.' Haven't I managed it? he wondered. He had a feeling that he, who had lived longer in Poland, was closer to the horrors of its past—was more weighted by its history. He agreed with her, and still he had a feeling that she made no allowances for the wrongs Poland had suffered, for its very real grievances in the face of crushing superior forces. She gave it no weight for being the underdog...

She expected more. 'What I want,' she had written back to him, 'is for a history—for a world view, because that's what it produces, isn't it?—to be devoid of states' interests, of judgments on the order of 'what was good for' Poland, or America, or whichever group of people (disregarding how bad for some other group), and whose goal would be to record the misery inflicted or the better conditions achieved, regardless of ethnic or national allegiance...All histories should be in essence histories of what was good—or ill—for humanity...'

But surely many historians—Polish, American, European—were objective and critical. Or was it that too few listened to them? After all, there were all those statues, and museums, and streets with names like 'Defenders of the Peace,' all those 'Combatants' Parks'—he had pointed them out himself. He had an image of Polish history reduced to the scale of the history of Szczotki Dolne, of the sole good being the advance of Szczotki Dolne in relation to Poland and the world. If Western historians had managed to get beyond that in terms of a broader association—Europe, the West— were they still at the 'Szcotki Dolne level' in terms of what was good for Russia, China, Africa? Would globalization bring about the broader picture, or only a change from nationalist interest to the interests of a cosmopolitan elite? He mused for a moment.

I won't take down the chart, he decided, but I won't expect my children to hold their great-great-grandfather's activities in great reverence either. He peered at the tiny miniature head of Michał Konstanty Radzimoyski on the chart. And here were his own grandparents, Jan Michał and Izabela, good people and upright, who brought their family safe through the war with uncomplaining resourcefulness. He couldn't be irreverent towards them, certainly. And yet his own children would be different. If I ever have any, he added to himself, drinking the last of the wine and heading for his computer.

"So you don't want me to invite Kalpurnia again?" said Pelagia to Konstanty as they sat the next day drinking tea in her peaceful garden amongst the tall pine trees. He shook his head, "Rather not. Very nice girl. Exactly the right type, I suppose. But no."

"You're hard to please."

"Yes."

"How can she be the right type, and be 'no'?"

"Chemistry?"

"What nonsense."

"No, I want a woman who is very intelligent, full of ideas, of warmth…who wants to listen to me, even when I'm boring. I don't know…"

"'Very intelligent' might be difficult; 'fairly intelligent,' I can come up with."

"It's just that I've met one like that…"

"Really?" Pelagia was all interest. "Tell me about her."

"No, for a lot of reasons… and she's not a possibility."

"Hmm…"

Konstanty could see Pelagia thinking, and wished he hadn't said anything.

"I know," she exclaimed, with an attempt to stifle a giggle, "it's Natalia Lanska's granddaughter, isn't it?"

"Let's change the subject."

Pelagia obligingly changed the subject, but continued to eye him. Suddenly, in the midst of a conversation about the health system, she broke off and stated firmly, "You need someone like Izabela, the one who designs furniture…some one very beautiful and charming. Too bad she's already married."

"Beautiful and charming—those are always married."

"True." Pelagia sat back in her chair and considered this fact glumly.

"I'm not sure beauty is really necessary, anyway," added Konstanty after a pause.

A long pause. "Wiktor can compose the music for your wedding."

"Pelagia! Please."

But really, thought Konstanty, as he drove home, rather regretting that he had let the conversation with his sister go so far, what is beauty? Perhaps because I'm a doctor, because I am acquainted with what's under the outer wrapping, it makes me too familiar with people as conglomerations of possibilities for high blood pressure, for heart failure, for the proper or improper functioning of all sorts of tubing and mechanics and chemistry. All bodies age, and most minds. I want a mind, he thought—but here he had to pay a bit of attention to the road, to downshift—I want a mind, he thought, shifting up again—that I will not outgrow. The necessities of the traffic prevented him from putting a face to the mind at once, or from considering that not too long ago the outer wrapping had not been a matter of indifference to him at all. But when, some time later, he began to think about Hania, he at once shook his head. Of course not Hania. Pelagia had known he wasn't serious, couldn't be serious, otherwise she would never have joked the way she had.

A civil war led to the abdication in 1668 of the last Vasa king, Jan Kazimierz. He was succeeded by two Polish noblemen. The second, Jan Sobieski, was born in 1629. He studied philosophy in Cracow, learned languages (including Tatar), and travelled abroad. His education, and perhaps his personality, fitted him for a better existence than he made of it. He went off with his brother to take part in opposing the Khmelnytsky Rebellion; the brother died and the rest of the story is contained in war: moving up the ranks to commander, he was in the Battle of Beresztec-zko—1651, the Battle of Warsaw—1656, the Battle of Podha-jce—1667, etc., etc., every year a battle—Hania typed on…*the Battle of Chocim—1673, (as a result of his victory here—and French bribes to the nobles—he was elected King of Poland in 1674).* Then more battles…*the Battle of Vienna––1683 ('The people kissed my hands, my clothing,' he wrote to his wife. 19,000 soldiers died)*…then more battles…*He died in 1696, his country in disarray, and is considered—*'oddly' Hania inserted, marking the word for Konstanty to note—*to have contributed to Poland's glory.*

Even while I am typing these things, thought Hania, I am thinking not of unending death and destruction, but of the fact that Konstanty wrote these words, looked at these words, and I am wondering when I will see him again. She knew that some days he worked evenings at the hospital, so it was much less likely that she would run into him on the stairs or at the grocery shop—or even that he might—she was silly enough to hope it—ask her out for coffee again. She had the more difficulty in keeping her mind off her imaginary romance in that the home atmosphere was unpleasant.

There seemed nothing to be done. Days passed. Maks' bad temper gradually declined into a simmering boil that allowed him to function normally and even be tolerably polite, but which boded ill, Hania realized, for some time when she was least expecting it. Fortunately, she had had the foresight to check her bed that first night. Three eggs were nestled at the foot, under the covers, just waiting for her to climb in and break them. But since then nothing had happened. Hania checked chairs before she sat down, her drink before she drank it, and kept Maks as much as possible in sight. He returned to learning the piano, even if he wasn't very cooperative, and insisted on changing the rhythm and the dynamics, playing everything fortissimo and looking at her to see if she would object. Sometimes she simply walked away and closed the door on him.

She tried to persuade him as much as possible to get out of the house, hoping that exercise might blunt some of the edge of his aggression. Her persuasion mostly took the form of bribery pure and simple. "Maks, come to the park and then we'll eat ice cream."

Wasn't that the tactic her mother had used with her? Hania thought, as they sat one day in café chairs beside the sidewalk, eating chocolate ice cream. After Babcia had said she'd never make a pianist, no talent at all, and Mama had been determined to prove her wrong: "Hania, practice one more hour and you can have a big bowl of ice cream." It was a very bad idea, using food as a reward regularly. Look at the results for her. She hardly fit in this wicker chair. Well, and why did people so nearly always repeat the mistakes that had been made in their own upbringing? Like Wiktor and her father being neglected as children, being furiously resentful of Babcia for the fact, and then turning off to their own children. Or herself, a stuffed child, stuffing another.

Respected Sir—she would write when she got home. She began composing her letter between spoonfuls, then pushed the bowl away, deciding she didn't really want it—"Is that instinct? That the accretions of experience, good or bad, have to be passed on? Is this the reason why humanity seems to have such difficulty breaking out of old patterns of behavior? One war leading to another and on and on, when avoidance would be possible if a little reason would be used because—"

That ice cream was going to go down Maks' shirt front. She half rose, scrabbled for a napkin. Too late.

"Maks," she asked another day, "don't you have friends you could go see or invite to play with you at the park?"

"All Warsaw kids go on vacation," interposed Kalina, "they've all gone to Cyprus or Egypt or Tunesia. Except the ones who went to the sea or to the mountains."

"Everybody goes on vacation but us. Why can't we go back to Żabia Wola? We could take Bartek. She'd like it."

"Yes, and come back again on the train with all the puppies? No thank you."

"Don't say we're going to the park again. It's too boring. I won't go. There's nothing but sandbox babies in the park."

"So we'll go sightseeing."

"Nooooo!"

"Come on, if you're good I'll buy you a nice treat. We'll go see St. John's Cathedral, where Stanisław Leszczynski was crowned king three hundred years ago." She had been typing about Stanisław that morning and her mind was full of his story as she got ready to go out. It seemed to her comforting, somehow. '*A man who would have been a good king for Poland but wasn't given a chance*,' Konstanty had called him. Stanisław had been a high-minded young nobleman when he caught the eye of the Swedish king, Charles XII, who had just invaded Poland. The king of Poland being on the run, Stanisław had been crowned in his place, but on Sweden's expulsion, he had had to abdicate and go into exile. The previous Polish king tried to have him assassinated, but he forgave his would-be assassins.—For which fact alone he should be honored, thought Hania.— Then he spent the next years playing music, painting, engaging in philosophy, and educating his daughter, who was unexpectedly invited to marry the French king, Louis XV.

So that was another marriage, sighed Hania. It was better not to dwell on such things. She picked up her handbag, collected Maks, and left the apartment, still thinking of the past.

Years later Stanisław had been persuaded to try to regain his throne. Konstanty had written that the French prime-minister, Cardinal Fleury, had sent him off for reasons having to do with the Austrian succession and

Bourbon interests in Italy and nothing at all to do with Poland. Poor Stanisław hadn't known that, of course.

Stanisław was getting on in years, badly overweight and not very healthy…

What had Konstanty thought on writing that, she wondered, did he feel the sense of repugnance some people seem to feel toward the obese? And yet his tone toward Stanisław was warm—

…he set out obediently for Poland in disguise, as an ordinary traveller, with a few companions, and was duly elected. Unfortunately, he was forced to abdicate again after a disastrous period of foreign intervention and the Russians' siege of Danzig. He had to flee on foot, through swamps and over great distances, all the time in danger of his life.

Hania and Maks were waiting at a stop light to cross the street. Maks tried to annoy her by repeatedly extending a foot beyond the curb.

…Having unwittingly served French interests, Stanisław was given the Duchy of Lorraine to rule, which he did with great success, making technical inventions, designing palaces and innovative gardens, promoting justice for the common man and religious tolerance, writing treatises on government, law, and philosophy; founding an Academy of Science and a public library; setting up a social security scheme for his subjects and a rudimentary but free health care system; and hosting many free thinkers banished from his daughter's court in France...

He had done all these things and been much beloved by his subjects, thought Hania, as she walked along with an eye on Maks. She'd asked Konstanty in an email if there were any statues or squares in his honor in Poland? No, he'd replied, he didn't think there were, not in Warsaw anyway. Perhaps because he hadn't won any battles? she'd asked, writing that she thought Stanisław made a good hero. She hadn't added that it made her own efforts to make the best of things seem more supportable to have a model. She liked the account of Stanisław's last days too:

He lived to be 88; in his last years he was rather feeble, but one of his former mistresses, whom he had shared with great goodwill with his prime minister, took kind care of him and he would sit by the canal with a fishing line, watching the passers-by. One morning his robe caught fire as he bent to light his pipe at the fireplace. An elderly waiting woman came to his aid and received burns as well. "Who would think that at our age we would burn with the same flame?" he joked with her, gallant to the end. His days were numbered but he remained cheerful: "you warned me not to get cold, you should have told me to look out for the heat," he wrote to the Queen of France, his daughter.

Hania hoped she'd keep her sense of humor that long. Judging by the look on Maks face she was going to need it. He was dragging behind her.

"Where are we going?" he whined, as they walked along Krakowskie Przedmieście.

"To the Old Town."

"The Old Town bores me."

"Yes. I know. You've told me so 23 times already. But we can't stay in the apartment all the time and I haven't been there for so long. And it's full of history. Look, see this church?"

The Church of the Sacred Heart loomed above them, its tall double flight of stairs protruding onto the pedestrian mall. "Chopin's heart is buried in there. Well, not buried, but sort of encased in a pillar."

Maks looked up at her, with a scowl. "That's horrible." He had stopped and was standing still. "Why do you tell me horrible things like that?" he said in a tone of disgust.

Oh dear, she thought, maybe she shouldn't have told him. One could never tell with Maks. It *was* unpleasant—carving up bodies for sentimental reasons.

"Come on," she said to Maks, "You're right. I'm sorry I mentioned it."

"No." Maks pulled at her hand. "I want to go and see it."

A beggar came towards them, an elderly woman, well-dressed and holding out her hand. A man, dirty and ragged, who had been sitting between the stairs, climbed hastily to his feet and came towards them too, hobbling on a cane. Hania distributed coins right and left, received elaborate, insincere blessings from one, and a look of resentment from the other, and hastened into the church. Here it was all white walls, and gilt, and an atmosphere of candles and the strong scent of incense. They crossed the nave quietly, so as not to disturb the scattered figures kneeling to pray. It seemed pleasantly peaceful. I could come here, sometime, and join them, thought Hania. They stared at the pillar for a long time. There was nothing, fortunately, to be seen, but obviously Maks' imagination was working. Hania wondered what went on in Maks' mind. Was he disturbed? Was this simultaneous repulsion and attraction normal?

"Where's the rest of his body?"

"In Paris."

"Oh. Who was he?"

"Chopin?" It was her turn to stare. How, living in a household of musicians from birth could he not know who Chopin was? But naturally, if no one paid attention to children they didn't know much. "He was a composer. One of the great musicians of the Romantic period. I'm sure you've heard his music. He was born here in Poland, but as an adult he lived mostly in Paris, because Poland was controlled by Russia then. About a hundred and fifty years ago there was a revolt and some Poles tried to get rid of the Russians. The result was that a lot of people got killed"—oh dear, here they were again...

"How many?"

Really, the child was a ghoul. "Mmm. Lots. Anyway," she hurried on, "what I wanted to tell you was that the Russian soldiers were so mad about the whole thing that when they found Chopin's piano in a palace near here, they threw it out the window, onto the cobbles." She saw she had his attention. "Come on. I'll show you where, if we can find the spot."

They walked down the street. "This doesn't mean that I want to go," said Maks suddenly, as if their little conversation had been compromising. "You're still my enemy."

"Your enemy, Maks? Would you put it so strongly as that?"

Maks looked a little uncomfortable but he added, his gaze in the distance, "Yes. You'll see."

"Listen, Maks," Hania began, and then stopped. Hadn't she already tried reasoning with him?

"There's a poet called Norwid who made a famous poem about the piano. At the end he says that 'the ideal hit rock-bottom.'"

"I don't know what you're talking about," said Maks. He was drooping along listlessly again, past the intricate wrought iron gates of the university, and the presidential palace—with scaffolding up again, because every president had his taste in paint—past Mickiewicz's super-sized statue behind the fence...he was walking slower and slower.

"There, Maks," Hania pointed, "In front of that church, St. Anna's, see, the king used to sit on a chair, on a high platform, specially made for him, during ceremonies. The former Tsar of Russia, Vasily Shuisky, and his brothers were brought here as prisoners from Russia, almost 400 years ago."

He wasn't listening.

"They spent the rest of their lives locked up in a castle."

He looked up quickly, but resisted the temptation to be interested. She gave up. There, standing before the Castle, in the Royal Square, was the tall column of Zygmunt III Vasa. They reached him and she stared up, contemplating the slightly bent figure. A jail-and-Jesuit-twisted man with a large cross in one hand and an up-raised sword in the other. It was a good statue, but the symbolism was offensive. They should take it down, Hania thought, even if it is a good statue, artistically speaking. Or they should break his sword or cap it, to show that no one approves of that mentality any more.

The base of the statue was crowded with skate-boarders, whizzing up and down, from plinth to cob-blestones, and a number of break-dancing teenagers were mashing their heads into cardboard to the sound of a radio. They seemed as far removed from old Zyg-munt as possible, but one never knew, perhaps such images left marks upon the brain and influenced behav-ior, later, in moments of trial...

Above them the brown-orange walls of the Castle looked down stolidly below the cheerful clock tower. They crossed the cobbled square with its pastel, candy-box houses. Not for them the expensive britchkas with their round, heavy horses awaiting customers. Those are the sort of horses I'd have to ride, thought Hania, as they threaded their way through the tourists, if I were ever to get on a horse. She spared a warm fellow feeling for the creatures.

They headed for the river, passing through the old market square, where the well-to-do sat under canopies, eating salads, and on to the embankment, where the young people sat on walls, drinking beer. Below, far below, on the other side of a highway, the river stretched out, gray and reserved and windswept, to a far bank where willows grew and nothing moved but possibly birds.

Hania leaned against the railing. Her ancestors, down how many generations, had stood thus and looked at the river. There wasn't any place in America where she could stand and think that. Did it matter? She looked down at Maks and considered putting the question to him, but he was caught up in watching the bicyclists go down the hill, and she didn't dare. In spite of his current intermittent enmity, he was close, he was here, he was her cousin, and New York and all her life there seemed very far away.

They turned back, and on Świętojańska Street, next to the massive pile of St John's Cathedral, they listened to a violinist, standing on the cobbles beside the crouching statue of a bear guarding the Piarist church. Someone, Hania supposed, from a symphony orchestra somewhere in Russia, or Belarus, whose livelihood depended on busking, illegally, in a foreign city. She was lucky in comparison. Two policemen were strolling towards them. The violinist hastily lowered his instrument, picked up his case, and moved off.

There was a window, selling waffles with cream. The scent was delicious, and Maks pulled her towards it. They ate, standing in the street; the cream dripped between their fingers, and the waffles were as good as they smelled. Well, thought Hania, this has really been a rather successful outing. We've walked a long way, and Maks hasn't really complained that much—since we got here—and maybe it had some educational value too. Really, she felt quite pleased. They finished their snack. Hania threw away the wrappers.

"Shall we go?" she said to Maks.

Maks backed away. "Who are you?" he said loudly.

"Maks," she hissed, "Stop that. It isn't funny. Come with me."

"What do you want from me?" he said, even more loudly, so that a middle-aged couple standing near, tourists obviously, looked at one another, clutched their cameras, and hurried away. "Why do you want me to go with you?"

"Maks! Stop that and come on!" She said angrily, her face turning red. People all up and down the street were stopping to stare.

"What's happening, child?" a brisk woman asked Maks, approaching and giving Hania a suspicious look.

"I don't know this lady, and she wants me to come with her," shrieked Maks, with totally convincing theatrics, "I think she wants to kidnap me."

The woman was joined by a number of other persons; they all turned and gave Hania indignant glares and began to talk at once.

"No," Hania tried to explain, growing more flustered by the moment. Piano concerts had given her poise, but nothing like what was necessary for such a situation. "He's just pretending! He's my cousin. Really ...I…"

No one listened to her explanation. There were five different opinions of what should be done and an argument was starting.

"Here are the police coming," said one of the group surrounding Maks. "You'll see I'm right," he added in an irritated tone to the others.

The police, the police, just great, thought Hania. What to do? What to do?

"Run, Maks! They're going to put you in *jail* for disturbing the peace!" she yelled over the hubbub of his rescuers.

"Aaaa!" shrieked Maks, and breaking through the circle, he dodged around the brisk woman and her helpers, pushed his way through a group of Japanese tourists who were clustered round a store window, helplessly observing the commotion, and ran down the street.

Hania whirled and ran after him. The Japanese tourists flattened themselves against the wall. Hania raced after Maks till they reached the end of the street and ran into the Royal Square. Maks stopped. Hania looked behind. No one seemed to have come in pursuit. She caught up with Maks, and walked past him without speaking. He fell in beside her.

"Maks," she said furiously, controlling her voice with difficulty. "I've tried to be your friend. But this was it. The outer limit. It's over. Finished. I'm not going to be your friend anymore. I don't care what happens to you. I don't care what happens to your stupid dog. It's over." She strode on, very fast. She just wanted to get as far away from the Old Town as possible.

"You mean you're really mad?" said Maks, trotting to keep up. He seemed surprised.

She stopped. "Yes! I'm really mad! I'm furious! I'm not going to do anything for you anymore." She walked on. "I'm not going to cook for you, or clean for you, or sit with you at night, or teach you the piano, or anything. You don't like me. Well, fine. I don't like you either."

To her surprise, he burst into tears. Real, genuine, grief-stricken tears. He cried all the way along Krakowskie Przedmieście Street; he cried, with heartbroken sobs, at the bus stop, where several women scolded Hania for her cruelty—"*Pani*, how can you treat the child like that? He'll make himself ill"—and all the rest of the way home, only stopping on the staircase to scrub his face with his sleeve. "I don't want Kalina to see me like this," he explained, sniffingly.

In spite of her year of teaching she really knew nothing about children, Hania thought.

11

Pity me, both old and youngling
I've been to a bloody wedding.
– 'Świętokrzyski Lament' (Medieval)

"Tata called," Kalina said, when they came in the door, exhausted and red-faced. And then to Maks, "What's wrong with you?"

Why, oh why, do I always miss them, thought Hania, tearing her mind away from the unpleasantnesses of the afternoon, and Maks' condition.

"What did he say?" she asked eagerly. I need to tell them that I have to be back in New York, that we're going to run out of money—because I've been using my own and what with paying for the groceries, and the electricity bill, and the train tickets…

"What happened to Maks?" Kalina asked Hania accusingly, when Maks wouldn't answer her. "What have you been doing to him?"

"I…" Oh, really, thought Hania, now I have to justify myself as well. "Maks can tell you that. But please tell me what your father said."

"I don't know; I wasn't listening."

"What?"

But of course, like father, like daughter, thought Hania in outrage. "Aren't you even interested in when they're coming back? It matters because of Bartek, after all—and I have..."

"Why are you getting so excited?" Kalina looked at her curiously. "I told them everything's fine, nothing to worry about, and they shouldn't hurry back. That's right, isn't it? We don't want them to come back, do we?" A pause, and then, very definitely,"I sure don't."

"No, no, we don't want them to come back," said Maks, continuing to sniff. "We want you, Hania. I'm sorry I did all those bad things."

"Right..." said Hania, and she left the children, went into the piano room, and sat down at a piano. She reached for the keys, and before she even began to think, her fingers began to play....

Suddenly she broke off. That was the piece she'd played at her last concert. A very small concert. She had played it perfectly and the applause had been half-hearted. She'd heard the audience's soft, startled cessa-tion of breath when she appeared on stage. Now she sat with her hands in her lap.

In three weeks she had to go back to New York. She would leave the children and return to her job. One had to make a living somehow. She doodled on the keys with one hand, rose impatiently, and went to the bookshelf. She ran her eyes over the list of titles hoping to remember something of use to her in this situation. There was Orzeszkowa's *On the Niemen*—that was an unusual riches to rags story in which the 19th-century heroine, against the background of Poland's last failed insurrection, considers leaving a position of compara-tive wealth and leisure for poverty and hard labour with the man she loves. I would gladly give up my compara-tive wealth for comparative poverty with Konstanty, she thought, but the question was hardly likely to arise.

She was not the heroine of a novel and her going or staying only concerned the children and herself.

And in either case, what was she going to do about Bartek? What was she going to do about Kalina? She had tried again to get the girl to go to a doctor but Kalina had refused point blank. And now she'd taken again to disappearing in the afternoons, not saying where she was going, and dressed in those outfits—those 'I'm a prostitute' outfits, there was no other word for them...And Maks? Hania, seated again at the piano, struck a quiet chord with her left hand. Well, it wasn't really her affair. In three weeks she'd be gone...she wouldn't have to worry about Kalina or Maks ever again, probably. She'd hear about them every few years through her father, who'd most likely get it wrong—she'd learn Kalina was a geology student when in fact she would be studying psychology. Maks would end up in a reformatory and no one would ever mention him. They would pass out of her existence.

The next afternoon Kalina put her head through the door of the piano room. "I'm going out." At least she said she was leaving these days, thought Hania—that was progress.

"Kalino! Wait!"

Kalina came into the room, looking defensive. "What? I have to leave. I'm going to be late."

"Late for what?"

"I have to meet someone."

Hania stopped on the point of asking "whom?" Kalina wouldn't tell her and she wouldn't like the prying. "I just—I know it's not my business, but I wonder if you really want to go out dressed like that?"

"What's wrong with the way I'm dressed?" Kalina asked angrily.

"It's just…" Hania began tentatively, "there are certain ways of dressing that make a woman look like she doesn't have a very high opinion of herself. Like she's begging for attention…"

"What do you know about it?" Kalina was instantly on the defensive, "Look at the way you dress—you call that having a high opinion of yourself?"

"I have to dress like this because I'm so overweight," murmured Hania, abashed. "I..."

"Well, if you have such a good opinion of yourself, why are you so overweight?"

Hania had no answer, and Kalina pulled the door shut and went off.

No, it wasn't exactly like that, thought Hania, trying to reason down her hurt; that wasn't really the mechanism. After all, there was Babcia. No one could say she had had anything but a superb opinion of herself, and yet she had been very large. Babcia had just liked to eat and she attacked the subject of food with the same impetuosity that she put into everything else. There had come a point for her, Hania supposed, when the pleasures of the table had come to outweigh the advantages of being less round. But then, for Babcia it had probably been a choice to let herself go. Hania hadn't made a choice. She could never remember exactly when she had ceased to be simply a far too chubby child and had become a seriously heavy teenager. She distinctly remembered the comments of other kids in high school, but by then she had been well on her way to obesity and any change had seemed impossible. She had had her music to concentrate on. She had concentrated to effect, blotting out every other unpleasant aspect of her life. It was only lately that she had begun to look at herself, to look about, and to think that she had ruined her life—no, that was too strong a phrase—that she had, rather, like most other people, in one way or another, put a serious impediment in the way of her own happiness.

What would her grandmother say to her, she wondered, if she were still alive?—now that she was adult, and perhaps they could have talked as adults. Would there have been any level at which they could have met? Would there have been one person in her family who might have empathized with her? Probably not, she thought, remembering some of her grandmother's more abrasive letters, but she would never know. Suddenly she wished very much that her grandmother were still alive. Now, she realized, she would never really know what she had been like. Tomorrow, she decided, she would go to visit her grave. She hadn't been yet.

Kalina was in a foul mood the next morning and only reluctantly and resentfully agreed to watch Maks, who said he didn't want to be watched by his stupid sister and had taken Bartek into the bedroom and slammed the door. Hania left the house with a feeling of escape. To walk along the street alone, to be unencumbered and have an hour of freedom ahead of her—it was wonderful, it was lovely, the sun was shining; she sat down on the bench at the bus stop to await her bus. The bus didn't come at once, and she began to wonder what Maks was doing, and why Kalina had suddenly become so unpleasant again, and what she was going to do about Bartek. Of course, in a very short time she would go back to New York, and then she would be free all the time, like this, and it would be wonderful and—very lonely.

A car had stopped in front of the bus stop and someone was speaking to her. It took a moment for her to come out of her thoughts. It was Konstanty, asking if he could give her a ride.

The car pulled back into traffic. She sat in the car and remembered what Kalina had said about her clothes and weight. She was going to Powązki Cemetery, she said. He suggested that if she had time to wait while he went into the hospital, he just had a brief errand there, and then he'd be glad to accompany her. Unless she preferred to go alone?

Prefer to go alone or with Konstanty? She almost laughed. Still, she was rather startled, made rather shy by his offer. She thanked him quietly.

Was it just his imagination, he thought, or was she losing weight? Maybe he was just getting used to the way she looked. She had quite a nice face, actually. Large hazel eyes and nothing objectionable about her other features.

They pulled up in front of the hospital. It was a pleasant-enough place, arranged around a courtyard with flowers and trees. "I'll just be a moment," he said, and was gone. Hania sat and watched a stream of elderly people, of women with swollen legs, of hobbling men with inward-looking faces, passing in and out of the building. She imagined them waiting at bus stops, going home, fixing dinner, washing their clothes and ironing them—they were all so clean—and doing the house-work, all in the face of illness.

Konstanty was back. He gave her his quick half smile. "I hope I wasn't too long. We can go now."

"I think that no matter what problems one had," Hania said with feeling, "a half hour spent in front of a hospital would make one think they were fairly small. It's like that piece of Solon I read once: 'If all our misfortunes were laid in one common heap, whence every one must take an equal portion, most people would be contented to take their own and depart.' I don't know how doctors bear it."

They were in traffic again. "It's not really that bad. What makes any problem seem worse is the sense of helplessness. Mostly we can do something for our patients. Not always, of course—and then it's good to have some other interest, some distraction. Most doctors have some outside passion that occupies them; for the women doctors it's usually their children. The male doctors go skiing or mountain hiking...I like history... But I'm sorry to hear you have problems that need to be reduced to size by the contemplation of worse ones."

The sympathy and the unstated question were almost too much. Almost she told him everything. Instead, she just smiled and said offhandedly, "No, nothing so terrible—just small worries about the children."

"I suppose their parents will be back soon."

Why did this fact no longer seem desirable?

They were approaching the cemetery, parking, passing by flower stalls. Polish people were always buying flowers for graves. Hania stopped. She couldn't afford one of those big formal bouquets—not to mention that she thought they were hideous—and perhaps one of the small pots would seem too skimpy. She could imagine her grandmother thinking "is that all?" in the one case, and "hmpf, what a waste of money," in the other. Konstanty was waiting patiently.

"I don't know," she said, "None of these seem right somehow."

They walked through the gates into the alleys of graves, quiet below the tall arborvitae and linden trees. Even the sound of the nearby traffic seemed muffled. Here were the birch crosses to the young, the piteously young, men and women who died fighting in the Home Army. "Age 17." Hania read on one of the markers, "I don't suppose he even understood what it was all about."

"The origins and reasons? No. Most soldiers don't. Or if they do, only their small, immediate part of it. They are cogs in wheels beyond their imaginings, no matter how well instructed or aware they may be...And not only soldiers. Take the First World War. Perhaps 37 million casualties, and the causes—I don't mean the train of events—are so unclear that historians can't agree on them; only that there was a great deal of nationalist feeling about."

They walked on. He said, "There used to be the graves here of some of the German soldiers who fell; some thousands of them in mass graves. But they were moved a hundred kilometers or so outside of Warsaw. I don't know why."

And here they were passing the tombs of the survivors of the 1863 Uprising. The graves were planted with hostas with tall pale-blue flowers; there was moss and cobblestones. What a lot of old rebels lived to be one hundred, thought Hania. Was that like musicians? They tended to be very long-lived too; it was good to have an interest in life. Were they kept alive by a passion of contrariness?

A short walk further and they reached the grave they were seeking. And now that they were here there seemed nothing to say or do. Hania stood contemplating the slab of marble. "Natalia Lanska, Pianist," it said, and her dates. I'd prefer to have "beloved wife and mother" on mine, thought Hania suddenly, not "pianist." Still, she was sure "pianist" was exactly what her grandmother would have wished. No doubt she had even directed it to be engraved thus.

She turned away, and Konstanty fell into step beside her. "I used to hear your grandmother playing," he said, "when I first came back to Poland from England. I would come back from the hospital—I was doing very long shifts in those days, conditions were worse than they are now—sometimes I would come in weary and discouraged, and I would hear your grandmother playing. I'm not musical, you know. I can't tell one Chopin piece from the other, but I always found it solacing and—uplifting, in a way. When she fell ill and stopped playing, I missed it. I've never found that recorded music has the same effect at all, even though it's supposedly more perfect—or so I've read."

"Yes. Live music is like a conversation with another person, recorded music is like words in a book. It's not the same thing."

"When will I have the privilege of hearing you play?"

"Oh, I don't play anymore," she answered dully and he gave her a look and obligingly changed the subject.

"Over there," he said, pointing an arm, "is a Muslim cemetery, and in that direction, the old Jewish cemetery."

"What will you do about the Second World War?" asked Hania, as if by an association of ideas. "I notice you've left it off in the material you gave me. Are you still working on it?"

"Yes. I'm thinking about it. Its closeness makes it difficult. My parent's generation lived through it—or didn't live through it in a lot of cases—and the numbers are so vast. The extermination of the Jews. I don't know if you realize we passed through the former Jewish ghetto on our way here? It's all Stalinist-and-later-era apartment buildings now." He gestured with an arm, "And then the non-Jewish population—2 million or more across Poland. During the Warsaw Uprising, over 150,000 civilians died in two months...In Poland—as in America and England, I think—we concentrate on our own losses; we forget the other civilians who died: Germany's more than two million victims, Russia's 13 to 17 million, China's 11 to 16 million. Over 60 million people across the world, and over half of them non-combatants—women, children, the elderly....We don't remember much about the bombing of German cities, or about Hiroshima, or the millions who starved in Bengal under British rule, or that our ally Stalin was a monster. It wasn't the liberating, saving, or patriotic event of later myth-making."

"You don't want, certainly, to exonerate the Nazis of their crimes. But the other participants shouldn't be exalted either. To paraphrase Churchill, you think that 'Never have so many owed their deaths to so few?'"

He was a little shocked at her irreverence, but smiled. "Something like that. Only, no, it's really that we're all responsible."

They walked in silence for a while, and then he continued. "To me the only heroes were—not the politicians or the fighters—but the ordinary people who risked their lives to save others—and there were many who did so. For instance, there was a young Pole named Matysiak I read about recently. He not only went into the Ghetto to bring out the Jewish girl he loved and her family—he then went back to rescue her dog. A couple I know kept a Jewish woman, a complete stranger, hidden in their apartment for two years—to the risk of their own children. I don't know that it's a decision I would have made. Of course, there were lots of denouncers too—that's the other side of the coin—but when one thinks that for every Jewish person saved ordinarily not one, but very many people, had to be involved, then one can see that Warsaw still holds numerous individuals—elderly people now—who showed the best side of their humanity."

"Yes." They were strolling slowly, very slowly, back towards the car. Hania broke another long silence. "Speaking of difficult subjects, do you think Churchill *did* help Stalin assassinate General Sikorski? Or is that just one of those conspiracy theories—Poles have a tendency towards those, I know."

"No. I don't know if it was Churchill. Or if it was an assassination. But I think the fact that the British have sealed the records for an additional fifty years is suspect."

"Fifty years. I wonder if I'll live long enough to know the truth?"

Not unless you lose weight, he thought, and then was angry with himself for the thought. It seemed so cruel, so harsh to have jumped to his mind like that. And she was really such a nice young woman. "Of course," he answered. "It won't make the news in America, but I'll send you a postcard, and we can dodder over to our old history books and scribble little amendments in the margins."

Konstanty dropped her off at their building. He had errands to do, he said. Hania, after a visit to a hospital and a graveyard and a discussion of war casualties, should have been depressed. Hania floated across the sidewalk and up to the door as if she were a part of the sunshine.

Aneta, the neighbor, was there, just going in. She watched Hania descend from the car and approach the entrance.

"So he gave you a ride?" She was watching the car drive away.

"Yes."

"He's nice, isn't he?"

"Yes." They went into the building and began to climb the stairs.

"Of course, I suppose he feels a lot of gratitude to your family."

Hania didn't really want to discuss her family or Konstanty with Aneta, but she couldn't help asking, "What do you mean?"

"It was because of your grandmother that they—the Radzimoyskis—got to keep that apartment. Everybody knows that. She had pull with the authorities. Didn't you know? Didn't you ever wonder how come only you—your family—and the Radzimoyskis have a full pre-war apartment, and for the rest of us they were divided? It was your grandmother. Who knows where the Radzimoyskis would have ended up otherwise, because in those days…well, you've heard how it was. You're lucky."

Hania could hear the note of envy, that bane of Poland, creeping into Aneta's voice. Even Aneta, she thought, whom she'd always thought pleasant, if simple:

et tu Aneta. Suddenly she felt quite flat. So perhaps his attention wasn't liking for her, but repayment, in sort, of a family debt to her grandmother? Well, of course, that made more sense. She said good-bye to Aneta and began to climb the next flight with such a weight on her heart that she suddenly realized—it's not a crush. Her legs didn't seem to want to move. She leaned against the banister. She was trembling and she felt sick. It's not a crush, she thought, I am in love with him, and I have every reason to be in love with him. He's a kind, caring, interesting man whose character has been known to me for a long time and whose family background vouches for his adherence to high standards. I'm in love with him. It's not just some crush that I'll forget about when I go back to New York and my usual activities.

But I'll have to.

She let go of the banister, straightened herself, and went on up the stairs.

She opened the door of the apartment to chaos.

"Hania! Come! Come quick!" shrieked Kalina.

Maks appeared, dancing about, waving his arms. "Bartek's having puppies! Bartek's having puppies!"

"Haannia!" called Kalina urgently.

Hania hurried down the hall and into Maks room. Bartek had chosen Maks' bed for her birthing nest. In the midst of heaped sheets and blankets, the dog was panting and straining. One small puppy—was it a puppy?—lay in a crumpled ball, another appeared to be emerging from the birthing canal. There was blood everywhere and green liquid. Hania felt her stomach heave.

"Aaaaa!" shrieked Maks, "Blood! Blood!"

"Is she all right?" asked Kalina, "Hania, do something!"

"Blood! Blood!" Maks shouted, hopping about.

"Maks! Be quiet!" commanded Hania, going to the bed. *Boże, Boże,* she knew nothing about dogs. "Imagine it's ketchup."

"I'm going to faint!" whimpered Maks.

Must be from Ania's family, thought Hania, her mind ricocheting. Surely the puppies were coming much too fast for normal? "Maks, you can't faint! Go find a hairdryer! Go!"

"*Do* something, Hania," said Kalina, "this one—I think it isn't breathing."

"Get that bulby thing we bought, Kalina, quick!" Kalina was gone and back in a flash, handing her the instrument.

Hania knelt beside the puppy. Indeed, it still had the sack over its face and appeared quite still. With a feeling of deep revulsion she wiped the sack away and began to suck the liquid from the puppy's throat with the bulb syringe. It didn't seem to be responding. She continued to aspirate and rub it. Maks had come with the hairdryer. Maybe it was breathing now? She wasn't sure. She handed the puppy to Kalina with instructions for her to warm it. There was the other puppy to see to. And another puppy was coming, *Boże.* She'd read what to do on the internet—had tried to prepare—but she'd never expected it would be so—so real. "Paper towels, Maks! Run!" He ran.

And now, oh horrors, there were the umbilical cords to be seen to. Tie them with dental floss and cut them with a dull scissors. That's what the material said. Three puppies—if the one Kalina was warming lived.

"It's moving," she said, "look! It's moving!"

Okay, so that was that. An hour later there were four puppies, two brown, one black, and one spotted, nestled beside their mother, nursing. Hania, Kalina, and Maks stood in a row, watching them.

Hania drew a deep breath. In a minute she could start cleaning. Maks would have to sleep elsewhere.

Someone was knocking at the door. Who could it be? More bill collectors? She didn't think she could deal with them now. Her hands were still bloody. Maks had already gone to see. She could hear him exclaiming excitedly to someone: "Bartek-had-puppies-Hania-saved-one-with-a-squeezy-thing-she-made-it-breathe-there're-four-of-them-there-was-lots-of-blood-it-was-horrible!"

Hania stepped into the other room. There was Konstanty, holding out her handbag: "You left this in the car."

"Oh. Thank you. I'm so sorry to have inconvenienced you. I can't..." she gestured helplessly with her stained hands.

He laid the handbag aside. "I gather you've saved the day again. Congratulations."

"Yes," she said rather wanly, "I'm the fix-it lady, the repairwoman."

"I'm sure you are," he smiled at her, and was starting to say something when Maks interrupted him.

"Come see the puppies! Come see!" he called, gesturing and hopping excitedly toward the bedroom.

Konstanty glanced at Hania.

No! thought Hania with an inward cringe. The bedroom's a total mess. It was a total mess at the best of times and now...She really didn't want him to go in there, but Maks was still beckoning, and there was nothing for it but to invite him with a gesture to follow.

Kalina had disappeared. The room was empty except for Bartek and her offspring. The puppies had squirmed into a heap beside their mother, who growled softly as Konstanty approached, but made no objection when Maks bent down and carefully scooped up a puppy. He placed it in Konstanty's hands. Konstanty held it up to eye level and examined it.

"A very fine puppy," he assured Maks, and Maks nodded with pride, took the puppy away, and handed him another.

Hania stood quietly in the middle of the room, twisting a paper towel around her fingers. She felt nervous and shy. Suppose he thought she'd made a mess of the umbilical cords? Or that it was poor management to have let the dog have puppies on the bed?

Konstanty, gently cradling the last puppy in his hands, looked around the room at the shambles of bedclothes and blood, at the discarded aspirator and towels, and his gaze came to rest on Hania. She looked like she was expecting him to criticize, he realized with surprise. And he had only been thinking how resourceful she was. He regarded her slightly flushed face for a moment in silence, uncomfortably aware of a mingled sense of pity and esteem.

"You did very well. Really. Congratulations." He handed back the puppy, and said cheerfully and rather briskly, "Let me help you tidy this up. This sort of a job is, er, my sort of job. I think you've probably had enough for today."

But Hania was adamant in refusal and increasingly discomposed, so he quickly took his leave and departed. She closed the door with relief, went into the other room, and sat down with a great variety of thoughts.

Always after a crisis or stress, the next day had a rather unreal feeling. Hania worked at the history, but the lines kept repeating themselves before her eyes.

*...Stanisław August Poniatowski, the last king of Po-
land, was kidnapped twice—the first time in 1733 while he was
still a baby, by a political opponent of his father's. He was not
born to the throne, but was groomed for the position by his relatives, the leading magnates of Poland. He was given a good education and sent abroad to study government (including to England,
which he admired, except for cock-fighting and the education system—'all about the cane.') He then went to St. Petersburg,
where, before returning to Poland to be elected king, he became the
lover of the future Empress Catherine.*

*In describing himself at the time, he laid claim to only
moderate looks and intellectual gifts, but considered himself de-
voted and loyal, sticking to his associates even when they wronged
him, and always 'infinitely grateful for any kindness.'*

Like me, thought Hania, remembering Konstanty's
smile the evening before. I shall always be grateful for
his kindness to me. Somehow she felt like crying. Fortunately, here was Maks to distract her.

He set a small, sleepy puppy down on her keyboard, and she had to quickly scoop up its warm body
to keep it from falling.

"Isn't it beautiful?" said Maks with deep feeling,
leaning over it, willing her to admire it as well. He
seemed almost friendly after the birth of the puppies,
and, in any case, very occupied with the creatures.
"When do they open their eyes?" When will they walk?"
he asked three or four times an hour, and ran continu-
ally to the room to look at them.

Kalina got dressed to go out. She stopped before
she left in front of Hania. "Is this better?" she asked.
Her clothing could have used eight inches more material in every direction thought Hania, but it was a big
improvement. She was touched that Kalina should have
taken her advice, even belatedly.

"Much better." And then she added, "I'm sorry about the other night. I thought we were good enough friends that I could mention the matter, but I didn't mean to upset you. I don't have the right to tell you what to wear."

Kalina didn't look at her. "I didn't mean what I said," she muttered.

Well, thought Hania. Well. One small success. The telephone rang and she picked it up, wondering who on earth. It was Konstanty, and, flustered, she could see Maks and Kalina listening with interest to their conversation.

"Dinner? Tomorrow? Yes, that would be lovely. No, no, I'll meet you there."

She put down the phone, feeling pleased, embarrassed, and worried.

"Are you going to marry Mr. Radzimoyski?" asked Maks.

"No, Maks, what an idea!" she exclaimed in dismay.

"I can lend you a nice halter top to wear," giggled Kalina.

She found a dress shop the next morning, one with a big sign saying it had dresses for plump *panie*. Nothing fit. There wasn't a dress in the shop that would go round, and the shop owner, irritated with her for being so unreasonably large as not to match the stock, finally just shrugged and refused to look for larger sizes or make suggestions. She retreated behind her counter and sat there sipping tea while Hania flipped dispiritedly through the hangers of dresses for women of fifty who'd put on a few too many pounds but still needed to go to the office. There was nothing appropriate, unless maybe this sand-colored dress with the crochet neck. That was almost pretty, but it would never fit. Still, she tried it on. It did fit. In fact, she looked almost—almost nice in it. She stared at herself in the mirror. Almost like she was a little slimmer, and the color was good, and it was crisp and fresh.

"I'll take it," she said to the shopkeeper, who rose, bored, from her stool.

"500 *złoty*."

Hania gasped. 500 *złoty*. She hadn't noticed the price tag. They could eat for quite a number of days with that amount of money. Oh, well…she would put it back. She was never extravagant, and to pay that much would be unreasonable. She began to return it to the rack, and then stopped. Was it unreasonable to want to look nice just once? That is, as nice as she could? Such an occasion wasn't likely to happen again.

"I'll take it," she said, digging in her purse for the money.

12

There's a wheel extending into the street, beside it a bell with a string; the infant was to be placed in this wheel and the bell rung...but when too many infants began to be abandoned in the wheel every night...a guard was stationed nearby...

—Jędrzej Kitowicz, 'On the Infant Jesus Hospital, Description of Customs during August III's Reign,' (mid 18th century)

She was to meet Konstanty at the restaurant; it was close, he had said. She dressed early, admired—almost—her image in the mirror, turned this way and that. It had been worth the price, this dress. And her hair was good—she had nice hair, thick and shiny. She would meet Konstanty in twenty-five minutes.

She came out of her room and looked for Kalina so she could say good-bye. Maks was sitting alone in front of the television. "Maks, didn't Kalina come back?"

"No."

But Kalina had said she would be back—she'd said so, Hania thought nervously. Still, it was early yet. She had time. No need to get upset. She sat down and twisted her purse strap into a pretzel. The minutes ticked by. It would take her ten minutes to get to the restaurant if she walked fast. She wanted to walk slowly, to arrive fresh and not panting in her pretty dress. However, if she had to run, she would run. Oh, why didn't Kalina come? She would go sit at the piano and play scales. She rose, and as she did she heard the sound of the door opening. It shut very quietly, and no one appeared.

"Kalina?" Hania asked eagerly, going into the entry. "Kalina, I have to leave…" And then she stopped. Kalina was leaning against the door, sobbing, silently, the tears running down her twisted face.

Hania went to her, "Kalina, what's the matter?"

Kalina shook her head.

"Come in here." Hania put her arm around the girl and guided her into the piano room. They sat down together on a bench.

"What is it?"

"I can't tell you." She continued to sob, gasping for breath.

Hania looked at her watch. Seven minutes. She could make it on time perhaps, but she couldn't possibly leave Kalina in this state.

Eight o'clock. He would be waiting, thinking she'd stood him up. How very funny. She felt like joining her sobs to Kalina's.

She told Kalina she'd be right back, went to the telephone, asked for information, and then called the restaurant. At the restaurant they said they would deliver her message if they saw anyone fitting the description, but they couldn't make any guarantees. That was all she could do. She hoped he'd forgive her. She collected a box of kleenex and returned to the piano room.

Kalina's sobs were quieting. Tears simply streamed down her face and she sat disconsolately. "Kalina, I want to help you, but I can't if I don't know what's wrong."

"At the church…."

"Yes?"

"There's…I've…We…"

"Yes?"

"I'm pregnant."

"Mother of God!"

Kalina smiled wanly through her tears. "No, not exactly like that."

Hania sat still. What did one say? Kalina was sniffing, between intermittent little gulping sobs. "Only now, he says…he wants to end it."

"Who is he?" Not a priest, thought Hania, please, not a priest. But there were priests who had children, every one knew that.

Kalina didn't answer.

"You say at the church. Is he a priest?"

"No." Well, that's one good thing, thought Hania with relief. A choir boy then. A pimply young fellow, experimenting with sex between soccer with his friends and cramming for a school exam.

"It doesn't matter who he is."

"Okay." She sat silently beside the girl, hoping her sympathy was felt and not knowing what to say.

Suddenly Kalina was talking. "He's the editor of a magazine they sell there. In the printing house by the church. It's an annex to the parish house. It's a magazine about family values, and homosexuals—how bad they are—things like that. He came out to the bus stop when we were sitting there once—two of my girl friends and I—not here, around here, it's quite a ways away—and he gave us these magazines. And we looked at them, and I said 'this is stupid stuff, I don't believe this—I know about family values.' And he said 'come into the office, and let's discuss it.' So I went. I thought he came from the church so it was okay. And then we talked a lot and then I started to go to see him every day, and later…anyway, he said he loved me…and then I learned he's married and has children, but by that time it was too late…" she shrugged.

"Does he know?"

"Yes…he says if I tell anyone he'll be in trouble and he thinks I'm too loyal to do that. And that it was a sin and it has to stop. But he said that before and then…it didn't end. Only now I know it's really ended."

Hania looked her question.

"Because he's started with my friend Paulina." She began to cry again.

"Oh…How old is Paulina?"

"17."

"So maybe she's beyond the age of consent, but you're not. It was a crime on his part, Kalina."

"I don't care. That doesn't matter."

But—thought Hania, and held her peace. No, it probably didn't matter right now.

"When…how long…how long have you known?"

"Since a little before you came. But it's three months old."

"Three months! Are you sure?"

Kalina raised her head and looked at Hania, making her feel her own naivety and inexperience. "Of course I'm sure."

"And you haven't said anything?"

"What is there to say?"

"Only…your parents will want to know…and, and, things like that…"

"I don't want them to know."

"But they'll have to...."

"Yes. But I don't want them to know when they could make me have an abortion."

Hania considered this. Would they? Could they? She had no reason to believe Ania and Wiktor were particularly good Catholics; on the other hand, she had no idea what sort of ideas they might have about abortion. She wasn't a particularly adherent Catholic either and yet she shuddered at the idea. "But you can't have an abortion in Poland…"

"They could make me go abroad."

Hania considered some more. "Not against your will. Would they?" Presumably Kalina knew more about her parents' ideas than she did.

Kalina hesitated. "No. Yes. I don't know. When they're not here it's easy to think I wouldn't give in …but if they were here it would be different. They can make me feel I have to do whatever they want so they'll be happy," she considered lucidly.

Yes, thought Hania, the Lanskis are good at that sort of manipulation.

"I can't tell them…" Kalina looked at Hania pleadingly. "Please, will *you* tell them for me? Not now, but later, when they come back...."

"You want this baby, Kalina?"

"*Yes*." There was passion and conviction in her voice.

But, thought Hania, you are too young to have a baby, way too young. You are fifteen. You have problems. You suck a pacifier. You aren't ready to be a mother. How will you support it? How will you look after it?

"In another month it won't matter. Then—will you tell them, Hania?…Not before though."

"But your parents will come back at the beginning of September. I have to be in New York at the beginning of September."

"Don't go. Please stay. We need you here—there's Bartek too."

Don't go?

Maks came into the room, whining. "What are you doing here? I'm scared in the other room by myself. It's time for me to go to bed. Why doesn't anyone take care of me?"

"Maks, I just told Hania about the baby."

"Oh, that." He wasn't interested. "Someone come with me to the bedroom."

Hania rose. "Yes, Maks, I'm coming."

The next day she felt overwhelmed by the tasks ahead of her. And there was Konstanty. She had met him on the stairs that morning as she toiled up to the apartment with two plastic sacks full of groceries. She had greeted him very shyly.

"Did you get my message?" she asked.

"No, I didn't get any message."

Oh, no. "I couldn't come last night. I'm so sorry. There was a crisis with the children and I couldn't leave. I called the restaurant. I hoped they would give you my message."

"It doesn't matter. Please don't worry about it." He was going on down the stairs, "I'm in a bit of a hurry, please excuse me, goodbye." He was gone.

Hania stood on the landing, watching his retreating figure. And I had this pretty dress, she thought, I almost looked nice. Now he's angry.

She couldn't give in to despair. She had other responsibilities; she went to face them. She would have time to make breakfast and an hour or so to work before she started making phone calls.

On a November night in 1771, King Stanisław August was kidnapped for the second time, his efforts at reform having annoyed a part of the noble class, which rebelled. His abductors, as they fled Warsaw with him, were undone by the dark, the mud, the fall of a horse, and incompetence. The king escaped with the aid of one of his kidnappers, whom he had persuaded to change sides after a long philosophical discussion. He wished to offer an amnesty to all the rebels but was prevented by Russia and Prussia...

Hania typed on, through the unwillingness of the nobles to compromise, to give up their right to rebel, their right of life and death over their peasants, etc., through the failure of reforms, until Russia, Prussia, and Austria, desirous of righting a balance of power among themselves, claimed that chaos prevailed in Poland and, in the first of their successive Partitions, which took more and more territory, divided part of the country between themselves.

....Stanisław August did what he could in the situation. He promoted the arts, sciences, and education (including for girls and including through Europe's first ministry of education). He also co-authored one of the first national constitutions in Europe. The Constitution of May Third was supposed to extend political rights to the bourgeoisie and make Poland more democratic, but instead it led to further rebellion by part of the nobility, another war, and the Second Partition of the country between Russia and Prussia. It is held against Stanisław that he eventually joined the side of the magnates, although he was trying to save what he could of the reforms. He was forced to abdicate and shortly died. He was a humane man, who tried his best for his country. Today he is often vilified.

There, another one who did his best in the face of difficulties, thought Hania, as she finished typing. She liked to read about people who'd made an effort to do what they could. She was trying too. What was that verse?

Do the work that's nearest
Though it's dull at whiles,
Helping when we meet them
Lame dogs over stiles.

She smiled rather wryly to herself. They were all lame dogs: herself, Maks, Kalina, Bartek the least of them. She went to attend to her own duties.

She had insisted that Kalina see a doctor.

"Why?" Kalina had objected. "I don't want to go."

"Yes. But I don't want to be responsible if anything goes wrong." This time she had a point of leverage and Kalina gave in with only token protest.

Hania searched through the phone book and found a private clinic on the outskirts of town. In a private clinic they wouldn't ask to see documents; there wouldn't be any questions about Kalina's parents, etc. So they were going, riding on one bus after another, with Maks, complaining bitterly, in tow because they couldn't leave him alone. Hania tried to concentrate on the views out the window. What a lot of theatres putting on 'Szekspir' and Irish plays; what a lot of movie houses; what a lot of apartment buildings and billboards again. They got off the last bus and began to walk.

Somewhere they were passing a churchyard. Was this the one? She slowed her steps, peering through the fence to see if there was a printing office inside. There didn't seem to be. The fence was sharply spiked, there was a security agency poster on the parish house—obviously the parish priest had never read *Les Misérables*, thought Hania—and there was a sign on the gate scolding the parishioners for not wearing good enough clothes to Sunday service. Hania stared at the notice in disbelief. Maks and Kalina were leaving her behind. Of course, there were all kinds of priests in the Church: some very good and some—not so good. She hurried to catch up with her charges. "Kalina, is this the church?"

"No. And please don't try to find it, because you won't."

Hania tried to imagine herself going in and speaking to the priest. What would she say? How would she begin? "Do you know, Father, what sort of a man...?" She couldn't even remember how one greeted a Polish priest. It wasn't just "good day." It was… "May He be praised...?" Something like that. But how did one say "goodbye?"

They came to the clinic and went inside. There was marble everywhere, bright cream paint, and fashion-model girls sitting at the reception counter behind new computers. Everyone was very pleasant and there was no waiting. Kalina disappeared into a room. Hania sat in a leather chair and Maks went to look at various medical posters.

"Maks, come sit beside me," she said, probably just too late.

"Well," he said matter-of-factly, dropping into a chair beside her, "I don't know why you don't want me to watch television. I think that"—he pointed to a poster graphically detailing a bladder operation—"is much worse."

She was inclined to agree, but adjured him to sit still and stop kicking the chair. "Look at that other poster—the one with the magnified dust mites."

She closed her eyes and tried to concentrate on Beethoven's *Sonata in F.* She opened them to find a woman, heavily pregnant, sitting beside her. The woman smiled and gestured toward Hania's midriff. "When's yours due?"

"Er…" The woman was going to be so embarrassed. "October."

"Everything's fine," said the doctor, appearing with Kalina and handing over a schedule of tests to have done. She's speaking to me, thought Hania, as if I'm Kalina's mother. Do I look that old? I'd have to be at least five years older than I am to have been a mother of Kalina's age.

They left the clinic and took the several bus rides home. Kalina seemed undaunted by the experience, thought Hania later, watching her around the apartment, perhaps even rather pleased by the attention. Perhaps that's what she wanted all along?

A postcard came the next day from Ania, tucked among the sheaf of bills that arrived almost daily. It was stamped "Switzerland."

Kochanie, We've just passed a wonderful week in the— somewhere illegible. *Lots of sun and good talk with friends. We're staying here with the Kueblers. I think we'll be leaving on Saturday. We miss you lots. Hugs and kisses. Mama*

Saturday, that would have been nearly a week ago. There was no telling where they might be now. Please don't let them be on their way to Poland, she thought.

One thing, after all, was certain. Whenever they arrived, she was going to be held responsible for what had happened. She didn't for a moment suppose the fact that Kalina had become pregnant before she came to stay would ever prevent Wiktor—and her father too, when Wiktor complained to him—from blaming her. It would certainly be all her fault for not looking after Kalina properly. And it wouldn't be entirely ill will; she didn't suppose either Wiktor or her father had ever considered questions on the order of the length of the human gestation period; they lived in such abstract worlds she doubted if they knew…Considering her own relatives, thought Hania, there was something to be said, in theory, at least, for the 'family values' people. If only the most rabid advocates weren't so likely to be people hiding some emotional disturbance of their own.

So what, she wondered, was she going to do about this editor of Kalina's? Could she just turn her eyes away and let him go on preying on young girls? Or did she have to take some action? And if so, what?

Later that evening Kalina came up behind her while she was searching the phone book for the names of editorial offices. "You can't do that!" she said.

"I wish I didn't know about it," Hania said, "but since I do, I don't think I can just let someone take advantage of young girls and not do anything to try and stop it. How many teenagers do you think this man will use the way he used you? From what you tell me, I don't for a moment suppose you were the first or that Paulina will be the last. I don't want to involve the police, but it seems to me that if I spoke to his superiors, he could be warned to behave himself, or an eye could be kept on him, or…I don't know…I'm not asking you to give me his name—I know you can't."

"No, so don't try." Kalina was being offensive again—and actually, Hania didn't blame her.

"I know this is really difficult for you…but think if other girls ended up in your situation. It isn't right, Kalina."

"What's wrong with my situation?" Kalina asked angrily. "I like my situation. I *want* a baby."

Then a moment later: "Okay"—she was almost shouting at Hania—"It wasn't the way I said, okay? He didn't know I'm fifteen. I told him I'm a university student and Paulina also. He didn't ask us to come into the office, we followed him. He didn't ask me to come back, I just came. There, are you satisfied?" She flung out of the room.

"Oh," said Hania. That put a different complexion on the whole. Adultery might be regrettable but it wasn't any of her business. Then for a moment, she wondered if Kalina was telling her the truth; turning it over in her mind she doubted and believed by turns; finally, she realized she would never know and that she had better drop the subject.

13

Let us plant roses, friend,
Long yet, the world is sure
To whir with snowy storms,
Let's plant them for the future!
– Seweryn Goszczyński,
'Planting Roses,' 1831

Everything was dreary, she thought with discouragement, typing away at the history. I am coming to a point in Poland's history where it becomes harder and harder to see events simply as something in the distant past, errors that modern progress will eliminate.

Tadeusz Kościuszko, friend of Thomas Jefferson and participant in America's war for independence, has a bridge named after him in New York and a mountain in Australia, and is considered by many to be a hero. He was born in Mereszow-szczyzna—an unpronounceable place even by Polish standards, thought Hania—*of rather poor parents, who owned only one village of serfs. He really wanted to be a soldier, but as no one—and he offered himself to various German courts—*—*would have him, he had to wait for the American Revolution. After taking part in this conflict, he used the money he received for his services to emancipate some American slaves; back home he contented himself with freeing his female serfs and reducing the men's labor…Then, in 1794, he headed a rebellion against the Russian occupation. Although he tried to encourage the peasantry to join by promising them some civil liberties, it was still a far cry from 'all men are created equal.' And the insurrection was a disaster. When the Russian forces reached Warsaw, they massacred ten to twenty thousand of the inhabitants (in revenge, perhaps, for the population's earlier attack on the Russian garrison, when two to four thousand soldiers were killed). The final outcome was the Third Partition, after which Poland had to wait another 123 years to regain its independence.*

Respected Sir, Hania wrote, *Given the divisions—social, linguistic, denominational—of all the peoples existing within Poland's shifting borders, the idea that a small group of people should take to the idea of dying, and worse yet, of killing, for the sake of 'Polish independence' seems unreal…The immediate results always so out of proportion with any possible benefits…not that I think killing is justified for any benefit…*

She considered, her finger over the send button: Should she send this? Perhaps he was getting tired of all her questioning. 'Delete,' she pressed.

Kościuszko had been captured by the Russians, but was pardoned by Tsar Paul I, along with 20,000 other political prisoners.

Serfdom was abolished in the Prussian partition in 1823, in the Austrian partition in 1848, and in the Russian partition in 1864.

Maks came to interrupt her. She looked up from her typing. "You never pay attention to me any more," he complained.

"I thought you were the boy who wanted to make me miserable." She wasn't in the mood for Maks's tantrums, but she regretted the words once spoken. Actually, he hadn't been making her life miserable lately and he'd even seemed fairly cooperative.

"But you're going to stay and take care of Bartek and Kalina, aren't you? So that's okay." He adjusted his glasses. "I don't have to make your life miserable."

She stared at him. Had she given that impression?

"Maks, I can't stay." His face began to take on an ominous darkness, but she couldn't deceive him. "I'd really like to help you, but I can't. I have to go back to New York in two weeks. But your parents will come back, and you'll be glad to see them, won't you? And school will start and you'll see your friends again…"

The phone rang. Maks was muttering something, but she didn't know whether it was "stupid, fat turnip," or "stupid, fat cabbage-head…" and she was glad for a reason to ignore him.

"Hello?"

"Haniu, *kochanie.*"

"Tato?" Her father.

"Hania, how are you?"

"I'm…"

He cut her off. "Hania, listen, Gerhardt just called and he says—"

"Tato, I don't know any Gerhardt."

Her father and Wiktor moved almost entirely in emigré circles of academics, writers, musicians, and scientists of vaguely Polish antecedents, who, although they seldom went near Poland themselves, had no interest in anyone who lacked a connection with the place.

"Kuebler. You know, Wiktor's friend in Berlin. Or Bern? So listen to me. Wiktor asked him to ask me to call you to ask if you wouldn't mind staying another two weeks?"

Why, thought Hania, did Polish people never do anything directly? Why was it always by involving as many intermediaries as possible? And then she thought— —two weeks more; a reprieve of two more weeks. And then, but my job?

"Tato, I have to be back in New York…"

"So I'll call this Szopecki and tell him that's all settled then, shall I? And he can tell Wiktor and Ania."

"Who's Szopecki?"

"I don't know. Gerhardt gave me his number. I think Ania and Wiktor are going to Turkey with him."

"To Turkey? What for?"

"To rest, I suppose, what else? You should go sometime. You know it's not good the way you never get out and see things."

"Yes, well…"

"So how are you? How are things? Did you know it's very hot here today?"

"Kalina's pregnant and I'm in love with a man who will never think of me." She could say it in perfect security. It would never go in.

"Good, good. So that's fine then. Did you know that Ania and Wiktor are going to a spa in Turkey? Wiktor's so tired after all the work he's done this summer that they need to rest. It's someplace called…let me see…well, someplace with a Turkish name."

"Yes, Tato."

"Mamo, it's Hania."

"Haniu, *kochanie*, how are you? Hold on a minute, I have to let the dogs out."

Hania waited for her mother to come back on the line.

"So, what's happening? How do you like Poland?"

"I like Poland very much. It's…just…I have this problem...these problems..."

"Say it straight out, because—wait a moment…" There was a conversation in the background, something about a truck and bales of hay. "Okay, sorry, I'm back on. Wayne's going out and I had to speak to him first. So, what's up?"

"There's this man…"

"In Poland?"

"Yes. I…"

"Oh Hania, you really don't want to get involved with a man in Poland. I hope it's not too late to tell you that?" Her mother's tone slid from worried to irritated, "You know, I really can't understand this fixation you have with Poland."

"That's not the problem…I…"

"Well, what does he do? Could he find a good job in America? You know, it's not all that easy with immigration. You wouldn't believe the problems we had."

"But I don't think he'd want to leave. In any case, that's not the point…"

"Not want to leave? Is he crazy? How could anyone not want to leave Poland?"

"Mamo, Poland isn't like it was. It's completely changed. Lots of things are good here…"

"Like what?"

"There's no death penalty, and the murder rate's quite low, and there isn't a huge jail population, and mostly people don't go around shooting each other, and men and women like each other, and if the health system's far from perfect, at least they're trying to provide one—but that's not what I called to talk about, I…" She thought of the moderate peasant prosperity of Żabia Wola, of the chic denizens of Krakowskie Przedmieście, of weeping willows draping the banks by the Palace on the Water. She would never make her mother understand.

"Hania, please. We can argue about Poland some other time—this is going to be a very expensive call for you. How's the piano playing?" But her mother wasn't listening. Hania could see her quite clearly across the distance; she had her hand half over the receiver and was giving instructions to her husband. Hania could see him too: a kindly man, who always wore boots and a Stetson, even to his wedding, even indoors. He called Hania a 'gal,' had nothing whatever to say to her, and tried to hide the fact by making jokes about 'Pollocks' and about taking her horseback riding.

"It's fine." She murmured, said goodbye and hung up. There was no one to talk to.

The phone rang again under her hand. She picked it up mechanically and was jolted by the sound of Konstanty's pleasant-timbred voice. Almost, she was too nervous to say hello back.

"I was calling to apologize for being so abrupt on the stairs this morning."

Oh, so he wasn't angry. She almost cried with relief. But, of course he wouldn't be angry with her for something she couldn't help. She'd have thought less of him if he had. She could reason like this now that he'd called.

"It's just that I had to get to the hospital rather quickly. I hope your crisis with the children wasn't too serious?"

"No. Not serious. Just…something I couldn't leave." She couldn't tell him about Kalina. What sort of a family would he think them? He would know eventually, of course, but by then she'd be back in the States, and it wouldn't matter so much…But why was she being so 19th-century? Teenage mothers were the commonest thing in the world. Still, she didn't think it would be a neutral fact to him.

"Do you have plans for tomorrow evening? Shall we try again?"

Hania put down the phone, her heart bubbling with gladness, and something like Tchaikovsky's *1812 Overture*—the part after the cannons—playing in the background of her mind.

He had said—she heard the smile in his voice— that this time, he would knock on her door, and they would walk together. He would come at eight.

At seven-thirty she was taking a shower. In the shower one hears nothing. She didn't like that. Maks had been unusually quiet all day. She turned off the water a number of times but she didn't hear anything. She was rinsing the last of the soap off when suddenly someone was knocking vigorously on the bathroom door.

"Who is it? What's happened?" she called.

It was Maks, squeaking, "Come, come quick! Burglars! Burglars have come into the apartment!"

"Maks!" she called, "Please leave me alone. I'm not falling for anything like that!"

"But come quick!" he was whispering loudly and urgently through the keyhole. "They're going into your room!"

"Maks, please."

Silence.

She dried herself and climbed out of the tub. Strange, when she first came to Poland the tub had seemed unusually high, in an odd European way, and hard to get into, and now she hopped right over without a problem. Maybe she had just got used to it, or maybe running after Maks was making her more agile. She had left her bathrobe in the hasty flight from Żabia Wola, so she had nothing to wrap around herself but an old beach towel she'd found in a cupboard. It made a rather insufficient covering, but she only had to reach her bedroom. She tucked the towel in modestly and was reaching for the door handle when Maks began to knock again.

"They're taking your clothes."

"What?"

The towel came undone and fell to the floor. She scrabbled for it, slung it around herself, and ripped open the door. Maks was standing there, head tilted slightly back, holding his glasses to his nose.

"Why didn't you hurry?"

"Maks, I don't like this sort of trick."

"Suit yourself, I warned you."

She hurried along to the bedroom. She had left the new dress hanging on the front of the closet. It was gone. She jerked open the closet door. There was nothing inside, not even hangers.

"Maks!" she shouted. "Maks! Where are my clothes?"

He appeared in the doorway. "I told you. Some burglars came in and took them."

"What nonsense. Tell me where my clothes are."

"I can't. I don't know where they took them."

Hania controlled herself with difficulty. "And what did they look like, these burglars? Like one seven-year-old boy named Maks?"

"No. One was sort of tall, and had blond hair, a nose like this, and a kind of squinty eye." He squinched up an eye. "The other was very large, with big arms, and…he was bald…They were wearing black caps."

"I suppose they were in desperate need of a size-vast collection of dresses." She glanced at the clock. Fifteen till. "Maks, it isn't funny anymore. Where are they?"

He raised his hands in a gesture of ignorance.

All right, she thought, they had to be in the apartment somewhere. She began to look. She tore her bedroom apart: looked under the bed, behind the closet, picked up the seat cushions. She ran into the next room, and searched it similarly, then Maks and Kalina's room. She threw boxes of toys onto the floor, jerked blankets off beds. Kalina was asleep on her bed, but woke up and said drowsily that she hadn't heard anything.

"Maks says burglars took my clothes."

"What nonsense," Kalina murmured, half asleep still, "he probably threw them out the window."

Hania ran and looked out all the windows. Nothing to be seen on the sidewalk. Where could they be? She ran, towel clutched around her, into the piano room, lifted the piano lids—nothing. Five till.

"Maaaaks!" she cried in despair, "Don't do this to me! Where are they?"

"Burglars took them. Maybe," he said, taking off his glasses and polishing them with an air she could only suppose he'd learned from a James Bond movie, "next time you'll pay attention to me."

She suppressed a strong urge to slap him. Two minutes till. It was hard to search while holding onto a towel, but she was a one-armed wonder.

The door-bell rang as she was straddling boxes in the *służbówka*.

She scurried to Kalina. "Kalina, I can't go to the door. Please, you'll have to go let Mr. Radzimoyski in— no, I mean, don't let him in—tell him what happened."

Kalina groaned but didn't get up. Hania leaned over and shook her. "Please, Kalina, please go now, before he thinks I've stood him up again."

Kalina stumbled to her feet and padded down the hall to the entryway. Hania, holding her breath to listen, heard her say good evening, and then:

"Hania says to say she can't come out tonight." A long pause.

What? Thought Hania, she isn't going to explain? She's going to leave it at that? Feeling intensely ridiculous, she called from down the hall, "Because somebody took all her clothes!"

She couldn't imagine how he would look on hearing such words. Would he laugh? Would his face take on a thoughtful look? Whatever, she was sunk beyond hope of recall.

Kalina was saying, in her sleepy voice. "Maks says burglars came in and took all Hania's clothes. She was in the shower, I think. At least, I guess that's why she's been running around half-naked, shrieking…But I don't know, I was asleep."

Aaaaah, thought Hania. I'm going back to New York and I'm never coming to Poland again. Never, never, never.

"Would you ask Maks to come here, please?" she heard Konstanty saying to Kalina. She retreated down the hall; she didn't want to know anymore. When she finally took her hands off her ears, she heard the door click open. She listened. There was a sound of thudding on the stairs, and then she heard Konstanty saying to Kalina. "Please tell your cousin that I will be back in fifteen minutes." There was the click of the door shutting again, and then Kalina calling, "Hania, Hania, he's gone and Maks has brought your clothes back! He put them in a bag and took them to the attic."

Kalina helped her iron the dress again. She was ready when the doorbell rang.

They were walking side by side along the street. "How did you convince Maks to give them back?" she asked.

"I reasoned with him. I told him that you were his friend and that you always tried to help him and he should try and help you. I told him I was sure he wouldn't want to make you feel bad…things like that."

"And it worked?" she looked at him in amazement.

"No," he shook his head rather ruefully. "I'm sorry to say, it didn't appear to move him a jot. Seeing which, I remained very calm; I told him I would call the police, that a detective would come and take fingerprints on the closet, etc."

"And that worked?"

"No. He said that burglars wear gloves and that his fingerprints would be all over the house—it wasn't proof."

"Ah, that sounds like Maks."

"So then I asked him if he'd heard of a truth serum? And he began to look a little less certain and asked if it were true. I couldn't lie to him, but I said I had a large syringe upstairs…" his hands made the gesture of a foot-long needle, "and that was sufficient… I wish it had been the gentler methods that worked; it would have fit my worldview better, but there you are…He's quite a character, is Maks."

"Ye-es," said Hania, without enthusiasm. "I suppose he'll grow up to be a big-league criminal, or a politician. Probably both."

He looked down at her and smiled, "That's a very pretty dress."

"Thank you." She blushed.

14

Some Poles hoped Napoleon would restore Poland's independence. In 1797 the Polish legions were formed in Italy and fought for Napoleon until only a couple regiments were left as soldiers of the Kingdom of Naples. (Amongst other employment, Polish troops had been sent against Italian peasant uprisings, against the Papal States, and, in 1802, to put down a slave rebellion in Haiti. So strange are the uses of soldiers.) In 1806, Napoleon reached Warsaw and established the Duchy of Warsaw. Polish volunteers rushed to his armies again. After Napoleon's 1812 disaster, Poland was again partitioned between the usual powers...

Hania paused, considering how to rewrite the next series of failed insurrections. One in 1830 was ignited when a group of cadets attempted to assassinate the Tsar's brother. Constantine escaped from a Warsaw palace in women's clothing, and later was willing to grant an amnesty, but, while some Poles wanted to negotiate, others were unwilling. The country fell into chaos and the resultant war with Russia lasted till September 1831. The constitution was suspended, repressive measures taken, and 9,000 persons went into exile. Then there was another uprising in Galicia in 1846, during which the peasantry turned on the insurgents; and––she began to type:...*In 1863, in spite of the fact that Poland had been enjoying increased liberty and growing economic and cultural attainments, grievances still existed, and another rebellion against Russia was attempted. It too was unsuccessful. The result was that 20-30,000 Poles died, 10,000 were sent to mines in the Urals, and 40,000 were sent to Siberia.*

Death and food for patriotic poets, Hania thought; all this dreary history was doing nothing to raise her spirits. Somehow she wanted to go far, far away—maybe to Siberia—and hide. But why? Yesterday evening had been one of the best evenings of her life; she and Konstanty had talked and he had even laughed and there had always been understanding, even when they disagreed, and no lack of topics. And yet she had risen today with a sense of despair. She was falling deeper and deeper in love, and she was quite aware that on his part—she swallowed—on his part…There was no 'on his part.' He might like talking to her, but he would be shocked by the very idea of a connection between them.

I am obliged to set a good example of happy maturity for the children, she chided herself, and I can't control my own emotions. She wanted to help them and perhaps they were less in need of help than she herself. Perhaps Kalina had been right in commenting on her size, and what did she know about relationships? She had never had a successful one in her life. Kalina had gone seeking love—never mind if it was also lust—after her own manner and seemed content enough with the outcome.

Kalina, actually, didn't seem unhappy at all. In fact, having got over her disappointment in her lover, her sense of betrayal, she seemed, if anything, relieved. Her ideas were all concentrated on the coming baby. The baby was to her, Hania thought, what the dog was for Maks: They needed affection and had enough sense to try for it by giving. In the face of their possibly greater wisdom, she felt uncomfortable that practical questions kept occurring to her. How would Kalina raise a child? How would she support it? But when Hania asked her what she intended to do about school she averred that she still intended to go, why shouldn't she? And when Hania mentioned the fact that there would be the birth six months into the year, and the baby to nurse, and the impossibility of leaving it to its own devices while she sat at school...Kalina had serenely replied that she was sure it would work out somehow, and what did Hania think of the name "Julia?"

Hania put aside her worries for her.

"'Julia's a nice name, but what if it's a boy?" And she couldn't resist adding, "like Maks?"

"No!" Kalina seemed truly taken aback. Obviously the thought had never occurred to her. "Hania," she said in a tone of horror, "do you think it's a...boy?"

"Could be."

"*Jejku!*"

A while later, Kalina asked her, "If it's a boy, what do you think of the name 'Mścigniew'?"

"Mścigniew? You wouldn't give the poor thing a name meaning 'Vengeful Anger'—Kalino, you couldn't do it!"

"Why not? I found it in a list of names. It even has a saint's day. See? December 19."

"A saint's day for Vengeful Anger? Still..."

"Okay, then, how about 'Igor?'"

"Igor...Igor...Igor Beavor. Why not?"

And one day, looking at Kalina full of her coming motherhood, Hania had a flash—of envy, of longing: She will have a baby, and I will grow into an eccentric piano teacher, with my hair in a wops on my head and strange clothing. I will be barren and childless, develop uterine cancer at fifty, and die early and unloved. She gave herself a shake. There were, as her grandmother said, no excuses; there was certainly no excuse for mourning over herself. She had work to do, and she rose with her usual determination and went to the piano room.

If she was going to be a piano teacher, she had better get at it. If she was going to stay then she had to make money.

It was after a phone call from Wiktor two days previously that she had finally made up her mind. He had called, just like that, out of the blue, when she had entirely given up the idea that he might phone.

"Haniu, *kochanie*, how are you?" She had been expecting a call from Konstanty; Wiktor's voice had taken her by surprise.

"Um...I'm...fine." She had such a mix of images in her mind, she didn't know what to start with first. But she made a stab at it. "Um...uh...um..."

"Good. Good. Listen, *kochanie*, I've just had this offer to stay and work here so we won't be back when we thought we would."

He didn't hear Hania's gasp but continued, "So since I know you have to be back in New York, we're trying to arrange for someone to come stay with the kids. But at the moment we haven't had any luck. There's an acquaintance of Ania's who knows someone who had a woman from some place in the countryside doing cleaning for her and she's going to try and get a number for us—but we don't know yet if she'll be willing to stay with the kids. If that doesn't work out we'll have to try something..."

"But...Don't you think you should be here—because of the children's schooling and...and…" Hania hadn't expected to have to tell them about Kalina over the phone. She had imagined telling Ania, one on one; still, she had to do it. But Wiktor was saying, with a tone of rather smug amusement:

"But after all, they're the ones that have to go to school, not us."

"Yes, but, but, I really think Kalina needs—needs her mother."

"Kalina needs her mother? She's a big girl."

"Yes, well, that's rather the point. She's..."

His tone was dismissive. "Now, listen, I don't know when we'll be able..."

But Hania broke in on him, fiercely. "Wiktor, is Ania there?"

"Ania? She's fine. Now, what I wanted—"

"Wiktor! You should come home because Kalina is expecting." There, she'd said it. She held her breath waiting for his shocked reaction. But he swept on.

"Well, we were expecting to be home too, but this is a very interesting offer and I really think it would be irresponsible of me to pass it up and—"

"She's expecting a baby."

But he was talking across her, over her, about a possible babysitter.

"Kalina is expecting a *baby* and Maks needs his parents too!" She said it loudly and firmly. He couldn't not have heard. It was only, as she heard him saying good-bye, that she realized how protected he was against hearing anything he didn't want to hear. Would he know, deep down in his subconscious, what she had just told him, or was it completely blocked out? She didn't know, and it didn't matter. Kalina and Maks had no one but herself. She found she was trembling.

The children at the private school in New York would never miss her. She picked up the phone and dialled a number. The principal was not pleased with her. In fact, although the school advertised itself as nurturing and supportive, she didn't feel supported at all. She felt like she'd had an earful and would never find employment in New York again. When the call was over she was free and unemployed and had an empty apartment in New York which she very much hoped someone would want to sub-let.

Then she called her father and asked him to call Gerhardt or Szopinski or whoever else he thought might be able to get a message to Wiktor to tell him she was willing to stay with the children.

Maks was watching her as she put down the phone.

"You're staying?"

"Yes."

"Good." Somehow he didn't seem very pleased. His tone was listless. "Mama and Tata aren't coming back?"

"Not right away."

He nodded, and turning, went away. She found him later sitting on his bed, with all the dogs beside him. He didn't look up when she opened the door. So it did matter to him then. She felt full of pity, but there was nothing she could do.

"I'm sure they wish they could be here," she said to his bent head. He shrugged.

Kalina shrugged too when she told her, but somehow Hania didn't feel that she was pleased either. Whatever they might say, however much they might protest, she realized, they wanted their parents and they had been expecting them back at the start of the year.

She felt so flattened by their reaction that she almost wished she could go back on her decision. But, she told herself, she had decided to stay for their sakes, not for her own, so what was she unhappy about? Because she too needed someone to want her, came the unbidden thought, and since she knew that she wasn't, really, going to receive anything from Konstanty, she had desired the children as substitutes.

She had to put these thoughts away. Perhaps the children would eventually give her what affection they could spare from elsewhere; in the mean time, she had practical matters to attend to—like how to make money.

The only thing she knew how to do really well was play the piano. She had a mental block about it, but that could be overcome. She had overcome many things to become as good as she was: she had practiced through fatigue—the endless hours—and boredom with some of the drudgery of the mechanics, and despair, when nothing would go right or some piece seemed impossible to master. She had learned one just went on. She got up, went into the piano room, and sat down at a bench. Once it would have seemed the most natural thing in the world to start playing; now, after over a year's break, it seemed strange. She decided on a Chopin mazurka—his most nocturne-like and not a very difficult piece, because she was out of practice, and also, because she was fond of it. She put her hands forward. How nervous she felt; suppose she had forgotten too much? She played. She imagined she was playing for Konstanty, who understood everything, too quickly, but wouldn't understand this—neither the music nor her pain, and so she put it all in, transformed it.

Stopped. So, actually, she could still play. That is, she had played this piece far more accurately in the past, but not, surely, with deeper feeling.

Maks was standing in the doorway. "Babcia used to play that," he said. "She played it differently. You made a lot of mistakes."

She was torn between a sort of wry amusement at his thinking he knew enough to criticize, and being impressed that he had sufficient musical memory to tell the difference between her rendition and his grandmother's.

"Thank you for those kind words, Maks. Maybe if I practice more, I'll do better."

"Yes. Do. I like it."

He sat down to listen; pushing up his glasses, he pulled his legs onto the bench and wrapped his arms around them. She took his presence as a compliment. She selected some music, put it on the stand, and began to work in earnest.

She would put an advertisement in the paper, she thought, and perhaps visit some music schools to ask if she could put her name up for private lessons. Would they allow it? She didn't know. If her grandmother had been here, all would have been so easy—well, logistically speaking, anyway.

After she had won her last competition, in Toronto, she had sent her grandmother a recording of her performance—and got back a letter beginning, '*I suppose you're expecting congratulations, but what can I say? I suppose the judges were rather deaf...Beethoven would be turning in his grave at your use of rubato in the...*' And only at the end, the little note, '*however much I deprecate your abuse of emotion, it at least makes a change from the mechanical perfection of too much of today's playing. If you keep working you may make a pianist someday*...' And that she had taken as high praise, because her grandmother rarely accorded anyone the honor of really playing the piano: "Rubinstein?—not a pianist. Horowitz?—hmpf." (On the other hand, she had been just as likely, for a younger pupil, to reach into the past for some previously disdained model of the art, to be held up as a pinnacle never to be attained: "ah, if you had heard Horowitz now...")

However, pianist or not, Hania wasn't so well known that she could expect pupils to line up for her at a moment's notice. And in the meantime, how did one make money quickly? She would have to buy books for the children when school started, and many other things. The apartment fees were unpaid and several other bills she guessed. They would shortly have nothing even to buy groceries with.

The line from the Scottish poet kept running through her head: '*Is there for honest poverty*?' Not amongst those who've tried it, she thought, as she considered their financial position. Could she sell something? What did she have to sell? She didn't think the puppies, in spite of Maks' hopes, were going to be worth their weight in *złoty*, so that left...

"Kalino," she said later, "what could we sell, and how?"

"Why?" Kalina looked surprised; obviously the thought that they might run out of money had never occurred to her.

"We need money."

"Haven't Mama and Tata sent you any all this time?"

Hania shook her head, and was about to say that she was sure they'd pay her back when they returned, but Kalina was already raising her voice in indignation: "Oh, that is so like them, so..."

Hania cut her short. "Yes. But that won't help. We need a practical solution here..."

"I know! We can sell Tato's piano on Allegro."

"Sell his piano!? We couldn't."

"Sure we could. We have to eat. You'd still have the other two."

"What's Allegro?"

"Oh, it's like e-Bay. I can show you how it works."

"Yes. Would you, please? I could sell some of my dresses perhaps—some of them haven't been worn much. My new one, for instance. It cost a lot. Maybe someone in the country is in need of a size-umpteen dress. It won't bring much, of course, but even fifty dollars would help. I'm sure there must be lots of women my size who have trouble finding things."

Kalina gave her a dubious look but refrained from saying anything, and soon they were seated together in front of the computer.

"So you see," said Kalina, "you'll have to get a Polish bank account first."

She had done that in the morning, and then she had gone to the park with Maks. It was one of the last hot days of summer, one of the final days for shorts and tee shirts and bare legs and little flirty dresses. She looked down the line of benches surrounding the playground, at the ranks of waiting mothers. Every woman had one hand up, holding a cell phone, talking, talking; each had one leg tossed over the other. They were bare legs, tanned, with polished toenails and little ankle bracelets. The playground was surrounded by lines of legs in thin strappy sandals.

There were only a few days left before school started, and as she watched Maks playing, she thought that she didn't know how he was going to stand the discipline. Neither he nor Kalina had ever suggested that he'd had problems at his former school, but she could see that he was a social misfit. Someone—stout older ladies, prim younger ones—were always telling him he was playing the wrong way, that he shouldn't go up the slide, or sit crossways on the swing, or go over the bars instead of across. Rebuffed by the Polish crowd, he tried the foreigners—and there were many at this park––and had no better luck. A woman with a big smile on her face and 'Colorado' in large letters across the seat of her trousers was engrossed in her own small child. Maks tried his few words of English on her, but she ignored him entirely. Hania was amazed at her own sense of wrath, her sudden surge of protectiveness for her cousin.

"Come on, Maks," she called, "let's go find more congenial company."

He came willingly enough.

"What's congenial company?" he asked as they walked along.

"People who like us and whom we like, that sort."

"Nobody likes me." The words were said without pathos or self-pity, just matter-of-factly. "Not even Mama and Tata. That's why they stay away."

Hania stopped. He couldn't really think that, could he? Maybe he did. What did one say?

"I...no, Maks, I'm sure you're wrong. They stay away because they have many things they have to do ...I'm sure they love you very much. Really."

"You're lying," he said, in his strange little voice. "I can tell. You're turning red. You told me I shouldn't ever lie and now you're lying. Ha ha." He seemed quite satisfied with the fact.

Really, she thought, maybe he just was too horrible to like.

It was two or three days later that she decided Kalina also had to be added to the too-horrible-to-like list. And she had been completely unsuspecting. She had seen Kalina and Maks bent over the computer screen one evening late, and they had quickly turned it off when she approached, but she hadn't thought anything of it, not really. That is, she had thought they were probably playing some sort of game she wouldn't approve of, because she heard them calling out numbers:

"5,000!"

"Kalina! Look, again!"

"5,500! 6,000!"

And a little later: "Yes! 6,500! Ha! Ha!"

"8,000! I can't believe it! 8,500!"

"What sort of game are you playing?" she asked.

"Oh, a numbers game," Kalina answered, innocently. "It's all right. I won't let Maks play anything he shouldn't."

No, she was quite unsuspecting. It was only when they returned from the park the next day, in the late afternoon, and she went into the piano room to continue her practicing, that she was struck. Something was different about the room. She had a moment of confusion. Very different. The piano was gone! The Steinway! For a moment she stood still, unbelieving. There, where it had stood, was a large empty space. Feeling chills up her spine, she backed out of the room.

"Kalino!" she called.

Kalina and Maks were sitting together on the sofa, looking very, very, innocent and conscious.

"Where's the piano?" She asked, still not understanding. "Did your parents come home? Did they have it taken somewhere?"

"It got stolen," said Maks.

"Stolen?" she gasped.

"No," said Kalina, "Maks, stop lying all the time! We..." She reached for her pacifier and began to suck it. A few sucks and she took it out. "We sold it."

"You did what?"

"We sold it on Allegro. We auctioned it off. They came for it today."

"You can't have!"

"Yes. For 9 million *złoty*. It was great!" said Maks.

"9 *thousand*, Maks!" corrected Kalina.

Hania sank down in a chair. "You sold your father's Steinway for 9,000 *złoty*?" 3,000 dollars. Less than that.

"You said we needed money. Well, now you have 9,000 in your account."

"No," said Hania, as calmly as she could. "Tell me it isn't true. Oh, what am I going to do?" She stood up again. Sat down.

"Listen. Do you have the number, the address of whoever bought it? We have to get it back."

"No. We don't." Kalina and Maks shook their heads, Kalina beginning to look a little more worried.

"Listen. A Steinway—that Steinway—is worth much more than that. Much, much more. And it wasn't yours to sell anyway. What do you think your father's going to say when he comes back?"

Kalina shrugged defiantly, "He should have left us some money, shouldn't he?"

"Yes, but that's not the point—I'll be responsible—I'll...Don't you see what position it puts me in?" She began to walk about the room, wringing her hands, "What am I going to do? Your parents will come back––and here they'll find that you're pregnant and the piano's gone and..."

"And which do you think they'll mind more?" asked Kalina in a derisive tone.

"I don't know. But I'm sure they'll think it's my fault and that I didn't look after you properly...and...Did you do it for revenge?"

Kalina shrugged, picked up the television remote and flicked it on.

"—Oh, there's no point talking." Hania left the children, went into her room, and turned on her laptop. Somewhere, hopefully, on the Allegro site, there would be the address and telephone number of the buyer. A little searching and she found it. The buyer was a Wojciech Kwiatkowski, and there was a cell phone number. She wrote it down and hurried into the other room to call.

She listened to the phone ring. He couldn't have come for the piano more than two hours ago. Perhaps she could catch him before it was unloaded. A curt voice said hello, over the noise of traffic. So it was still being transported; it must be going somewhere outside of Warsaw. She took a deep breath.

"Hello. Is this Mr. Kwiatkowski, who just bought a piano?"

"That's right. Who's this?"

"I'm"—she hesitated, what was she? She plunged on—"I'm the cousin of the girl who sold the piano to you. The problem is, er, the problem is that it wasn't her piano to sell. So, I'm really sorry, but, er, I wonder if you could bring it back? It belongs to her…"

"I bought this piano from someone named Hanna Lanska. Is your cousin Hanna Lanska?"

"No, I am. But…"

"You advertised the piano on Allegro. It was you?"

"Yes. No! I mean, yes, it was under my name, but…"

"There aren't any buts. You sold me a piano. I've got it."

"But I didn't"—well, yes, it had been on her account—"I mean, it wasn't mine to sell."

"Lady, don't give me that," His was getting offensive. "I know what it is. You've found a buyer who'll give you more and now you want it back. Forget it. Even if you try through the courts, you won't ever see this piano again." The line went dead.

Hania dropped the receiver back in its socket and strode down the hall to her room, banging the door a little as she shut it. What was she going to do? But the man was quite right; there was nothing she could do.

Well, she thought after a time, she could go on with her work; that would be better than pacing about the room to no purpose. She sat down, calmed herself, and went back to her typing. She was almost at the end. What, she thought, in a state of nervous exasperation, was she going to do when she no longer had this task to take her mind off things?

15

...Who feels strength's elation
Let him fight the elements, let him make probation,
When the fire catches, water's no salvation.
– Hieronym Morsztyn (c.1581-1623),
'Cold Love'

She was typing lickety-split, but in counterpoint to all these words was the thought about the piano—that piano which had been a real and solid presence, and whose absence from the piano room was so conspicuous. How could they? How could they? What will Wiktor say? How could they?

And yet, after a couple of hours, her interest gradually fixed itself on what was before her. Konstanty had made a number of comments.

The first socialist party was formed in 1892. The most famous of its later leaders was Józef Piłsudski, a freedom fighter——or terrorist, depending on one's point of view? Hania added in a note for Konstanty—*who in 1904 formed an armed organization (Japan helped some with the arms and Austria with training) for the purpose of assassinating Russian functionaries and sabotaging the state. The estimated casualty figures for the organization's peak year vary from several hundred to 1,000 Russian officials. In 1908, Piłsudski also took part, along with his future wife and three future prime ministers of Poland, in a spectacular train robbery. They made off with a fortune.*

And yet, thought Hania vaguely, there's the Piłsudski museum here, and a Piłsudski square, and a Piłsudski statue…She would take the subject up with Konstanty, next time she saw him.

When World War I broke out, Piłsudski formed the Polish Legions, and—with an eye only for Polish independence—took them into the conflict on the Prussian and Austrian side, assuring the British that he only meant to fight Russia. Unfortunately, although the country regained its liberty at the end of the war, this did not mean the end of strife. The areas of the former partitions had mixed populations; before the borders were settled, acts of violence and armed uprisings took place in Cieszyn/Tesin in Czechoslovakia; in Greater Poland (where a speech by the pianist Paderewski may have sparked an insurrection against the Germans)…

—Tsk, thought Hania, as if this vaguely besmirched her profession—

…and in Upper Silesia (three uprisings) before it was decided to divide the territory. There was also a fight over Lviv—25,000 soldiers died. And a war with Russia over western Ukraine in 1919. Depending on the historian, Poland saw its chance to expand its territories, secure its borders, or make a pre-emptive strike. Russia had its own views of expansion. By the time the Bolshevik army was turned back, 100,000-150,000 Russian and 60,000 Polish soldiers were dead. A victory was claimed by each side and a division of the territories made.

And yet, Konstanty had written in the margin, *when I see the issues that people were willing to kill for—actually kill other human beings—my hands drop. I know that conflicts are carried on, usually, by a small portion of the population; I would like to believe that few parents truly feel that a border, or any other issue, is of more importance than the lives of their chil-*

dren. I would like to believe that the only 'patriots' are thoughtless young persons, or the ruthless minority who make use of them.

How strange, thought Hania, reading and suddenly concentrating. Those are almost the exact words I was going to write to him once. These last paragraphs had been written recently; he'd handed them to her the other day. He hadn't written earlier sections in quite this tone. It had been obvious he'd always disliked bloodshed, but he hadn't expressed his distaste for his country's actions in quite this form; there had been a little reserve. Was even he, descendant of the past establishment, coming to feel that settling differences by violence should be as outmoded as cannibalism? Maybe her questions had moved him to take a less conventional view? Her natural modesty asserted itself: no, he must have arrived at this point on his own.

It is distressing, too, that the Polish victors should have behaved at times so like their previous oppressors. But why am I surprised? Repression is known to beget repression, and insecurity frequently leads to fighting. It is only that I would be pleased for my country to have the high ground of magnanimity. Not to mention that the after-effects of the uprising in Greater Poland are sometimes cited as having contributed to Hitler's rise to power. These words were crossed out. Presumably he'd decided his own views were irrelevant to the subject. And surely the next sentence was a speaking commentary on the times:

...Perhaps it was not as surprising as it may seem that one of the largest organizations in inter-war Poland—with one million members—was a society promoting the establishment of Polish colonies in Africa...

In May of 1926, Piłsudski staged a coup, with the avowed intent of 'purifying' government, and thereafter, remained Poland's virtual dictator until his death in 1935.

It was the phone ringing that made her leap up and open the door again. Maybe it was Wiktor or Ania.

"It's for you," Kalina held out the phone.

Oh, thought Hania, maybe it's Konstanty. She took it with her breath held. She had half expected him to call today, and then she'd forgotten, because of the piano, but now the piano ceased to exist and her whole being was concentrated on the telephone. It was Konstanty. He was asking her what plans she had for the next day.

She was thrown off guard, hastily cast about in her mind for tomorrow's plans, and began to stutter: "I…I told Maks we'd go to Wilanów. I read that one can take boats on the canal—I thought it might amuse him and I haven't seen the palace." But that was before she learned about the piano. Oh, why couldn't she just have said, no, I don't have plans? Why was she so slow?

"If I can find which bus to take…"

"Would you like me to drive you?"

Oh. And she'd have to take that wretch Maks with her after what she'd said…

"Yes. Yes, thank you. That would be very kind of you."

Konstanty put up his cell phone and went back into the hospital. His step did not quicken but his heart was unaccountably light. There was his colleague Kowalski, with his neat haircut and too much cologne, who always annoyed him by having too ready smiles for him, and calling him '*Pan Doktor Prince*,' and being just a shade too curt with everyone else below the rank of director. Today, however, Kowalski couldn't faze him; he gave him a much more benign nod than ordinary; he smiled at a nurse he rather disliked; he went into his office. Some tune kept jiggling about in the back of his mind as he talked to a patient. He sat at his desk and wrote out a prescription.

The voice of his patient, a heavy, elderly woman, broke in on his thoughts. "Well, Doctor, I don't know what my heart's beating to, but from what you've been telling me, it's not the cha-cha."

He looked up in surprise and she regarded him with some amusement. Had he been humming? That tune? He, *Pan Doktor Prince* Konstanty Radzimoyski? What was happening to him?

"Well, well," said the woman with a smile.

Hania had done her best to prepare Maks for the outing by telling him a little history: "the palace was built by Poland's famous warrior-king, Jan Sobieski, three hundred years ago," and reading him the riot act: "behave or else." Still, some of Hania's nervousness must have shown the next day, because as they were fastening their seat belts in Konstanty's car, Maks leaned forward and assured her earnestly, in a loud, conspiratorial whisper: "Don't worry. I'm going to be good today."

She saw Konstanty's mouth twitch as he started the car, and she had to smile too; she turned around and said, "Thank you, Maks."

Maks nodded, and leaned back in his seat, preparing to chat confidentially, man to man, with Konstanty. "This is an old car," he said.

"Yes, but it runs pretty well."

"I'd buy a BMW."

"That's a nice car."

"Why don't you buy a BMW?"

"Well, I don't think I can afford it."

"Why?" said Maks with curiosity, "are you poor?"

"Oh, moderately," Konstanty replied with good humor, and glanced at Hania, who whimpered "Maaks..." and looked out the window.

But Maks was thinking the matter over in the back seat. After a moment of silence he spoke again, slowly, consideringly, obviously without ill intent: "You're poor...and Hania's fat...I guess that makes you alike, doesn't it?...Maybe you should get married."

"Maks, please!" Hania cringed against the window in an agony of embarrassment, unable to look at Konstanty.

But Maks wasn't finished. "Then you could have a baby. Like Kalina."

There was a moment of silence. Then Konstanty began loudly and decisively to talk about the palace.

"A certain 18th-century English visitor to Poland claimed there were a number of noble houses here where the inhabitants lived better than anyplace else he'd seen in Europe. I imagine Wilanów was one of the places he had in mind. It was owned by the Sieniawskis at the time, although the Saxon king, August III, was living there."

So now he knows about Kalina, thought Hania, through waves of hot blushes. But then he already knew. He wasn't surprised at all. It was so kind of him to keep talking when no one was listening. She had to pull herself together.

"Sobieski's sons must have hated that August not only took the throne from them, but was living in their father's summer residence. Still, unlike in many other European countries, such shifts were common in Poland. Few noble families managed to live on the same estate for many centuries. My own ancestors lost Radzimość twice, and only regained it the second time through marriage. They were frequent visitors to Wilanów in the 18th-century; there are old letters mentioning various entertainments at the place. One time, for instance..."

He carried on determinedly in this vein to drown out any more ideas Maks might have, and Hania was eventually able to recover and made an effort to join in so he wouldn't think her affected by what had passed. Somehow they reached the palace and parked in the lot.

As soon as they were out of the car, Maks made matters worse again by sidling up to Hania and saying in a loud puzzled voice, "Why are you angry? What did I do wrong?"

"Never mind, Maks." She had herself under control now, "Look, you can see the palace from here. Isn't it beautiful?"

"No. It looks old."

But she didn't let him express more of his opinions; she bored him mightily with a patter of talk, so that he disconnected from the two adults and stared about the park as they all walked together toward the gates. But Hania, even as she talked, was thinking, I am fat, I am fat, and this man walking beside me knows it, and even if he is being polite and ignoring the fact, Maks has brought it to mind...She made a gigantic effort to try to shake off the mood, to concentrate on her company and surroundings instead of on herself.

Well, she thought—trying to take some pleasure after all in the scenery, in the heavy greenery of late summer at the penultimate moment before the arrival of autumn, in the white palace laid out round the courtyard lawn before them, the gold of the tower finials and medallions glinting down at them—well, King Jan Sobieski built this place for his wife, whom he adored—

whom he worshipped—and Marysienka wasn't exactly a nymph in figure either. She was pretty hefty actually...

They went inside. She hardly dared look at Konstanty, but she had to say something. They stopped before a statue of Sobieski on a small horse, trampling over two prostrate Turks. "There," she said, "that's just the sort of statue I think could be dispensed with."

Actually, Sobieski was no lightweight either.

"Why is that man crushing that little horse?" said Maks, looking at the statue from a different angle. "I don't think that's very nice."

Konstanty laughed. A tour guide turned and gave the three of them a reproving glance, and a museum employee stepped forward and asked them to move on. Konstanty, who was not used to being treated in that manner, whose ancestors had danced down these very rooms, stared in astonishment and then moved on with Hania and Maks.

This trip is just one long embarrassment, thought Hania, looking at museum exhibits with unseeing eyes and trying to make intelligent comments about marble urns. I wish I could go home, I wish it were over.

It was over. They were shepherded out of the building by the last of the attendants and stood again on the gravel walkway. "There's the park too," said Konstanty, who had a feeling that all was not well with Hania but who thought it would be rude to cut the expedition short on his own initiative, "if you're interested in seeing it?"

"Yes, I'm afraid I promised Maks a ride in a boat."

"That's right. I'd forgotten for a moment. Let's go then." He headed toward the ticket counter again.

He wants to go home too, thought Hania, but he can't say so without being rude. The idea added immensely to her discouragement. The three walked past the ornamental grape vine with its great leaves, through the formal garden with its clipped arborvitae and fountains, down toward the bank of the lake canal—even the sculpted cherubim on the balustrade were fighting, Hania noted with dismay. A short stroll along a wooded path brought them out by the water. The bank, inhabited by a few ducks, jutted steeply downwards from the walkway to the water. One gondola was receding into the distance with a boatman and a party of tourists; another was pulled up, resting partly on the bank. No one was around. It was rather chilly here; a slight breeze, unfelt in the park, swept the damp off the water and blew it toward them.

"I don't know if we have to wait till the others come back..." said Hania uncertainly.

"Why don't we take this one?" said Maks, pointing at the boat, and beginning to slide down the bank.

"No, Maks, wait, perhaps there's someone in that building over there."

Konstanty went in search of a boatman. The door opened to his knock, and Hania could hear Konstanty asking someone if they might be taken for a ride.

"Yes. But not that lady," said a man, emerging from the boathouse, and making no attempt not to be overheard. "Sorry, but she's simply too heavy."

Konstanty told the man quite peremptorily to be quiet and strive for intelligence, at which the man shrugged and retreated into the boathouse. Konstanty knocked on the door again.

Hania, aching with shame, started forward to say that it didn't matter, she really didn't need to go with them, it was only for Maks, etc., when a cry made her turn abruptly about.

While her back had been turned Maks had jumped into the boat, and the movement had freed it from the bank. It was floating out into the deeper water. As the distance widened, Maks stood up in the boat.

"Help!" he shouted, looking with anguished eyes at Hania. "Help!"

"Sit down!" shouted Konstanty, too late.

Maks took a step toward the edge of the boat and fell forward, against the gunwale, so that he was half bent over the gunwale and the gondola dipped danger-ously toward the side. "Hania! Help!" he shrieked in terror. The movement had shoved the gondola further into the current and the distance from the bank was widening with the seconds.

"Can he swim?" asked Konstanty, but Hania had already ripped off her shoes and was down the bank and diving for the water. She couldn't wait. Maks could hardly dogpaddle. If he went in he would panic and it would take too long to reach him.

Konstanty on the bank had a moment of hesita-tion: is it necessary, is it kind? Then he too tore off his shoes and jacket and dove into the water. It was very cold.

Hania was a good swimmer and a few powerful strokes brought her up to the boat. She caught hold of Maks, and with Konstanty's help—O *boże*, he was there too!—was able to right the boat, pull Maks' terrified iron grasp off the gunwale, push him down onto a seat, and wade with the boat back to shore. They wallowed out of the water, Konstanty with his usual gravity, she like a hippopotamus, or so it seemed to her, and pulled the gondola back up onto its perch.

The boatman was watching them with crossed arms from the top of the bank.

"Told you so," he said with glum satisfaction to Konstanty. "You can explain yourself to the security guards."

And in fact, two security guards were hurrying towards them.

The security guards were happy to exercise their functions, and expostulated at great length on the illegality and large consequences of damaging and appropriating property within the park, etc.; a discourse punctuated by the boatman's cries of "Amen" and "I told him so," and "what sort of people are they?" and "what sort of an idea?"

"Your name?" the security guard was batting a pad of paper with a pen.

"Konstanty Radzimoyski."

The guard hesitated, pen over paper. Konstanty began to wring water out of his clothing. Hania wished she were dead.

The guards abruptly lowered their tone, asked rather politely if they could see identification papers, considered, hemmed, admitted that it had probably all been an accident as the gentleman said, suggested that the gentleman and his family probably wanted to get home quickly and change their clothes, said "good-day" quite civilly, and took themselves off.

Hania, Konstanty, and Maks walked through the woods, past the fountains, the topiary, and the flower-beds, through the entrance gate—how the tourists stared!—and, in silence still, across the grass to the parking lot. The wind that had been hardly noticeable before struck them with icy claws under the green leaves of the trees.

Hania didn't dare look at Konstanty and her face was grim and set.

If Hania had smiled at him, had looked up to share the moment, Konstanty would have seen the funny side. As it was, he felt a vague and unaccustomed sense of dissatisfaction with himself, of humiliation, that made him speak shortly.

"I should carry a blanket in the car, but I don't have one, I'm afraid."

"I'm sorry, we'll get your car wet."

"It doesn't matter."

"I didn't get my boat ride!" said Maks, loudly.

"It doesn't matter, Maks," said Hania quietly.

"I'm cold!" he whined.

"Let's all get in," said Konstanty, unlocking the doors.

They got in. Konstanty started the engine. "It has to run awhile, I'm afraid, before the heating will kick in." He set the car in reverse, and as he turned his head to look behind, his glance fell on Hania and was arrested there. Her face was averted. Really, she looked like she thought he was the biggest fool in the country. So he was. He certainly hadn't arranged matters very well that day.

A heavy jolt and grinding of metal threw them forward. Konstanty never swore, not ever, but certain impolite words flashed across his mind. He jammed on the brake, opened the car door, and stepped out. He had backed into a passing Mercedes, and the owner, a youngish and bull-headed man, emerged with every display of rage and evidence that he wished to do battle. Konstanty listened politely while he was called several unspeakable names; he stood unmoved, his gravity only increasing, while the other man danced about, swinging his arms, almost but not quite aiming blows. This dignity eventually had its effect. The other man ran out of epithets, and became aware, as people quickly do in Poland, that the moral upper hand was not his. He subsided into head-shaking and huffing.

"Do you want to call the police," said Konstanty, "or shall we just fill out the insurance forms?"

The man grumbled a good deal, and agreed to do the forms. By the time they had filled out the papers— (Maks, in spite of Hania's efforts to control him, was bouncing at the car window, asking excitedly, "are they going to fight? Are they? Will the police come?")—the man had ceased to be angry and even suggested a garage where Konstanty could get his car fixed. "Not too expensive...I suppose yours is only liability insurance," he added rather smugly, looking at Konstanty's older vehicle. Then he shook hands and departed.

Konstanty got back in the car. Hania didn't say anything. She wanted to say, "I'm sorry, if you hadn't brought us here today none of this would have happened..." but she didn't trust herself to speak. They drove home in complete silence.

On the staircase Maks ran on ahead, and they could hear him knocking on the apartment door, hear it open and close. Hania and Konstanty went on up more slowly. Hania hoped that none of the neighbors would see them. Konstanty considered the possibility and decided he was really past caring. They stopped outside the Lanski's door. Hania had been gaining resolve as she climbed. She had to say something. She took a deep breath.

"I—I'm so sorry. None of this would have happened if it hadn't been for us." She was having difficulty speaking. She gestured toward his wet clothes. "A-and the car. I'll pay for the damage, of course."

"You'll do no such thing. It was entirely my fault. I was the driver, not you." He looked at her, unsure. Was that a tear, or only the lake water still? Her hair clung in wet strands to her cheek. He put out a hand and gently smoothed it back.

She froze at the gesture, and he did too, startled at himself and at her reaction. She raised wide eyes to his. He stepped back. "You'd better get dried and changed." He had his foot already on the stair up. "Goodbye."

"Goodbye." She turned quickly away and went through the door.

16

He who bravely bears the punishments of fate
And all his cares, and changes not
Either in evil times or good,
Him I call a man and thank him for his manliness.
Hieronim Morsztyn (c.1581-1623), 'A Man'

Hania went indoors, took a warm shower, put on dry clothes, sat down in a chair with a cup of tea, and stared into space. She was curiously numb. She couldn't bear to think over the last hour, and only shook her head when Kalina asked her curiously what had happened. She didn't feel like talking at all.

For some reason the words 'Marysienka was fat too' kept repeating in her mind like a broken record. And other little bits, that she remembered typing not too long ago, recurred too. Jan Sobieski wrote passionate letters when he was away from his wife. One he began '*my most beautiful little wifey, greatest consolation of my heart and soul!*' and continued, 'I hope that *notre amour ne changera jamais en amitié...it has seemed to me that I could not love more or deeper, but now I admit that not more—because it is not possible to love more—but je vous admire ever more, seeing perfection and such a good—and in such a beautiful body—soul.*'

A beautiful body? Few persons looking at portraits of the queen would think that. That was the effect of love. It was possible then, for love to transform the outline of the beloved into beauty. Still she would be foolish, very foolish, to think the *amitié* between herself and Konstanty would ever be transformed into *amour*. One had to protect oneself and be reasonable. And yet he had put out his hand.

So there it was; she had tried to keep her mind off it but she couldn't. The memory was present all evening. She went to bed with it, dreamt about it, woke with it in the morning. She relived the moment over and over, so that all day long, whatever she was doing––fixing breakfast, sweeping the floor, playing the piano, talking to Maks—she was conscious of his hand putting back her hair, felt the brush of his fingers against her skin.

He will call me today, she thought, or he will write an email, and she waited for it, both patient and impatient, holding off from the moment of hearing his voice, of seeing his words, and yet savouring it in advance.

Konstanty did not write or call. In the evening he drove out, in his damaged car, to Konstancin, to his sister's house. She had a number of guests, as usual, including Kalpurnia, who greeted him with just that precise calculation of distance and familiarity that he expected. Here, he thought, as he sat on a sofa beside her, is a woman who would never see in me anything but the sum of my social parts; here is a woman who would never cause me to jump in a lake.

He began to make conversation. How oddly thin she is, he thought, as he talked of other things. Pelagia too. I wonder if she's becoming anorexic? No, surely not, he considered, as he watched his pretty sister laughing with her guests, hers wasn't at all the personality.

And Kalpurnia's personality? Oh, Kalpurnia didn't have a personality, only guidelines set down by her circle. Unkind, unkind, he told himself, she's really very nice, and to make up for his thought, he turned and smiled at her, but fortunately didn't have to speak again, as his attention was claimed by another guest.

Pani Topocka was the sort of woman whose respectability stood out around her like an aura. She was a sturdy woman in her sixties, with her hair in a chignon, flat shoes, and a serious expression, a woman whose life work was to ensure the erection of statues and the inscription of plaques for as many acts of sabotage or insurrection as she could find. She was now organizing a monument, Pelagia said, to the women from the Konstancin area who had participated in a World War II plot to poison German officers in city restaurants. There would be an unveiling ceremony and Father Wysocki was going to speak and give the blessing.

The guests were enthusiastic and as they talked around him, Konstanty sat bemused, imagining what the monument might look like. It would have a column, surmounted by a large cross, with an engraving of a plate and silverware and the words 'In honor of the glorious act of patriotism performed by the women of Konstancin, whereby 5 German officers were sent to the hospital and 15 seriously incommoded.' And below there would be a Latin inscription: 'Caveat Eater.' Well, no. He swallowed his laughter in a hasty sip of too hot tea. He would save the joke for Hania.

And then he remembered that he had been trying hard all day not to think about Hania. He also became aware that Kalpurnia was approving the monument and asking that her name be put down for a subscription. He was going to be asked next. No, not asked, but everyone would look at him, or consciously not look at him, and he had better seek now for a mode of escape. This wasn't the place to speak his mind, or to embarrass *Pani* Topocka by suggesting that he didn't think any act of violence should be commemorated. He made as if to stand, but his brother-in-law entered the room at that moment, and, out of a polite respect for his—regrettable, but we think about it as little as possible, as some of the guests would no doubt summarize it—nationality, the conversation instantly switched to other topics.

Konstanty sank back in his seat. It was very pleasant here, really, in this comfortable room with the large fire in the chimney, the guests with their air of breeding and polite speech; one felt secure; there was a restful lack of stimulation and all the choices were already made for one. He didn't need to think about a certain girl, who could not, somehow, be whittled away to her essence, her eminently desirable mind, leaving her excess weight—and excess baggage in the shape of regrettable relatives—quite to the side.

And yet, if it was possible to rid oneself of national sanctities, to re-evaluate who and what were worthy of honor in Poland's past, then why couldn't one free oneself of convention in a personal matter? If it was obvious that human happiness could be better served by a more penetrating view in the one case, then surely there were other areas where old ideals could profitably be abandoned? Wasn't that what Hania, in other contexts, had been telling him? He had a momentary image of walking through the door with Hania— and he stood up abruptly, without even knowing why, and went to stare into the fire.

Hania squinted at Konstanty's handwriting:

For Poland, World War II had three main results. One was the immense loss of life and material destruction. Another was the shift of its borders westwards: Russia took its eastern lands, the Potsdam Agreement gave Poland territories to the west in compensation, and mass migrations of populations ensued. The third was Poland's domination by Russia again, and the imposition upon it, for the next half century, of Communist rule.

She had only a small stack of pages left. He would leave one more section in the Lanskis' mailbox; she would correct it and hand back the manuscript and then, she supposed, the intercourse between them would be entirely reduced to a nod and a sentence or two at chance meetings on the staircase. She felt bereft at the thought of giving back his handwriting. She had carefully preserved all his emails. Yesterday, when five days had passed since their outing to Wilanów and she realized that he was not going to call or write, she had opened them, and read them one by one. She hadn't been fooling herself, she thought; there were a great many of them and they did show a growing intimacy. And he had invited her out once to coffee, and once to dinner, and he had taken her to Powązki and to Wilanów. Still, there wasn't anything that gave her the right to suppose he had more than friendly feelings for her—even that last gesture, she had to admit, could fall in that category, and it was only she who was so stupid as to make something of it. The thought was bitter.

She had only the children to distract her. School had started, and she had spent hours traipsing round stores for their supplies, dragging a reluctant Maks, who suddenly decided he didn't want to go to school.

"I don't want to go," he stated for the tenth time as she picked up a book for him. "I don't want that book. Don't buy it."

She wasn't as sympathetic with him as she might have been. She had her own preoccupations. "I have to. You have to. Sometimes in life we have to do things we don't like."

"Oh, ha. You never do."

"How do you know, Maks?"

He changed tack abruptly. "I won't go and you can't make me."

This was a declaration of war, and with Maks, the merest hint had to be taken seriously. Hania had to put aside thoughts of Konstanty, of the weight of Polish history, of a difficult passage in a Chopin étude, of notebooks and textbooks and pencils, of tonight's dinner, of four puppies, and pull her mind out, like Hercules emerging from the Augean stables, into the moment.

"What is it you're particularly afraid of?"

"I'm not afraid. I'm just not going."

"Okay. Good. That makes it much easier for me. I was going to help you with your homework so you'd be the best student in the class and everyone would look at you and say 'there goes the smartest boy in the school' but now I won't have to. That's good." She made an effort to appear relieved and pleased.

Maks said nothing for a moment, and then, with disgust, "Kalina says I can't cheat until I know how to read."

"Well, there you are." Goodness, yes, all Poles can read.

Maks kicked at pebbles and scowled at her. "Okay. You can teach me that much. But no more."

"Okay. Agreed." Obviously her ideals were shrinking.

"You see?" said Kalina, some time later, "We had to sell the piano. How else would we have managed?"

Hania had to admit that Kalina was right. She wasn't finding it easy to attract students. Two little girls had come. One was skinny and uninterested; she had a blank look in her eyes and reminded Hania of a rubber pencil. The other was skinny, uninterested, hard-driven by her mother, and fitting piano lessons in between English, German, French, math, ballet, and tennis lessons. Neither wanted to learn, but she did her best with them. They nodded politely and looked out the window or at the clock while she explained the beginnings of music theory.

Lessons with Maks went much better. Not only was he making real progress at the piano, but he was learning to read with great rapidity as well. Maks, Hania thought curiously one evening, as she stared at his head bent over a book in which he was carefully deciphering words, was the one bright spot in her desolate existence.

On the other hand, since she had to walk with him to school, and meet him afterwards, it made it impossible to seek other work.

Then Kalina came back from school one afternoon, threw her knapsack in a corner and herself onto the sofa, and announced that she wasn't going to school ever again.

"What happened?" asked Hania, regarding her darkened face and trembling lip with trepidation.

"They think because they're teachers they can speak to us any way they please; they can humiliate us and make fun of us and..." Here the rest of the sentence was lost in tears.

Hania waited a moment, then asked "Which teacher, and what did she—or he—say?"

"My Polish teacher. She's really mean," Kalina said between sniffs, as she hugged a sofa pillow. "I had her last year too. She likes to make fun of people. But last year she didn't pick on me, because there was this really stupid boy in class, and she always went after him. But now he's gone and..." Kalina shrugged.

"What? She calls on you and you don't know the answer?" Hania guessed, trying to imagine what a Polish classroom was like.

"No. I know the answers...." Kalina pulled some threads out of the pillow. "She makes remarks about my looks." Sniff. "Like today, she says, 'What's wrong with you? Why are you sitting there like a sack of potatoes? Straighten up.' I mean, it's not her business is it, how I sit? And yesterday, she didn't like something in my essay and she says 'the only thing sloppier than your writing is the way you look.' And all the kids laughed... I'm not going again."

"That's horrible. That's unacceptable. I'll go and talk to the director. Maybe you can go into a different class."

Kalina shrugged. "It won't do any good." But she looked rather hopeful.

Hania went back to her typing, wondering how much of Kalina's problems with her teacher were the result of leftover thought patterns from Poland's past.

...The Communist regime, which was forced upon Poland by the Soviet Union after the war, ruled the country with a heavier or relatively lighter hand for over forty-five years...Perhaps initially the enthusiasm expended on rebuilding the country distracted those not directly affected by the excesses of Stalinism

(there were some tens of thousands of victims)...When Stalinism ended in Poland, there was a brief period of euphoria during which censorship was relaxed, and more could be written and debated than before, but by the end of the fifties, the party was again tightening its claws.

Hania had an image of the national emblem, the bareheaded Polish eagle—the Communists had removed its former crown—coming down out of the sky to sink its talons into the country. She deleted the line, and wrote instead: '*the party reaffirmed its hold on society.*'

Although politically, the severities of the first half of the fifties never returned, general living conditions were difficult during the entire period: for many people these included appallingly crowded living quarters and long queues for staples...The rights of citizens, enshrined in the constitution, were flouted as a matter of course by the police and the courts.

The next day, Hania, feeling considerable apprehension but armed with a sense of duty, pushed open the glass doors of a modern school building and went in. She had called yesterday and asked for an appointment. She was to meet the directress at eleven. It was five minutes before the hour. The hallway looked like school hallways everywhere, with notices up, and some class's identical drawings behind a glass display case. There was a vague hum of muffled voices behind classroom doors. In the office, a couple of bored secretaries were drinking tea and reading magazines. They gestured towards an inner door but told Hania she'd have to wait. She stood and waited. Eleven. Eleven five. Eleven ten. She tried to catch the eye of one of the secretaries, and finally one looked up with half a glance and shrugged. "Okay, go on in *pani*." Hania opened the door and found a middle-aged woman in a suit, shuffling papers. She did not look up on Hania's entrance.

Hania began uncertainly, still standing. "Hello, I'm Hania Lanska, I called yesterday..."

The woman still did not look at her. "Sit down," she almost snarled, "you can see I'm busy."

Hania sat patiently, hands folded in her lap, her astonishment at the woman's rudeness growing as the minutes ticked by.

Finally, the woman put aside her papers, leaned back in her chair, and looking somewhere in the corner of the room, with her nose in the air, said "What is it that you want?"

"I came because my cousin has a problem with her Polish teacher and as I am looking after..."

"Who are you?"

"My name is Hania Lanska and I'm..."

"I don't care what your name is. What business do you have here? Are you a parent?"

"No, I..."

"Then on what basis have you come here to complain? How is this possible?" The woman was tapping briskly on the desk with a pen. "*Pani*. I am very busy. Please don't bother me anymore." She pulled some papers in front of herself again and pretended to read.

Hania began to feel rather heated. "I may not be a parent, but I know improper behavior when I see it! Kalina's teacher's behavior is unacceptable. And so is yours." She began to rise.

"How dare you be so uncivil to me!" the directress snapped.

"I suppose," said Hania, "that I shall have to seek help higher up." She turned to go.

"Well," said the directress, suddenly smoothing her hair and adopting a different tone, "there's no need to get all upset. Please sit down."

Hania sat, her heart beating in outrage. The directress shuffled some papers. "Lanska, Lanska," she murmured, "that name sounds familiar." She suddenly rose and went to a filing cabinet.

"Ye-es. I have a note here..." There was a considering silence. "Where are her parents?"

Hania had to admit she didn't know.

"You don't know? How can you not know?"

"They're travelling."

"It doesn't matter," said the directress, with an impatient gesture, "We'll have a phone number in our records, somewhere."

Did they have cell phones? Of course they would. But Kalina had said not. Kalina had lied, thought Hania.

The directress waved a slip of paper. "You haven't been looking after her very well, have you?" she added with only a hint of triumph.

So, thought Hania, as she and Maks went into the Łazienki Park later that day. She walked with forced calmness and a feeling of hollow tranquillity. I have messed everything up. I have tried to help and I haven't. The school would contact Wiktor and Ania. And what would they do when they couldn't avoid the truth? Would they just call and make a scene or would they call her father and make a scene and expect him to pass it on? Would they come back? Somehow, she didn't think they were likely to handle the news in any very constructive manner. Now that she had decided to stay with the children and her life with them had settled into a routine, with its own small pleasures and compensations, the thought that it might be disrupted was very unsettling. What was going to happen? But there was nothing she could do.

And in the back of her mind, always, as a subtext to every other thought, was the idea: Konstanty doesn't want to have anything to do with me.

The trees were turning gold and red and darkening, the paths were patterned under their feet with the points of the oak and chestnut and broad maple leaves. The air was cool and full of the threat of colder weather to come. But today, in the September haze, the park was still beautiful. If they turned to the right after the duck pond, and passed over the bridge, they would come out on the far side of the lake and have the Palace on the Water ahead of them, perched on its island, with its lovely proportions and pillars and statues.

Here, high above them, the white Belweder mansion, where Piłsudski had once ruled and Lech Wałęsa had spent his term in office, presided over a vista of lawn and lake. They went down the hill, leaving the city behind, and walked along the wide clay path by the bank of the pond.

Hania said nothing, and Maks did not break the silence, but he kept glancing at her now and then. They stopped beside a weeping willow tree. Its graceful arms brushed narrow yellow leaves against the water. Ducks paddled in and out among the branches and a white swan floated up, dipping and bowing its arched neck.

"Why do you look so unhappy?" Maks finally asked Hania. "I haven't done anything terrible today, have I?"

"No, Maks."

"Then what?"

"I feel old and ugly and fat."

A pause, while Maks considered this, and they began to walk again, the swan gliding beside them.

"I guess you are old," he said at last, "but you have a nice face. I like your face."

"Thank you, Maks, that's kind of you."

"Swans are fat too."

They circled the park and returned home. There was no doubt about it, she thought as they walked back up the hill, she was losing weight and gaining in condition. She wasn't even breathing hard. She had been doing so much walking it had cut her appetite too. She had no desire to eat all day and she was definitely less heavy. But what did it matter now? Even if she could skip up the stairs, she thought when they reached their building, Konstanty wasn't coming down.

She went into the piano room. Kalina came home and opened the door.

"Well? Did you talk to the directress? What did she say?"

"I'm afraid I didn't do any good. I think she intends to call your parents."

Kalina stood still for a moment in the doorway, her school bag bulging over one shoulder, her stomach protruding over her jeans. Hania couldn't read her face.

"They had to know sometime," she added tentatively.

"But not from the school!"

"I'm sorry, Kalina," Hania whispered.

Kalina shrugged. "Fine." She turned away with an air of unconcern, closing the door rather too forcefully.

Hania began to play the piano. *Ave Maria*, with her own variations.

In the apartment above, Konstanty crossed to the window and unhooked it, pulling it open enough so he could lean out. The cold autumn evening came in with its scent of rain and leaves. He struggled to catch the music. The notes came to him individually, in little groups, some he missed. He imagined Hania in the room below, at the piano, with her brown hair down her back. He didn't know why he hung on each note so. He had made it clear to himself that he wasn't interested in the girl. And because he had seen, in her eyes, that moment when he had touched her cheek, that she––he didn't want to think about it. He straightened abruptly, brought the casements together sharply, and, feeling unhappier than he could remember feeling, snapped the latch into place.

Maks came into the room. He stood beside Hania with his no-nonsense air. He was probably up to some mischief, she thought.

"You love the piano, don't you?" he asked.

"Yes. Once I loved it very much. I hardly thought about anything else."

"Do you love the piano more than you love me?"

She was startled. Did he have some premonition of loss? Had Kalina told him something? Did he think she loved him? Did she?

"It's not the same thing, Maks. One could never feel for music the way one feels for a person." There, she had admitted it. She held love highest. If she had had a choice between love and a career as a concert pianist she would have chosen love. Hands down. She wasn't going to have either, but that was another matter. "Yes, Maks, I love you much more than the piano." And it was true. She reached out to give him a hug but he recoiled from her grasp, adjusted his glasses, and said, "So that's okay then...Are you going to teach me something new? Or am I just going to stand around here all day?"

17

Solidarity, a mass movement of 11 million members, was characterized by the determination of ordinary citizens simply to turn their backs on the regime in power, and is especially memorable because, for the first time in centuries, Poland had produced a truly revolutionary movement. Through restraint and a willingness to negotiate, the movement led entirely peacefully to the collapse of communism in Poland and to the reestablishment of independence. In the wake of the Polish revolution, Communist regimes were sent—peacefully—packing in one country after another across Eastern Europe, in what is called the Autumn of Nations, or the revolutions of 1989...

Hania finished proofreading the last sentences she'd just typed about the growth of civil society—resolutely keeping out of her mind such mental associations as had to do with the old system and apartments and people who might or might not have behaved one way or another out of gratitude—and booming economics (but not, of course, that everyone benefited). There, that was it. There wasn't any more. She deleted the last period. Put it back again. There was really nothing more to be done on the work. She just had to send it off to Konstanty and that would be that. She opened the email:

*'Respected Sir...*There was no place at all to say any of the things she wanted to say. It had been nearly three weeks now and there had been no exchange between

them other than her return of new sections and his acknowledgement of the same. His silence told her as effectively as shouted words that he had decided to put an end to their friendship. She felt humiliated and slightly sick looking at the words. She took a deep breath. Hearts didn't really break. *Respected Sir, Here is the remainder.* She pressed send.

Sometime she would have to give him back the handwritten papers, but that could wait. Maybe she could mail it to him, and then she wouldn't have to meet him. It was Saturday morning, one of her gormless little piano students would be coming, and then there was housework to do, and piano practice. She could certainly keep herself busy. Kalina and Maks had gone off to the park to try to give away the puppies. She crossed her fingers that they would be having luck.

And here it seemed her wish came true. A couple of hours later, just as she noticed that it was starting to rain, starting to pour in fact, and wondered what was happening with the children, they burst into the apartment, shaking off water-drops and bubbling with glee and excitement.

"What?" Hania cried, leaping from her chair, and seeing their empty arms, "Did you give *all* of them away?" What a relief.

"Better!" exclaimed Kalina with a laugh, "We sold them!"

"You what? How?"

Maks was bouncing up and down, digging wads of bills out of his pockets. "Look how much! We sold them for four hundred *złoty* each. To nice people in fancy clothes."

Hania looked at him in amazement. Kalina giggled and held up a cardboard sign. It said, 'Rare Breed! Chien Bâtard.'

"We didn't want to say just 'mongrels' in Polish, so I wrote it in French. And people kept coming up and saying 'what's that? And I said 'Shen Batar' from Ulan Batar, I think, sort of like Shih Tzuh of the Manchu and everyone said 'oooh' and 'aaaah' and wanted to buy them."

"Look. We've got 1200 złoty."

"Rany Boskie! But..."

Well, what was there to say really?

They grinned at each other, laughed, Maks skipped about and sang. It was a moment of camaraderie and solidarity.

Then there was the sound of a key turning in the lock of the apartment door. Their heads all turned and they gazed in surprise at the door. It swung open, and first a large suitcase was thrust in and then Wiktor followed—a man with a neat gray beard and an expensive, rumpled overcoat.

He didn't appear particularly happy to see them. They stood in a group staring, while he reached outside the door and pulled in another suitcase.

"Your mother will be here in a moment," he said rather gruffly, not particularly looking at any of them. "She's getting things out of the car." The charm was definitely not turned on.

Ania walked in then, blonde and pretty and dressed in slightly too young clothes. She had a look of irritation on her face.

The meeting was awkward. No one really knew what to say.

Wiktor and Ania came together and rather sidled over to the group and made perfunctory kisses all around.

"Er…um..." Someone had to say something. "Did you have a nice trip? Did you come by car?" Hania asked. She couldn't very well say, "Why are you here?"

"No." answered Wiktor shortly. "It was a terrible trip. Very inconvenient."

"Oh...um..." She felt the need to act as hostess, somehow. "Could I get you something? Shall I make some tea?"

"Coffee," he barked and turned and headed for the piano room.

Hania watched him go. When she looked back, Kalina and Maks seemed to have faded away somewhere. Ania was saying to her, in an aggrieved tone over her usually rather saccharine accents, as she hung up her coat, "You know we had this really strange phone call from the school. Of course, we don't believe a word of it. I won't even tell you what they said, it's so ridiculous. But as responsible parents we had to come back and it's very, very inconvenient, because Wiktor is so busy, and we can only stay the weekend, we'll have to drive all the way back Monday night, and Wiktor's very upset about it, but I said, we have to come, because how will it look if we don't?

How will it look? Thought Hania, that's what matters to you?

"And we can go right back..."

But here she was interrupted by Wiktor, saying in a voice that began like quiet thunder and ended in a rather high shriek.

"Where is my piano?"

"I...I sold it."

"You what?" Wiktor's eyes were bulging and his voice was shrill, "You what?" he shouted.

"Because Kalina's pregnant and we needed the money."

Ania clutched at her heart, her throat. "It's true! She's pregnant! I can't believe it!" Her voice was shriller than Wiktor's and much higher. "She's pregnant! How could this happen? How?!"

Wiktor continued: "How could this happen? My piano!" He strode about in circles muttering and gesticulating. "My beautiful Steinway grand..."

"My daughter is pregnant!" shrieked Ania, stamping her feet.

"My piano!" shouted Wiktor over her screeches.

"My daughter!"

And then they both stopped and turned to Hania. "You! It's all your fault!"

Konstanty held out his cup to his sister, and she poured a stream of hot golden tea into it, then added a slice of lemon with tongs. The finished history lay to the side of the tea tray, on the polished surface of a small wooden table. They were sitting in the large living room, with its view of lawns and trees and a number of recently planted azalias. Somehow he didn't see any of it. The white pages of the history were a sort of specter of Hania. "*Respected Sir,*" she had written, "*Here is the remainder.*" Nothing more. It was probably the shortest note he'd ever had from her. Well, and what more did he want? Nothing. Nothing, of course. He hadn't seen her for nineteen days now. He had never meant to hurt her, and knew, perfectly well, that he had. He had liked her but had never intended that she should have feelings for him. He hoped she would get over it quickly.

He looked at his watch. It would be exactly nineteen days in another two hours.

"You're very quiet today," said Pelagia.

"No, no, I'm just the same as always," he answered distractedly. He had known that she admired him—that walk in the cemetery, that dinner out. But he was rather used to being admired, so he hadn't been careful—hadn't thought about what ideas she might get...Or, yes, actually, he had. So why had he continued to seek her out?

"Did you write all this, or did that—what's-her-name, the fat one?" Pelagia was flipping through the history, reading here and there. "I like this bit," she said appreciatively, pointing to a passage.

"She's not fat!" Konstanty nearly snapped.

Pelagia looked up at him in real surprise. And quickly back-tracked. "I'm sorry," she said quickly, "You know I can never remember anyone's name. Hania Lanska. That's it."

"It was a joint effort," added Konstanty rather stiffly.

"She seems to have talents."

"Yes."

A long pause. "I like large women," said Konstanty. But a voice prompted, no, you like one girl, who happens to be overweight.

"And why not?" asked Pelagia's husband in his deep voice as he came into the room, "Your sister likes large men." He sank his enormous frame into a chair beside his wife. He had put off his banker's suit for the weekend, but he still looked like what he was: a very well-fed, well-pleased man of money.

Pelagia gave him a rather irritated glance. "I like *one* large man. Sometimes."

After Konstanty had left, she remained sitting on the sofa, leafing through the pages of the history. She handed a few pages to her husband, and he read them calmly, balancing a glass of wine on one broad knee.

"I can't use this," she muttered glumly, sinking back against the sofa cushions.

"Well," said her husband, "I rather agree with him. But no, I suppose you can't. You'll have to snip and trim it."

And Konstanty, driving back to Warsaw through the rain raking cold claws across the windscreen and the brown falling leaves, struggled with an urgent desire to talk to Hania, see Hania. But he stifled it. It wouldn't be fair to her.

There, that was it, thought Hania, looking around the room. It hadn't taken her long to pack, even though her arms and her fingers were stiff and clumsy with nerves. Down the hallway she could hear Ania and Wiktor in Kalina's room, having hysterics. Every once in a while she would hear Kalina's voice, rising higher than theirs, then sobs. Then Wiktor shouting. Then Kalina's voice telling them, in her clear, lucid, no-holds-barred tone, just what she thought of them as parents. Well, she was enjoying herself, thought Hania, rather bitterly. She was finally getting the attention she wanted. It wouldn't last. But she was making the most of it. Only there was Maks—who was completely left out of the action. The last time she'd looked, she'd seen him slumped against the door, whimpering against it—"I sold the piano. I did that. I've been bad too." But no one was listening.

She had called to him softly. "Maks!" But he had ignored her. And when she had tried again, he had made an impatient 'go away' gesture in her direction.

She had gone back to her packing. Wiktor had told her to leave. He had said a lot of other things she didn't want to think about, and Ania had backed him up with nods of her head and shakes of her head and tears. She pulled the strap of the bag over her shoulder. The only thing left were these notes belonging to Konstanty. She put them uncertainly under her arm, and headed down the hall.

There was no point in saying good-bye to Ania and Wiktor. Their last words had been on the order of "get out!" Kalina was fully engaged. But she had to step over Maks to get past him as he lay with his ear against the door. She knelt down beside him.

"Goodbye, Maks. I have to leave now."

"Goodbye." He hardly looked up.

She straightened, and went on down the hall and out of the apartment. As she pulled the door shut, she dropped the papers, and they scattered across the landing. She had a wild desire to drop down beside them and burst into tears. Instead, she bent with shaking fingers and gathered them together. She had better give them back now and have one less thing to worry about. She left her bag on the landing, climbed to the next floor, and rang the bell with her heart thumping.

After a pause the door opened, and Konstanty stood there, looking surprised and serious. "Please come in," he said courteously, stepping back, but she shook her head.

"Here," she said, "I just brought these back. I have to go now. Goodbye." She pushed the papers toward him. He took them and started to say something, but she held out her hand, "Goodbye." He took her hand, and held it a moment longer than necessary, so that she had to make a slight effort to get free. "Goodbye," she said again, pulling her hand loose, and she was backing away, turning, going down the stairs.

"Wait," he said, but not very loudly, and she didn't stop; he could hear her feet on the steps and the sound of something heavy bumping against the banisters.

He closed the door, and leaned against it, breathing hard, his heart racing.

Hania lugged her bag along the street to the bus stop in the pouring rain and wind. The bus stop had a shelter and fortunately, it was empty. She sat down on the hard bench. It was cold and her clothing inadequate. She was wet, and her hands and feet slowly turned numb, but she hardly noticed. She had been rejected by everyone. The outer weather was nothing compared to the great inner cold seeping through every part of her being. She struggled against it, tried to make plans. She didn't even know where she was going. The bus didn't come. She put her face down in her hands.

When she looked up, she saw that Kalina and Maks were running across the street toward her.

"Hania!" they shouted. "Hania!"

"Are you really going?" said Maks.

"Tata told us!" said Kalina. "I can't stand him!" she shrieked. "He never listens! I told him I was the one who sold the piano! I told him!" Kalina was obviously still riding the adrenaline of altercation.

"Don't go," said Maks, looking subdued, "Please."

"It's all right, Maks," she said, "I have to go."

"But..."

"Kalina, Maks, you can see I can't stay now. But thank you for coming..." Really, it had made a tremendous difference to her. "I'll always remember our summer together, and...and I'll always be your friend."

They nodded, standing in front of her. She rose and gave them awkward hugs. "You'd better run back. You'll freeze without your coats." They turned and ran.

She sat back down. Still the bus didn't come. She blew in her hands.

Konstanty couldn't settle down in the apartment. He turned on the television and flicked through all the channels and turned it off. He opened his laptop, and then closed it again. He went into the kitchen to make himself some tea, and forgot why he was there. He went to the window and stood there, looking out at nothing. The rain spattered against the window. An occasional car passed, and an occasional hurrying umbrella. The pavement glittered gray in the descending dusk. In a moment it would be dark. Wasn't that Kalina and Maks running across the street? He watched without much interest as they ran into the building. Hania wasn't with them. Hania was downstairs. He found himself trying to imagine what room she was in. Maybe she was standing at the window, just below him. She would look out into the street and see the same things he saw. Why did the thought increase his pulse so? She would look down the street at the crowns of the lindens and the piles of leaves around the trunks, down on the tops of the cars, and along the street to the bus stop. Someone was sitting at the stop with a large canvas bag. He looked again.

Konstanty, who never ran, whirled away from the window and ran out of the apartment, leaving the door open, and taking the steps down three at a time.

Here was the bus at last, thought Hania with relief, and rose to meet it, oblivious of the water sluicing off the shelter roof onto her head. She hefted her bag to her shoulder as it came up.

"Don't get on! That's the wrong bus!" someone shouted as she lifted her foot to the step.

She moved back. Konstanty had appeared at a run around the edge of the bus. She stared at him. He slowed to a walk but seemed to be panting. The bus moved off with a roar.

"Oh," she said with difficulty, her jaw clenched against cold and emotion, as he came up to her, "now I've missed the bus."

"You didn't want it anyway," he answered.

"Didn't I?" she muttered doubtingly, "I'm going..." Actually, she didn't know where she was going.

"Where? I met Kalina and Maks on the stairs." He tugged at his tie to loosen it and got his breath under control. "They told me you were leaving."

"Yes. S-so I guess any bus to someplace I can stay. Any cheap hotel, I guess." She was shivering uncontrollably. "Which bus should I take then?"

He had come unaccountably close. He was standing still, and his breathing was now only just slightly hurried. He didn't look exactly calm, but collected and rather amused. He answered deliberately, "None."

None? What did that mean? And why was he here? She stared at the wet pavement. She couldn't meet his eyes. She couldn't bear that note of tenderness she imagined. It must be pity. She had such a lump in her throat she was afraid she would start to cry. That would be the final humiliation. Another bus was coming up. They always arrived like this, in clusters.

"Don't go," he said.

"This isn't the right bus either?" She sniffed.

"Completely the wrong bus."

"I'd b-better w-w-walk then..." she murmured between chattering teeth, and leaned sideways for the handle of her bag. He reached out a hand and stopped her. "You don't want to do that."

She took one quick look upwards, and saw that he was watching her with a look of—a look of—a look of all her dreams. She had a moment of panic. It was her imagination, of course. It must be.

She stepped hastily backwards.

"You aren't going to run away from me now are you?" He stood watching her with an expression of mingled fear and laughter—that would serve him right. He'd been so blind not to recognize at once what really mattered.—And yet, she somehow didn't run.

"I..."

"Hania...You're just exactly what I want. I can't let you go—not by bus, not by foot, nor...taken off by pneumonia...Come. We have lots to talk about but here it's too cold. Come." And then, more firmly, but smiling at her, "Come." He shouldered her bag, and took her hand—somehow she didn't pull away—and together they crossed the street.

And then they were in his car, heading to Konstancin. "So," he said to her adverted face—she still couldn't look at him, but sat staring at her hands clasped in her lap—"You'll like my brother-in-law, he's a very decent fellow, and my sister—you'll grow quite fond of her when you know her well...They'll be happy to have you. There's lots of space. But anyway, I shouldn't think you'd be there long...Your aunt and uncle won't stay in Warsaw, and you'll want to be close to the children. They really need you. So we'll have the wedding at once, don't you think? I can't see any reason to wait..."

She glanced up at him then—one quick look— and he smiled, and turned his eyes back to the road, and she sat and looked out over the dashboard unseeing, and somewhere in the back of her mind, the music began to well. A hint of melody—delicate, sweet, searching, and underneath, chords starting quietly and building slowly, with the triumphant laughter running in rippling trills throughout. A piece of music entirely her own.

THE END

SOURCES

Translations from Polish and French are mine unless otherwise noted.

Chapter 2:

*'they carry cytars...' Theofylaktos Simokattes quoted on www.płatniarz.com, (accessed August, 2006).

Chapter 3:

*'As the country's climate...' Pomponius Mela quoted in Małgorzata Fabianek and Małgorzata Nesteruk, *Straszna Historia, Ci Sprytni Słowianie*, p. 7.

*'and therefore...' Procopius quoted in Aleksander Brückner, *Tysiąc Lat Kultury Polskiej* (Księgarnia Polska w Paryżu: Paris, 1930) p. 27.

*'grain...' Ibn Jakub quoted in Brückner, op. cit., 166.

* Lines 121-123 of *Goethe's Faust*, Part I, translated by Louis MacNiece, (Oxford University Press: Oxford, 1951).

*'drank...' Bishop Thietmar quoted in Jasienica, *Polska Piastow* (PIW: Warsaw, 1966) p. 72.

*'exuberant lifestyle,' Jasienica's words, op. cit., 72.

* Brückner, op. cit., 101.

Chapter 4:

*8,000 maidens...the Anonymous Gaul, quoted by Bruckner, op. cit., 71.

Chapter 5:

* Mermaid statue; Trojden's castle and surroundings; see Marek Ostrowski, *Wars's Gaze, Triptych Warszawski* (Ostrowski: Warsaw, 2006).

* Goebbels and pitch...Jonathan Tennenbaum, 'Revolution in Music: A Brief History of Musical Tuning,' reprinted on the website of the Schiller Institute, from *Fidelio* magazine, Vol. I, No. 1, Winter, 1991-1992.

* Erasmus on John a Lasco, from *Studies in the Book of Common Prayer*, Herbert Mortimer Luckock, 1833-1909 (Longmans, Green, and Co.: n.p., 1900), p. 38.

* 'the peasant is not your slave...'; 'songs'...Andrzej Frycz Modrzewski, *On the Improvement of the Commonwealth*.

*On the lot of the peasants, quoted by A. Ernt-Świetlicka and C.Świetlicki in '*Folwark. Szlachecki i Chłopi w Polsce XVI Wieku*,' at www. republika.pl, (accessed August 2006).

* On Lafayette, from *Lafayette*, Harlow Giles Unger (John Wiley & Sons Inc.: Hoboken, N.J., 2002) pp. 177-9.

Chapter 6:

* The papal nuncio Julius Ruggieri on Zygmunt August, quoted in Jasienica, *Polska Jagiellonów* (PIW: Warsaw, 1983) p. 379.

Chapter 7:

* Archbishop Tillotson quoted in Walerjan Krasinski, *Zarys Dziejów Reformacji w Polsce*, vol. II (Zwiastuń Ewangelicznego: Warsaw, 1905) p. 36.

* Text of the *Konfederacja Generala Warszawska* on the website of the Archiwum Główne Akt Dawnych

Chapter 8:

* Henri III's stay in Poland and flight from Cracow described in *Les Reines de France au temps des Valois, 2. Les Annees sanglantes*, Simone Bertiere, (Editions de Fallois: Paris, 1994) p. 261-262.

* Adam Mickiewicz, *Pan Tadeusz*, translated by Kenneth R. Mackenzie (The Polish Cultural Foundation: London, 1990) p. 120.

*On Bathory's supposed madness, Krasinski, op. cit., footnote on p. 30.

*Accounts of the Czaplinski Affair vary. Execution: Kuropas, Myron B., Saga of Ukraine, The Age of Heroism, Vol. 2, MUN Enterprise, Chicago, 1961, p. 34.

Chapter 10:

* Stanisław Leszczynski's last days and quotes from Simone Bertiere, *Les Reines de France au temps des Bourbons*, *Le Reine et la favorite*, (Editions de Fallois: Paris, 2000) p. 602.

Chapter 11:

* Figures for Second World War deaths vary widely.

* Wacek Matysiak...mentioned in Ilona Flutsztejn-Gruda, *Byłam Wtedy Dzieckiem* (Norbertinum: Lublin, 2004) p.135.

Chapter 12:

* Cock-fighting and caning, Adam Zamoyski, *The Last King of Poland* (Jonathan Cape: Great Britain, 1992) p. 49 (from *Mémoires secret et inédits de Stanislas Auguste*); self-portrait, from *Mémoires secret* quoted by Zamoyski, op. cit., p. 58.

Chapter 15:

*Polish colonies in Africa, Maciej Ząbek, 'Colonial Aspirations in the Second Republic and the Imperial Culture of Inter-War

Europe' in *The State and Development in Africa and Other Regions: Past and Present, Studies and Essays in Honor of Professor Jan J. Milewski*, (Warsaw, 2007).

*A certain 18th-century visitor…letter of 1750 of Sir Charles Hanbury Williams to Henry Fox, quoted in Zamoyski, op. cit., after the Earl of Ilchester and Mrs Langford-Brooke, *The Life of Sir Charles Hanbury Williams* (Thorton-Butterworth: London, 1929).

Chapter 16:

*Jan III Sobieski, *Listy do Marysienka*, letter of 9 June 1665, in the Virtual Library of Polish Literature, UNESCO.